KILLINGS AT LITTLE ROSE

Finley Martin

KILLINGS AT LITTLE ROSE

Finley Martin

The Acorn Press
Charlottetown
2019

ACORNPRESS

P.O. Box 22024
Charlottetown, Prince Edward Island
C1A 9J2
acornpresscanada.com

Edited by Jane Ledwell
Designed by Matt Reid
Printed in Canada

Library and Archives Canada Cataloguing in Publication

Title: Killings at Little Rose / Finley Martin.
Names: Martin, Finley, author.
Identifiers: Canadiana (print) 20190149892 | Canadiana (ebook)
20190149906 | ISBN 9781773660394
(softcover) | ISBN 9781773660400 (HTML)
Classification: LCC PS8626.A76952 K55 2019 | DDC C813/.6—dc23

The publisher acknowledges the support of the
Government of Canada, the Canada Council of the Arts and
The Province of Prince Edward Island.

To my daughter, Arja Romaniuk, whose
many admirable personal characteristics
inspired the Anne Brown character.

PROLOGUE

July, Charlottetown, Prince Edward Island

Eighteen-year-old Jacqueline Brown sat in the family room watching old *Monty Python* skits. The title of the next skit flashed onto the screen: "The Pet Shop." Her face brightened. She paused the recording and shouted, "Mom, come quick. This is a good one. Come quick. You'll love it."

Anne Brown poked her head into the room and followed her daughter's beckoning hand. She slipped between the arms of a large, comfy upholstered chair and leaned back. Her smile was pleasant, hopeful even, but sadness hung about the corners of her eyes.

"This is sooo funny," said Jacqui, as her finger pressed "play."

The TV screen sprang to life as a gentleman entered a British pet shop.

"I wish to complain about this parrot what I purchased not half an hour ago."

The proprietor looks puzzled. "What's, uh... What's wrong with it?"

"'E's dead. That's what's wrong with it!"

"No, no, he's not dead, he's... he's restin'!"

"All right then, if 'e's restin', I'll wake 'im up!" he said and began shouting loudly at the cage. "'Ello, Mister Polly Parrot! I've got a lovely fresh cuttlefish for you if you show..."

"There! He moved," interrupted the proprietor.

"No, 'e didn't. That was you 'itting the cage!"

"I never!!"

"Yes, you did!" The customer begins to yell and bang on the cage. "'ELLO POLLY!! Testing! Testing! Testing! This is your nine o'clock alarm call!" He pulls the parrot out of the cage and thumps its head on the counter. He tosses it in the air and watches it fall stonily to the ground. "Now, that's what I call a dead parrot."

Death... dead. These were funny words in the mouth of a comic.

But the words struck Anne with the same force as a hand slapping her face, and they jogged images and memories that spilled helter-skelter into her head. For her, the deaths were recent memories. Emotions had not yet calmed. Wounds remained raw.

She had seen so much needless destruction, so many unfulfilled dreams, so much hatred unburied, so many festering secrets, and so many futures unlived that she sickened at the enormity.

And what was the upshot of it all, she wondered. Little more than a troupe of dead bodies. No excuses. No what-ifs. No sober second thoughts. No replay. Now just images slipping silently into history...

History.

That word snagged Anne mid-thought.

Was it all over? Really over now?

Tragedies had converged with such suddenness that the aftermath seemed to have lost all resolution and sense and meaning.

Anne scoffed at her own naivety.

There is no happy ending to murder, she reflected. Nor is there a soul-saving moral or tidy wrap-up. Dead is dead... and that's the end to it.

Anne felt something well up inside, and she recalled her uncle, Bill Darby, her mentor and friend for his last six years at Darby Investigations, and the advice he once gave her: *A smart cop keeps life in the top drawer and work in the bottom one. It's the only way to get through this messy business.*

Another bit of good advice I didn't take, thought Anne. Her tears had started. She knew the sobs would come.

"No, no! 'E's pinin'," said the proprietor.

"'E's not pinin'! 'E's passed on! This parrot is no more! He has ceased to be! 'E's expired and gone to meet 'is maker! 'E's a stiff! Bereft of life, 'e rests in peace! If you 'adn't nailed 'im to the perch 'e'd be pushing up the daisies! 'Is metabolic processes are now 'istory! 'E's off the twig! 'E's kicked the bucket, 'e's shuffled off 'is mortal coil, run down the curtain and joined the bleedin' choir invisible!! He's f*ckin' snuffed it!...THIS IS AN EX-PARROT!!"

Jacqui heaved uncontrollably in laughter and looked toward her mother, but her mother was no longer there. She heard a car door shut and an engine spring to life.

Suddenly Jacqueline recognized her poor judgment, and a surge of mortification swept over her.

It had been too soon, she thought. Much too soon.

1.

March 15, Four Months Before
Little Rose Harbour, Prince Edward Island

Bernie White was probably the only person on Prince Edward Island distressed by the unexpected spring thaw. In the dim light of the building, his face was a jumble of gravity, worry, and confusion. His damp overalls clung to him, he felt the chill, his hands were grimy, his hair matted.

A calamity surrounded him, and the anxiety of having to make his next call sickened him. He looked around one last time, hoping for some relief, something positive, something hopeful, but there was nothing.

Then Bernie pulled a cellphone from his pocket and tapped in a number. Water dripped freely from the ceiling. As he waited for someone to pick up, he sloshed nervously through several inches of water covering the concrete slab of the factory floor. His free hand wiped a line of sweat from his forehead. A streak of grime took its place.

"Jean Gauthier, please. It's important. Tell him Bernie White is calling."

Jean Gauthier was sitting in his Halifax office, a hundred yards below the crest of Citadel Hill and the cannons that once protected the entrance to Halifax harbour. His window revealed the steep slope of the city toward the waterfront and a grand view of the harbour. His office was among a suite of offices which comprised the headquarters of M. Gauthier & Son, a company of considerable influence in Canada's east-coast fishery.

"Yes, Bernie. What is it?"

"Bad news, I'm afraid. No way to soften the blow. Pipes burst. The factory is awash. Quite a mess here."

"What the hell happened?"

"Pipes froze. The sudden thaw flooded the place. I found it this morning. Someone reported water seeping out the doors."

Jean Gauthier flushed with anger but held his tongue. He knew he would regret it if he unleashed the tirade struggling to leap from his mouth.

The phone silence grew longer, and Bernie's anxiety mounted. Finally, he burst out, "Listen, Jean, I did my job the way I always have. I cut the power to the pump when we closed the place down in November. I drained the pipes. I filled the traps with antifreeze."

Bernie paused to let his remarks find a receptive spot in Jean's mind, but Jean said nothing.

"Look," said Bernie, "I even hired Luc LaVie to give me a hand with the winterizing. Check with him, if you want. Remember, I've been doing this for the past fifteen years. It's not something I'd forget."

The silence continued.

"If somebody fucked up, it wasn't me," said Bernie. His tone was defensive and punctuated with finality.

"Was there a break-in?" said Jean.

"Main doors were locked when I got there. Had to use keys to get in. Other doors were secure, too. Windows latched. There was nothing strange on the outside. I can't imagine how anyone could get in."

Another silence.

"Do you want to sack me?" said Bernie.

"No. It looks like it's happening all over again. I don't blame you. What's the damage?"

"Plumbing in the factory is shot to hell. Upstairs piping for the toilets and kitchen is gone. Plus repairs to walls and floors. It'll cost thousands."

"Get some estimates from local contractors. Do it today. We've only got six weeks left before lobster season opens. Call a locksmith, too. Have him replace all keyways and padlocks. We'll limit key access and step up security as well. Maybe you can bring Luc back sooner or hire an extra man."

Jean hung up the phone and stared sullenly out the window. An oil tanker lumbered across his view of the harbour. Michel, Jean's father, hovered at the doorway to Jean's office. He hadn't heard the whole conversation, but the tone in Jean's voice had indicated something wrong.

"What's going on?" asked Michel Gauthier as he stepped into his son's office. His words sounded more like a command than a question. Michel would have been called "old" by some, but not likely to his face. He had fished off Nova Scotia's east coast for years and saved frugally before venturing into business on his own. He had lost his youth but not as much strength and acumen as had most deskbound men his age.

"Nothing, Papa. Nothing important."

"Cut the bullshit, Jean. Just tell me."

Reluctantly, Jean related the gist of Bernie's phone call.

"A smart businessman recognizes when he's fucked up. He cuts his losses and moves on. I told you this venture into PEI was a bad decision. You insisted. So I let it go. You have to make your own mistakes—I know that—but you'll never become a successful businessman if you don't learn from them."

"I'll handle it, Papa."

"Get rid of that fucking factory at Little Rose Harbour. Sell it and move on to something with better prospects. Don't waste your money... and mine."

"I said I'll handle it, Papa. Don't worry. I'll handle it."

"Then do it," he said, and muttered something about places of bad luck as he turned and walked away.

2.

Saturday, April 30th

Sullivan's Point was a headland among the saltwater estuaries that lay between the villages of Gaspereaux and Annandale, on Prince Edward Island's east coast. Sullivan's Point lay less than a mile from the open sea, and, like much of the exposed coastline, the vegetation had suffered relentless salt spray and crushing nor'easters. Its shoreline was a shambles of matted eelgrass and seaweed, bits of plastic buoys chopped by propellers, and a few carcasses of seal pups slain by starving coyotes.

The Grant homestead had been built on Sullivan's Point a century before, and no other building could be seen from there. Woodlands and fields grazed the crests of hills. It seemed a wilderness, even though the road to the point led to the cannery only a mile and a half away and to the village of Halkirk, a bit beyond that.

Little value remained in the Grant property now. The eighty-year-old house had been vacant for decades. The roof leaked and timbers were rotted. It bowed and sagged, especially along the front porch. Windows jammed, doors stuck, and a mouldy odour seeped through broken panes of glass. Nearby was a fallow garden, recognizable only by a dozen raised earthen rows. Past the garden lay a small graveyard, fenced off with hand-hewn hemlock posts and rails. A few mossy gravestones memorialized the original settlers and their descendants. Newer graves had been marked by crosses, now in disrepair, and depressions in the ground suggested unknown remains. One recently tended grave had a cluster of crocuses near its head, and they were about to bloom.

Beyond the house and the garden and the graveyard spread a stretch of scrubland. At one time that acreage had been cleared for farming, but it was too exposed to the sea. Later, trees had been planted, evergreen and deciduous, ornamental and practical, but even that effort proved neither decorative nor useful. Neglected, the trees grew misshapen and underdeveloped, and served no purpose beyond a windbreak for a drafty old house.

It had been a queer morning. Early fog had poured downriver in thick, damp billows and flooded scrubby fields and briars. It had slipped through huddled spruce thickets, beaten to dwarfish size by decades of sharp winds, and then drifted seaward. A foghorn wailed near the cape, and countless fishing boats rumbled toward the lobster grounds.

Just before mid-morning, a light breeze sprang up and dispersed the fog. The sun gained strength and a draft of warmth overtook the landscape. Finches and warblers rose from the shadows of bushes but scattered at the noisy intrusion of several flatbeds and a dump truck rattling up the dirt road from Halkirk toward the Grant homestead.

Within twenty minutes a construction crew had offloaded a grader, two bulldozers, and several small tracked vehicles. By noon, machines had levelled the old house and two outbuildings. A front-end loader dropped the rubble into a dump truck. Work crews manned chainsaws and clear-cut the scrub trees in the forsaken orchard. A dozer pushed trunks and limbs into a remote part of the old farm for a burn pile. When the job was completed in a few more days, the land would be cleared, cleared of everything except the old burial ground. That would remain undisturbed.

Willy Munro, operator of a skid loader, mounted the cab of his vehicle, started the engine, and raised a stump removal bucket on the hydraulic arm of his machine. The bucket was a funnel-shaped steel digger that narrowed to two sturdy beaver-like teeth. He reckoned he could rip out a couple dozen stumps before the day's end. In two days he could clear the whole lot—that is, if the new owner could afford it. Willy didn't work for nothing. He recalled a job a few years back when, after he had finished his work, the client claimed that he hadn't okayed the extras. He made a mental note to phone and double-check how far back through the scrub he should work. Then he lowered the digger, shifted the control levers, and braced himself for a jolt. When the loader lurched forward, the digger's teeth tore into the soil.

The first stump was tougher than he had expected, but he knew that trees exposed to frequent gales put out sturdier root systems than sheltered trees. They would be no match for his hardy little machine, and one by one he broke the roots loose. The stump itself was next. Several jabs with the digger's teeth loosened the soil around it. Another jab and lift and the stump let go. A final thrust upended it. A clumpy mass of soil, root fragments, and decaying vegetable matter dangled from the base. Willy drove the skid loader forward. The stump cleared the hole, rolled off the bucket, and fell to the ground. A clump of soil broke away from the base of the stump.

Then he saw it. It startled him. It was filthy with clay and faded in colour. His first impression was that it was a flower, but that was a ridiculous notion. He stopped his machine, turned it off, and stared again, more closely. It was small and bluish. A bag or cloth or something.

It was then that a more believable prospect snagged in his mind.

What if it's a bag of old coins... or silver... or jewellery?

Willy had heard tales of old-timers who hid their money in places no one else could find, especially during the Great Depression. They didn't trust some relatives. They didn't trust some neighbours. And they didn't trust banks.

Willy slowly emerged from his cab and pretended to examine the track and sprockets underneath his loader. Then he looked around to see if anyone might be watching.

Finders keepers, he thought, as he slowly approached the up-turned stump. Willy looked around one more time. Then he reached out for his prize.

It was a small bundle bound with rags, about the size of a loaf of bread.

A nice pile of cash.

He grabbed the bundle. One more furtive glance around. Then he pulled the treasure from its lodging.

A corner of the cloth had caught in a snarl of small roots and held stubbornly. Willy's fingers slipped from the bundle, and it fell. The cloth of the stained old parcel fell apart as it dropped to Willy's feet.

Willy looked eagerly down at his windfall. The shrivelled remains of a human skeleton the size of an infant stared back up at him.

3.

Friday, May 3rd
Little Rose Harbour

Bernie White, general manager of M. Gauthier & Son's only fish-processing factory at Little Rose Harbour, walked across the paved lot.

Bernie's cellphone clamoured with the jingle of a Vegas slot machine. He glanced at the caller name and grimaced as if interrupted from some important task. It was Jean Gauthier, the new owner.

"Yes?" said Bernie. "You've hired someone? She'll be out when? That's kinda soon isn't it? We're really busy around here... up to our eyeballs in work. First week of fishing and all... Not much time to babysit her... all right... all right... all right... I'll make some time. What do you want me to do with her? Orientation? Okay. She can have access to what? Anything she asks for? Are you sure that's wise? No... no... I don't have any problem with it. None at all. No problem. I'm just sayin' it's risky to give someone off the street the run of the place. Right. Later. Right."

Bernie disconnected and stared at his cellphone as if it had soiled him. Then he turned around and headed back to his office.

Bernie's eyes drifted toward several trucks parked not far up from the door to his office and a couple of others lined up on the far wharf. A few belonged to buyers from competing processors. Queens County Packers owned one of them. Two old men sat idly on its weigh platform. He knew Spit and Squeak. In fact, he knew everyone who walked the wharves at Little Rose.

4.

Two old men at the weigh station prepared for the last inshore fishing vessel to slip through the narrow slot in the breakwater and rumble into Little Rose Harbour. It swung its bow to starboard, gunned the engine in reverse, and nudged alongside the wharf. Crewmen tossed the lines up. The station men caught them, snugged the boat against the wall, and tied it off.

Five crates of lobster lay on the open deck of the boat. Two deckhands, one of whom was the captain's wife, the other her adult son, waited until they saw Sampson Pitt and Wesley Peake peering down at them.

Both men were in their mid-sixties, friends since childhood, and former fishermen. That's where all comparisons ended.

Wesley was tall and wiry. He had lively eyes and a puckish grin. A conspicuous dimple drew eyes to the centre of his chin. His face was long, his jaw receded, and a thin crop of corn-silk yellow hair sprouted from the crown of his head. Usually he covered it with a cap, but the day was warming, and he had tossed the cap aside.

Sampson was short and gruff, a bachelor with the qualities of a bulldog: a flat-nosed face, a wrinkled brow, and a compactness that suggested a reserve of strength and agility that he could still call on.

Few men in their community managed to retain any remnant of the noble and distinguished names their parents had given them at birth. Abridgements and nicknames abounded locally. Wesley's name ordinarily would have shortened to Wes, but a childhood illness affected his vocal cords, and the scratchy sounds that subsequently came from his mouth led others to dub him "Squeak."

Sampson was too grand a biblical name for the runt of his mother's litter. However, another inadequacy fated him even more: a speech defect and a resultant stammer. Sampson struggled even to correctly pronounce his own name. Consequently, whenever he attempted to say, "My name is Sampson Pitt," it came out "Sampson Spit." And so from childhood on he was known locally as "Spit." Numerous fights toughened the boy in elementary school, but after he won a few of those scraps, the teasing ceased and some self-respect returned. Oddly, his nickname persisted, but Sampson Pitt no longer took offense at it.

"Th-th-there ya go," said Spit, swinging the boom on the wharf crane until it settled over the boat.

Squeak hit a button for the crane's motor and shifted a lever. The motor groaned; the cable lowered to the boat deck, and the crew slipped a bridle of hooks under handles of the crate. The motor groaned again. The tray rose to a loading platform and scale, and Spit unhooked it.

"125 p-pounds," he shouted down. Three men should have manned the weigh platform. They were one man short.

Spit uttered a mild oath under his breath and slid the tray back into the box of a refrigeration truck. Large blue letters and the picture of a smiling lobster on the truck read *Queens County Packers*. He grunted, then lifted and swung the heavy tray over a holding tank and dumped the lobsters in. A few shovels-full of crushed ice followed.

Fifteen minutes later, the remaining lobster trays had been raised, weighed, and stored. The boat pulled away and headed for its berth. Spit and Squeak sat down on the loading platform, puffed cigarettes, and bided time until the offshore boats from Fishermen's Bank and the Ridge and Cape Louis made it in.

"Wh-what do ya make of it?" asked Spit.

"What d'ya mean?" said Squeak. The wind had backed easterly and with it came a cool draft. He grabbed his hat and drew it firmly down over his balding head.

"I mean the d-dead k-kid they found on Fig's family homestead. What else would I mean?" Spit swiped the back of his hand across his nose and snorted. He seemed angry.

"It troubles a fella. That's all I can say."

"S-same with me. Everyone's talkin' about it."

"It don't make no sense." Squeak spoke with a bewilderment that begged confirmation. He peered at Spit then returned to the yet unsolved cryptogram in the morning newspaper.

"Depends how you l-look at it."

"It's a puzzle. That's true." Squeak was disappointed in Spit's ambiguity and looked away. Then he added, "It's been a long time."

Spit nodded and stared for a long time eastward for a sighting of the next vessel.

"Wonder where Fig is? He's late. Not like him."

5.

An hour later an RCMP cruiser swung into the paved area next to the factory. The police car stopped, facing the approach to the harbour. Constables Tim Bittle and Freda Mumford turned to their back-seat passenger, Newton "Fig" Grant.

"Thanks for your cooperation, Mr. Grant. You've been helpful. If the investigators have more questions, they'll let you know."

Fig nodded and without comment exited the vehicle.

Fig Grant was taller than most, a large brooding man with features weathered by relentless sun, salt spray, and icy winds.

His white hair was cropped short on a flattened crown and his jaw was broad, both contributing to a near-perfect rectangular head. Large ears lent him an air of attentiveness. Dark eyebrows brought hardness to his eyes. His chest was broad, his hands large and strong.

He cast a shadow of unpredictability, much like a bristling dog approaching strangers on a narrow lane.

Fig made his way toward the refrigeration truck. Spit and Squeak sat up a bit when they spotted him.

"Slept in, did ya?" said Squeak.

"With one eye open," said Fig with a wry grin. A meagre smile transformed his face from pensive cloudiness to disarming candour and, for a brief moment, Fig seemed almost boyish and handsome. Then the cloud lowered again.

"What did they want?" asked Squeak.

"They wanted to know about the baby."

"What'd ya say?"

"I told them about Mary."

"D-did you tell 'em the r-r-rest?" said Spit.

"No point. Best let it go."

"Ya think they'll let it go?" asked Squeak.

"It's been a long time. Too long."

"I th-thought it was snatched," said Spit.

"So did I. Guess I was wrong." Fig's face darkened, and he scowled. His face darkened further. Then his tone lightened, and he said, "They was diggin' into other things, too... sneaky like."

"Like what?"

"Shine... stills... stuff like that. I had to admit it, though. I had no choice..." said Fig.

Squeak looked up. He felt an unsettling chill. He leaned forward apprehensively.

"I had to admit... that I've had a taste or two from time to time... but had no idea who might 'a ran it off."

Fig laughed at the worried expression that had mounted Squeak's face. Then his finger jabbed toward the water past the channel buoys.

"Two more comin' in. They're ours. Look lively, now," he said.

6.

Saturday

Anne Brown arrived early. It was not yet seven when she drove into Little Rose Harbour. She wanted to get a sense of the place before she plunged into her new assignment. So she bypassed the factory's parking lot and drove toward the wharf.

At first, she was surprised by the bustle and noise. Quite a contrast with Charlottetown, probably still half-asleep, she thought.

Few fishing boats were tied up. Most working vessels were off-shore and had been for hours. Those with mechanical problems tugged at their lines and waited for mechanics or spare parts.

Forklifts ferried tanks of ice or loads of pallets along paved lanes. Generators hummed, machinery clanged, and steam filled the air near the plant. Rackety exhaust fans expelled fumes and heat; freezers churned out a feed of crushed ice and sent it rattling down chutes. Stationary pumps sucked cold sea water into holding tanks to freshen live lobster, and vehicles driven by retired fishermen, factory workers, truckers, buyers, and sellers drifted past her.

Several concrete wharves made up the harbour. Together they formed a slot and breakwater between the open waters of Northumberland Strait to the east and Rose Creek to the west. The space between the wharves had been dredged. Channel buoys marked a safe course in, and a two-lane road marked the only way out. It wound north to the village of Halkirk, through which Anne had driven on her way into Little Rose Harbour.

A string of shacks, where fishermen stored bait tubs, nets, traps, and spare gear, lined the southern dock. A half-dozen buildings belonging to M. Gauthier & Son stretched along a dock nearer the road. Each wharf had power winches for lifting heavy gear, engines, or tubs of fish and lobster.

Anne noticed few, if any, idlers hanging about. Hard work and industry appeared to be the standard, and she guessed that local layabouts would find no hiding place from opportunities to work. On the other hand, perhaps they could find opportunities to make easy money here.

Anne made her way back toward the factory and parked her car.

She had too quick a sit-down orientation with Bernie, the factory manager, before he introduced her to the office staff. Then he pointed her toward the women's locker area, where Anne hastily changed into the clothing required for work on the factory floor.

At eight o'clock sharp, work should have begun inside M. Gauthier & Son's lobster factory, but the only signs of commerce were the hiss and whimper of the boiler waiting to swallow up its first batch of lobster, the hum of industrial lights, and the sputter of water hoses dampening the floor.

It was not a quiet place, though.

Most of the racket came from three dozen women gathered in small social groups around the factory floor. The women could be a boisterous lot when idle, and their hoots and hollers filled the vault-like building with chatter and laughter, and their echoes added several choruses to the din.

Despite young and pretty girls among them, as a whole, they were an unattractive group. They had pulled their hair back and soundly tucked it under hairnets. Shapeless white gowns gave even the most pleasant figure an amorphous look. Calf-high rubber boots eliminated any remnant of gracefulness, and there was no point in makeup or perfume because, in minutes, the steam of cookers, the smell of boiled lobster, and the sweat of tedious work would dull any effort to look attractive.

Some of the women complained impatiently among themselves at the delay and speculated thornily about what was going on. They wanted to get to work, but Bernie had said that he had an announcement to make beforehand. It took Bernie's best boatswain's voice to be heard over the chatter, but after a few moments they settled down, and then he began.

"We'll get you working in a minute, girls, and yes, you'll be paid for the delay, but I want to make a little announcement."

"You're having a baby?" shouted Myrna from somewhere in the crowd of women.

"Naw, he's just piled too many desserts under his belt," said Sadie. Everyone laughed. So did Bernie as he raised his hand and motioned for a little more order.

It wasn't until he raised his arm that anyone noticed the woman just behind him. She moved ahead and stood next to Bernie. She cut a small figure. She was a bit over five feet. She looked almost waif-like in her shapeless garments, hairnet, and rubber boots.

"This here's Annie... Annie Brown."

Anne winced at the diminutive rendering of her name. It made her feel even smaller than she was, but she smiled anyway. *Play the game*, she thought.

"Annie's an engineer. She's going to be working here for a while."

"Got no trains on Prince Edward Island," said Karen. "You plannin' on running a track through here?" There were a few titters from the group. Bernie ignored the comment.

"Annie's an industrial engineer. She's been contracted by management to look for ways to improve what we do—machinery upgrades, reorganization, product or property expansions, efficiency. She'll be getting her hands dirty on the line, trying out the production stages. She'll be here for a week or two, I expect. Get to know her... show her the ropes... give her a hand... just as if she were a regular new worker. That's it, girls. Have at it."

Bernie took Anne's arm and led her toward a large swarthy woman. Bernie introduced her as Enid Clements and explained that she was in charge of the steamer, the first step in the production line. Anne shifted her clipboard and papers and offered her hand. Enid gave a firm shake and explained the procedure.

Live lobsters from holding tanks are dropped into the boiler. High-pressure steam is injected at a hundred degrees until the cooking time completes. Anne recorded the details of Enid's demonstration and timed each segment of the process. After cooking, the lobsters were exposed to cold water for twenty minutes.

Enid Clements at sixty was the oldest worker at the plant and had worked through three changes in factory ownership during the past twenty years. During the noisy operation of the boiler, Anne probed Enid about the company, but Enid had nothing negative to say about the factory or, for that matter, about any thing or anyone. Her attitude surprised Anne. It was unusual. An uncomplaining worker. Or perhaps only a cautious one.

Anne liked Enid in spite of her reserve. So she didn't press her for information. Anne knew she'd have a more relaxed opportunity to chat with Enid later. Anne discovered that she had reservations for lodging at the same place as Enid.

7.

Bernie White would have said that he was ensuring the security of the business that the Gauthiers had entrusted to his management skills. He would have said something like that if he had got caught. However, there was little chance of that happening right now. All the workers, even office staff, were busy with some task at this early hour as he found his way into the women's change room and stood in front of the locker he had assigned to the new girl, Anne Brown.

There wasn't much in the locker. Street shoes, a light jacket, and a small handbag. He grabbed the handbag, his fingers fumbling through the contents: a package of tissues, lipstick, a few cosmetic doodads, an open pack of chewing gum, hair clips, a cellphone, and a wallet.

Bernie pulled the wallet from the purse. He fingered through her driver's license, credit cards and bank cards, and three or four other cards from retailers. A zippered compartment revealed a few hundred-dollar bills and two fifties. Strangely, there were no photos. He tried the cellphone, but it was password-protected.

The sound of footsteps rattled along the hallway.

"Bernie, you up here?"

Bernie hastily jammed each credit card into its individual slot in the wallet and closed the locker door.

"Yeah! What do ya need?"

***

Anne spent two sessions with Enid at the boiler before she moved on to the sectioning table. Two women worked there. One introduced herself sullenly as CeeCee Dunne. A skinny redhead didn't look up and didn't speak. Their job was separating the tail, claws, and body from the cooled lobsters. Anne joined them and drew howls of laughter at her dainty, awkward efforts to tear the lobster neatly and quickly into four parts. Anne realized her attempts had been pitiful and clumsy, and laughed with them. It soon became apparent, however, that her co-workers' amusement smacked more of derision than conviviality, and their disapproval did not diminish as Anne's speed and skill improved.

Anne stepped back away from the table for a moment and retrieved her clipboard. She recorded the time it took to section each lobster and the number of lobsters sectioned at their station over a fixed period of time. CeeCee looked annoyed. She stepped back from the table and grabbed Anne's clipboard. Anne ignored her.

"You're timing us," she said.

"That's part of my job," said Anne.

"The hell it is. That's an invasion of privacy," she said. "You can't do that. It's against the law... the labour code or something."

Anne's lips twitched. She wanted to say something but didn't. A rattle in her head muttered something about "arguing with a lamppost." In spite of that she had a special job to do and, as she caught sight of Bernie heading over, she thought it more prudent to let someone else settle this dispute.

"What the hell's going on here?" said Bernie. "Back to work."

"She can't do this," CeeCee said, jabbing her finger at Anne's timing entries.

"She can do what she's paid to do, and she's been paid to do this," said Bernie.

"It's not fair."

"Back to work," he said, his sternness eroding CeeCee's bluster.

"Back to work!" He spoke with enough force to break their hesitation.

CeeCee and the redhead turned and grabbed two more lobsters from the tray. CeeCee slapped hers down onto the steel table with a crack and viciously tore it apart. She glared back at Anne and tossed the dismembered parts into a tray. Bernie led Anne to another station.

"A couple of hotheads. Don't pay them any mind."

Cookie Doherty and three other women worked that table, where the bodies were taken apart. Cookie, it became clear, was a close friend of CeeCee. Kate Chapman, a younger worker, made room for Anne alongside her, and that kept Anne away from any subtle payback Cookie might contemplate.

Anne found work at this station more complex than the previous two. It required several machines and the energy of half a dozen women to complete numerous tasks. First the legs were detached and fed through a wringer machine that squeezed lobster meat from shellcasings. The gib was removed, the body shaken, and the carapace deboned to make delicacies like lobster paste and tomalley.

After several hours on her feet, Anne was exhausted and filthy and smelled of stale lobster. She wanted a shower desperately, but that would be a long while off. The fifteen-minute break was spent with Kate Chapman on an unoccupied bench outside. CeeCee and Cookie and the redhead kept their distance as they shot vengeful glances in their direction.

"Thanks," said Anne.

"For what?" said Kate.

"You know. Giving me a less awkward position at the table." Anne nodded toward Cookie.

"They're okay most of the time. Gave me the gears a bit last year when I was working part-time. But it went away… eventually. Better to steer clear of them altogether if you can. They kinda think they own this place."

Anne took a sidelong glance at the trio. Veteran grumblers,

she thought. Perhaps she should give them a wide berth. Payback wouldn't help finish her job here.

***

CeeCee, Cookie, and the redhead met Anne's glance head-on. They sat on their bench like three crows peering at a bird's egg in an unguarded nest.

"What do ya think she's up to with those notes she's making?" asked CeeCee to no one in particular. Her long bleached hair had been neatly twisted up inside her hairnet. Her dark eyebrows knit together in bewilderment.

"You have to know somebody to get a job like that," said Cookie.

"Those jobs should go to locals," said the redhead. "She probably knows some high-and-mighty from Ontario or someplace."

"You're right there," said Cookie, "but my thought on the matter is that she's here to make us work harder than we do now... and cut jobs... our jobs."

"That sounds about right. That little bitch," said CeeCee.

8.

The rest of Anne's morning was uneventful. The other workers she met were helpful and friendly and she continued to work her way through the production process. Outside of the usual questions about Anne's background, and if she knew this or that person from somewhere, there was little opportunity on day one to dig into questions more pertinent to her investigation. It would draw too much suspicion. And when they weren't probing her history, they were consumed with local gossip, some spicy, some humorous, and some disturbing. Perhaps the most fascinating tidbit centred on the discovery of a dead baby at an abandoned farm a few miles away. Apparently, the baby had been dead for many, many years. Whose baby? Where found? What happened? The air swirled with a blur of names and places. Speculation followed, and this old and mysterious death led Anne to drift into her own thoughts, her continuing struggle with the past—what to leave behind, what to hang onto?

Perhaps some memories had too strong a grip on her, she thought. Perhaps they were keeping her from reaching out for her future. For years, her best friend had been Dit Malone. Over time Anne's feelings had grown toward love for him, but she resisted the impulse. She never really told him how she felt. Perhaps she was uncertain herself. Then it became too late. He married Gwen Fowler, someone who was not uncertain. Later, Ted Billings, a physician, had shown interest. She liked him, but Anne still had the brakes on. Then came an opportunity that Billings couldn't pass up, a chance to do something more significant than family medicine. So with Anne's apparent ambivalence tipping the balance, Ted accepted an offer to join Doctors Without Borders in Syria. His departure brought back memories of Anne's deepest heartbreak, the death of her husband, a war correspondent killed in Kosovo.

More recently, though, Anne felt as if she might be able to park some of her past. She had met someone. Now she felt hope—hope and the possibility that a meaningful relationship may lie ahead. Whenever she saw him, she caught her breath and felt a rush of emotion. Whenever she thought about him, she felt warm, even a little giddy, and found herself smiling at nothing at all.

She scribbled a few notes onto her clipboard and moved down the production line. Two tables were set up for cleaving, splitting, and removing meat from lobster claws. Anne was able to get into the rhythm of that job. She almost enjoyed it.

***

A bell signalled the lunch break. By then, Anne was feeling a bit more confident about her newly learned skills.

She also felt as if she were becoming part of the group. A good deal of that feeling came from the buoyant, good-natured company of women at her lunch table. Enid was one of them. Kate was another. Two or three young and rather new workers sat with them. Enid seemed like a mother figure for Kate, but without the smothering authority that comes with that role. Kate was timid, plain, and unsure of herself. It seemed no time at all before the signal to return to the processing line.

Again, Anne changed tables and joined the "hash pickers." Separating the lobster's knuckle and thumb was tolerable enough, but digging out that knuckle meat was a struggle. Her fingers and hands ached and cramped, and she felt one or two of her joints growing numb. For some of her experienced co-workers, the litany of swear words which slipped involuntarily from Anne's mouth became their unexpected amusement and pleasant diversion.

The second-last stage of processing, tail splitting, seemed like an afternoon snooze compared to knuckle picking. Then came the last stage, packaging. It varied with each customer's special need and, in this case, packaging was set up for flash freezing two-pound bricks of lobster meat.

When five o'clock struck, most of the girls grabbed their time cards and punched out. A few stayed behind to clean gear, sanitize tables, and hose residue from the floors, but Anne headed straight for the door, fresh air, and a bench to collapse on for a moment or two before heading for the boarding house she'd arranged to stay at. Being on her feet for so many hours was exhausting, and it had been a good many years since she had done such arduous and tedious work.

"You get used to it," said Kate as she exited the factory and joined Anne on the bench. Kate knew how Anne felt. It had been a year since her first day at the plant. Kate had just left high school.

Anne lifted her head up for the first time. CeeCee passed at just that moment.

"Did anyone time *you* today? See how you'd like it," she said.

Anne was too worn out to reply. Kate scowled at CeeCee as she passed but said nothing. "She's got a point," said Anne. "It's tough work. I work out a lot at the gym, but it's not the same."

A steady stream of vehicles sped out of the parking lot and roared up the road toward Halkirk and points beyond. Kate walked slowly with Anne toward the remaining cars.

"You going tonight?" asked Kate.

"Where?" said Anne.

"To the dance."

Anne looked up in surprise. "Oh, god, no. I haven't been to a dance in years."

"It's at the community centre just outside Halkirk. Live band on Saturdays. It's fun."

"I've had enough excitement for one day. Oh crap!" Anne stopped in her tracks and stared at her car. Four flat tires. "Crap! Crap! Crap! What the hell am I going to do now? Four friggin' flats!"

"Don't worry," said Kate looking at her watch. "Mossey's Garage. They're open until five-thirty. They'll fix you up in a jiff... I can drive you over there right now."

Misery and frustration faded from Anne's face. "Thanks. Let me grab my suitcase first."

Anne grabbed her travel bag from the front passenger side. As she did, she noticed a folded handbill under the wiper blade. She slipped it into her pocket, tossed a suitcase into Kate's back seat, and got in.

"All set," said Anne, "and thanks."

As Kate pulled out of the parking lot, Anne turned and looked down at the line of wharves. The harbour had grown as quiet and still as a picture postcard. Only a few movements caught her eye.

"Who are those guys?" she asked.

Kate swung her head quickly down and back again. "Just a couple of old fellas from the area. The big guy is Fig. The scrawny one is Squeak. The short one is Spit."

"A lot of nicknames around here, aren't there? You got one?" Anne asked.

Kate looked at Anne a bit startled. Her face grew bright red. "No," she said and turned her attention to the road, "But you may get one before you leave Little Rose."

***

Kate pulled up to the door of Mossey's Garage. Anne's face screwed up with concern.

"It'll be okay," said Kate, and added, "Anne, won't you come to the dance tonight? I don't want to go by myself. Please!"

"I'll think about it, but I really doubt that I'll be up to it tonight. I'm worn out."

Please... please, I'd really like company," said Kate. "Can I call you? Maybe you'll change your mind."

Anne felt the burden of Kate's inability to recognize the subtleties of "no."

"You can call me... but the answer will be the same."

"Okay, I'll call... and thanks."

Anne's eyes rolled in frustration. "Anyway, thanks for the ride," she added.

Bob Mossey's Garage in Halkirk could have been the setting for a 1930s period movie. The pumps in front looked like they hadn't been used in twenty years. The building itself looked abandoned. The white paint on its wood frame was stained and peeling. A crumbling concrete pedestal marked the spot where something had once stood, and the remains of disfigured cars and rusting truck frames lay strewn across the asphalt pavement of a nearby lot.

Inside, a small woodstove would have pumped heat fuelled by a few sticks of kindling during cold spring mornings. Along the wall a half-dozen grey and balding heads would have perched side by side on metal chairs, sipping coffee and sizing up other locals popping in with news or gossip or car repairs.

Today, however, the stove was cold and the chairs empty. Bob Mossey was about to close up for the day when Anne walked in.

Bob Mossey was a short man, surprisingly bright-eyed for late afternoon, and he moved with a gait that belied a workman in his eighties. Nor did he waste time. No sooner had Anne explained her dilemma than he hopped into his truck and drove off, leaving her standing alongside her luggage and with assurance that her vehicle would be looked at straightaway.

9.

Late Afternoon, Village of Halkirk

The name Halkirk Manor would generate more cachet than a lodge called Finnerty's Boarding House and, because it had such an impressive Victorian façade, ample rooms, and a historical connection to a renowned ship's captain, Jane Finnerty rebranded it with the upscale title.

The day before, Anne had phoned for reservations. Now, she toted her luggage the short walk from Mossey's Garage to Halkirk Manor. She mounted the manor's steps to a spacious veranda, and Miss Finnerty, the proprietor, greeted her as she pushed open the heavy, engraved wooden front door.

Miss Jane Finnerty was a spinster in her mid-fifties and reputed to be a fountainhead of local gossip. Jane smiled a rather polite smile, more businesslike than cordial. She stood taller than Anne and bent stiffly at the waist to shake hands.

"Welcome to Halkirk Manor," she said, "but I thought you had a car."

Anne mentioned a minor breakdown and that it was being taken care of.

"I see," she said. "Anything serious, dearie?"

"I hope not," said Anne. Jane paused expectantly for more. Anne looked down at her luggage and back up at Jane.

"Oh, of course. I'll show you to your room. Right this way, please."

Jane Finnerty was neither an attractive woman, nor a homely one. She had long brown hair, pulled gently back and fastened into a loose roll. Her nose was long and narrow with a prominent bump just below the eyeline. Her mouth was broad, her lips thin and tight. Her most striking feature was her eyes, luminous hazel with yellow-green flecks of gold that drew envious attention but left dissatisfaction because her eyes lacked engagement. They peered back softly and intently, but rarely blinked or divulged feeling. They were hungry eyes, those of a bird of prey, Anne thought.

Anne was impressed by the layout of the manor's lobby. The receiving area was roomy. A rather broad staircase lay straight ahead. To her left was what looked like a sitting room. To her right was a dining area dominated by a long wooden table covered with linen. The table was set for six. At the foot of the staircase and to the right Anne saw a small desk and receiving area. Behind that was a door that Anne presumed led to the kitchen and pantry and some closets.

Jane guided Anne to the desk.

"How long do you plan on staying in the area, dearie?"

"It's undecided. I'll pay for five days in advance, if that's all right, Ms. Finnerty."

"Please. Call me Jane. We don't stand on formalities around here. Let me see. Five days at eighty dollars a day... plus tax... puts it at four sixty. Meals are extra, but I'll just add them to your bill when you check out."

Anne pulled out a card from her wallet. "Debit," said Anne.

Ms. Finnerty looked down her nose. "That's your charge card, dearie, and I'm sorry, but we've had problems with Interac and cheques recently. So we only accept cash now. If you don't have the full amount, you can give me the balance when the banks open Monday."

For a moment Anne felt rather stupid and confused.

Anne stared at her wallet. The positions of the debit and credit cards had been reversed, something she had never done, something she would not do, all of which suggested that someone had been into her wallet recently. The unanswered question was why—idle curiosity, basic nosiness, or distrust of her motives for being at the factory—and who.

Ms. Finnerty may have suspected Anne suffered from some degree of slow-wittedness because of her sluggish reply to the suggestion for cash payment. Finally, however, Anne extracted three hundred dollars from a zippered compartment and handed it to Jane.

"I'll need a proper receipt for tax purposes," said Anne coolly.

"Of course, dearie. No problem at all," she said, scribbling out a receipt from a tablet of blanks on her desk. "And thank you for your understanding. Will you be dining here this evening?"

"Yes, I believe so."

"We serve dinner at six sharp. Breakfast starts at seven. I'll show you to your room."

Anne's room was one of five on the second floor. It was spacious and decorated in a twentieth-century motif. The bed was a large four-poster. The chairs, dresser, and side table were Depression-era pieces. The bathroom was cramped, but it had a shower stall. Anne flung herself onto the bed for a moment or two and then headed for a long, steamy wash-up.

The shower was exhilarating. The hot water cascaded off her shoulders and sounded like laughter, falling onto the tiles below. The shampoo foamed and the soap lathered and Anne scrubbed and washed away the smell of sweat and fish and the stress of a difficult day. Even the needlelike drill of the showerhead was invigorating. It made her feel alive and purposeful, and her mind drifted toward the expectation of feeling pretty and even being desired once again.

She slipped on a pair of jeans and a fresh, button-up, red-checkered shirt and rolled up the sleeves a bit. She blow-dried her hair. The conditioner had left a bit of sheen that caught in the lowering afternoon light through the window. Her brown hair had some natural curl to it. Two hair clips held it loosely along the sides of her face and let it tumble down the back of her neck and onto her shoulders. She looked in the mirror. Human again, she thought, then sighed and smiled.

With the restoration of normality and the affirmation of humanity, however, came the obligations of employment. Her eyes fell upon the clipboard she'd carelessly tossed on the chair. That triggered a reminder that she needed to make a call. She picked up the phone on her bed stand. A light on the receiver lit as she did so. She began to dial a Charlottetown number, hesitated, and returned the phone to its cradle. She fumbled through a pile of clothes on the dresser, found her cellphone, and dialed the same number again.

"M. Gauthier & Son. Hello," said the voice at the other end.

"Mr. Gauthier, please."

"This is Mr. Gauthier. Who is this?" he asked.

Anne looked skeptically at the phone in her hand. Then she heard confusion in the background.

A new voice came on the line, this time a more familiar one. "Anne, this is Jean. I'm putting you on speakerphone. You were talking to my father a moment ago. Okay, go ahead."

"Misters Gauthier, both of you. Just checking in. So far no one has questioned my cover story."

"Bernie is accepting the situation?"

"Seems to be still in the dark so far."

"And you're sure that's the way you want it?"

"Absolutely."

"And the workers?"

Anne heard something unexpected near her door. A minuscule sound, difficult to identify.

"And the workers?" Jean Gauthier asked a second time.

"Oh... most are pretty tolerant or ready to roll with the punches. Three or four have their noses out of joint, but I'm guessing it will work out. Too early for big ideas or real progress, but I'm confident the job can be completed in a week. I'm coming to Charlottetown late tomorrow to fill in some blanks. Is that okay?"

"Sounds good. Look forward to it. Dad will be here, too. He'll likely help out any way he can."

Anne's ears always perked at small noises that seemed out of place. She thought she heard something again. A squeaking sound. And it was nearby.

"Gotta go," said Anne softly as she disconnected. But she continued talking into the phone. A bit louder now.

Jane Finnerty held her ear close to the door to Anne's room. She had seen the flicker of the light on the switchboard at the main desk and was overcome by curiosity. It seems she was always overcome with curiosity.

Time and again Jane's mother had railed against her daughter with the old proverb "Curiosity killed the cat," but, fact is, inquisitiveness had fed Jane quite well over the years. Jane had grown quite plump with gossip. In her younger years it had made her popular as a prime source of "dirt" on locals. Later, Jane realized that knowledge of comings and goings-on is power. And some knowledge can be most profitable if not broadcast over the countryside.

Anne rambled on to an imaginary Mr. Gauthier.

"Yes, I'll look at that report when I get back to town. When will that be? Soon... That's right... Maybe even tomorrow... Be sure you have all the supporting documents you need. The accountants are sticklers for detail, and they may want multiple copies. Oh... and don't forget that authorization..."

As she spoke, Anne had been walking slowly toward the door to her room.

Jane noticed a slight increase in Anne's voice and surmised that she was growing nearer. When neither fight nor flight is a wise choice, pre-emption often is. So Jane firmly knocked on Anne's door.

When Anne opened it, she still held the cellphone to her ear. She looked quizzically at Jane Finnerty.

"Didn't mean to disturb you, Ms. Brown."

"We'll talk later, sir," said Anne and pressed the icon to end her call. "What can I do for you, Ms. Finnerty?"

"Just wanted to make sure that everything in the room was satisfactory... and to tell you that dinner's in fifteen minutes."

***

Anne made a second call on her cellphone, this time a real one, to her daughter Jacqueline. She had no misgivings about her daughter's ability to look after herself while she was away. Anne just wanted to hear a friendly voice, one that she could feel at ease with. It was just the tonic she needed after her own day of impersonating someone she was not. Afterwards Anne sorted her dirty clothes into a bag for cleaning and, in doing so, she found the folded handbill she'd taken from her windshield. She opened it. But it was no handbill. Bold hand-printed words read, "STOP. GO HOME OR ELSE." Anne sat on the edge of her bed and pondered its meaning. Did it refer to her work as an industrial engineer? Or could it mean that someone had discovered her real purpose in being at Little Rose Harbour? Anne felt a growing unease.

Anne dawdled longer than the prescribed fifteen minutes, only to find that she was the last boarder to enter the dining room. Serving dishes and large bowls already were circulating counterclockwise around the table. Anne felt a bit embarrassed; more so when Jane tossed her a schoolmarm scowl that bespoke the sin of tardiness.

"Sorry," she said and took the only remaining seat.

"Well, well. You'll not be getting dessert then, will ya?" said Enid with a wink at Anne.

"I have to watch my weight, anyway," said Anne with a forced laugh and a glance toward the reddening face of Jane.

"Our new guest is Anne Brown," Jane said to the diners. "She'll be here for just under a week or so, and perhaps joining us for meals as well. Anne, this is Enid Clements."

"Yes, I met Enid at the factory. She introduced me to work on the cooker."

"And the gentlemen here include Jack Pine, a Newfoundlander who came to work locally a few years back..."

"G'day," said Jack.

"...and Tom Edison Bean. Tom was a fisherman in his heyday. Now he's an inventor."

Anne and Tom nodded toward each other.

"Men of few words," said Enid, "and a godsend for that," she added.

Then everyone dug into their dinner before it cooled. The main dish was fried breaded haddock. Each guest received one fillet, but there were ample boiled potatoes and turnip. The biscuits were fresh, molasses on the side. Dessert was jello topped with a tablespoon of whipped cream. The coffee was fresh and the tea properly steeped. Anne had never acquired a serious taste for tea, traditional or herbal, but coffee was just the stimulation she needed at that moment.

Conversation continued over hot cups. Jane led.

"So, Anne, I know you work at the factory, but what exactly do you do there?"

"I'm only there temporarily. I'm an industrial engineer doing some research for the owners."

"Research... I see," she replied with a hint of confusion. "What kind of research would they require after all these years?"

"The owners are new. So I suppose they're looking for ways to improve production... efficiency... quality... things of that sort."

"Is your husband able to make up for your absence on his end?"

"I'm a widow, but I have a daughter... almost grown now."

Anne began to sense that Jane's line of questioning was developing into something more than idle chitchat.

"Is Brown your single name, dearie?"

"No, it's not."

"You do have Island roots, though."

"Distant ones, but what about you? Is there a Mr. Finnerty about?"

Jane shook her head, and her lips formed to ask another question, but Anne, tired of Jane's probe for information, took the initiative.

"The reason I ask, Jane, is that you have such beautiful eyes.

They must have tempted one or two handsome young men."

"More than one or two, I should think," said Jack Pine with a snicker he instantly regretted.

"And just what d'ya mean by that?" Jane said, rising up out of her chair like a snake preparing to strike.

"Didn't mean a t'ing, luv. I'm just sayin' that you musta been some pretty years ago... and still are... still are, if I do say so me-self."

"Well, if everyone's finished, I got dishes to clear away... and not all evening to do it." Jane loosed an indignant grunt. Her brow darkened, and she noisily snatched two empty serving dishes from the table and made for the kitchen.

10.

Enid, Jack, and Tom hastily fled the dining room and the flaring eyes of Ms. Jane Finnerty for the relative safety of the veranda. Not wanting to be abandoned, Anne followed and shut the front door behind her.

It had been a very warm day, and now it had become a most pleasant evening. The boarders felt content at the end of their work week. Anne felt content on a full stomach and the freshness of her shower still lingering. A light coastal breeze filtered around Halkirk Manor carrying the scent of the sea and early summer flowers. A few passersby waved; some spoke; others paused and relayed news that had not yet made the rounds.

"Did ya hear," said one, "that George Halloway got drunk and wrecked his car last night? Ran into the Mounties, he did. I mean he drove right into the side of their patrol car on Main Street. Dumbest thing ever."

"Dumbest thing I ever heard," said Tom to Jack, "was this fella over Cardigan way. Stole a farmer's horse, but the horse didn't take to him. It bit him and run off. So then the fella thinks he's been cheated, and he takes the farmer to Small Claims Court for damages and loss of wages."

"Evenin', Jack," hollered another. "S'pose ya heard that Jay Dee got boarded by Fisheries? Caught him with undersized lobster... for the second time."

"He'll get a good fine for that, now," said Jack, and added, "They say he's been fishin' others' traps, plus his own. I think he's 'bout due to be fetched up good."

"It's quite a news service here," said Anne and looked at Enid with an amused grin.

"Most of it will make the *Eastern Graphic* by Wednesday, but the juiciest news wants to move faster than the speed of type or good sense, if you ask me."

"I kind of sensed that on the production line. It was hard to break the ice with the girls when the hot topic was that dead baby they uncovered near here."

"Something juicier will replace it come Monday. Mark my words."

"How long have you worked at the factory, Enid?"

"Been there near thirty years now."

"Then you must be looking forward to retiring soon."

"Retirement is for people with government jobs. They can retire. The rest of us work," she said with a wink and a chuckle.

"That must be a worry."

"It is if a person thinks much about it, which I don't. No point worrying on what you can't change."

"Seen a lot of changes over the years?"

"Oh my, yes... good and bad."

"Someone mentioned that the factory almost didn't open this year."

"Would have been a real hardship if it had happened. Thank god they took care of it quick."

"Took care of what?"

"Frozen pipes and water damage... a lot of it."

"An accident?"

"So they say."

"Is that what you think?"

"Accidents happen, but this seemed more than an accident to me."

"Why do you say that?"

"Take Millie Smith, for example. She don't drive in the winter.

She lays her car up in her garage in November and doesn't drive it again until March. Now, if her car catches fire in February, how likely is that an accident?"

"Are there many *accidents* like that at the factory?"

"Over the years there's more than one would expect."

"Why would that be?"

"I've got curiosities, but not many thoughts on that topic... but what about you? Family... boyfriend?"

"I have a daughter, nearly grown. I'm a widow..."

"And boyfriend?"

"I'm working on that, Enid. I'm working on it," said Anne. "What's the story on Ms. Finnerty? "A bit of a strange bird, is she?"

"Dearie?"

Anne looked puzzled. Enid clarified.

"They call Jane 'Dearie.' For obvious reasons. Not to her face, of course. If I called her that, I'd be driven out and looking for new quarters. She doesn't take to criticism well. Now I'd best be going in," she said.

Enid departed. Anne was left in the company of Tom Edison Bean and Jack Pine, who were still mulling over news on the grapevine. Anne was content just to listen for a while. Finally the conversation turned to mutual interest when Jane Finnerty's name was mentioned.

Anne hadn't pried much out of Enid, so she thought she'd try the men.

"What's the story on Jane Finnerty?" she asked, her eyes fixed at a point halfway between the two men. Both looked at each other, but Jack began first.

"She's a strange one, she is. A bit like a cat. She purrs nice when she wants something, but is just as likely to scratch if ya even t'ink about crossin' her."

"I'll say one thing for 'er. She knows what's goin' on around here. She knows it all," said Tom.

"That's right. No doubt about that," said Jack.

Mossey's Garage was within sight of Halkirk Manor. As Anne wondered about the fate of her car and the dreaded repair bill, she watched Bob Mossey lock his front door and head toward the boarding house. A set of keys dangled in his hand, and he jingled a steady beat with them as he strode over.

"Here ya go, Missy. Car's fixed. Doors locked. You're good to go."

"That's great, Bob. How much do I owe you?"

Bob thought for a second and said, "Ten dollars will do."

Anne looked surprised.

"Ten dollars?"

"Ten dollars," said Bob. "There was nothin' to it, missy. The tires was just deflated... not slashed. I just charged ya for the service call and to put some free air in. It was just a message you were gettin'."

"How do you mean?"

"It was a warnin' more 'n' anything else, ya see. If your tires was cut, now that'd be another story altogether."

"This happen often?"

"Oh, I sees it from time t' time," he said, pocketed the tenner, and strutted away with the swagger and nimbleness of a twenty-year-old.

"Nice fella," said Anne.

"The very best," said Jack. Tom nodded.

"You have family, Tom?"

"They've all passed," he said reflectively. He seemed to drift away. His hands lay folded over a prominent belly. His face was a kind one but with a fullness that made his eyes almost vanish from his face. A web of red capillaries coloured his cheeks.

"How'd you come by your name... Tom Edison?"

He stirred a bit and slowly returned. "It was my father's doing. My father had a great admiration for that American inventor. My father was a tinkerer himself. He turned out new gizmos and refined old devices. Useful things. People were more resourceful then. If they had a problem, they fixed it themselves or found somebody local... like my father... to do it. I picked up his talent, and now I tinker in a corner of Jane's basement, but there's not much call for my skills, nowadays."

"And you, Jack... what do you do?"

"I just fish. It's what I always done in Newfoundland, and now I duz it here."

"You have your own boat?"

"Naw... I works as a hand on Hec Dunne's vessel, *Hell to Pay*... and have done for five years."

"Family?"

"Me wife run off. I come here wid m' daughter, Alvina, but she grew a wild streak, too. She run off a couple years ago."

"I'm sorry to hear that."

"But I knows where she's at. She's living wid another girl not far from here and works at the restaurant. We talk the odd time, but she has her own ways now."

Anne's phone vibrated against her side and rang a musical phrase. She looked at the caller name. It was Kate. She answered.

"Hi, Kate. What's up?"

Kate wanted Anne to go to the dance.

Kate's voice was excited. "It starts at nine and gets rolling by eleven. You'll love it. Lots of nice people there. Cute guys, too. Maybe you'll meet somebody interesting. Can't go wrong. It'll be a nice way to wind down from work, won't it? I'll drive. Please..."

Anne felt sorry for Kate, who seemed to have few close friends locally. But Anne was adamant and dragged out her best arguments for having a lazy Saturday night right where she was now.

"Thanks for the invite. Love to go but too tired after work. Just starting to recover. Have I told you that I've just started seeing somebody? Maybe another time, okay? Just not tonight. Thanks again, Kate, but no. Really."

No line of reasoning could convince Anne. None. And she made that as clearly and as politely to Kate as she could.

11.

Evening, Local Community Centre

Kate drove her car as if she were a novice. She sat ramrod straight, both hands gripping the wheel, her eyes floating attentively from road to rear-view mirrors and back to the road. Her full attention grappled with the consequential job of driving. All of which made Anne quite nervous.

"So glad you could make it!" said Kate. "Don't know if I coulda come by myself. You wouldn't think so, but I'm rather shy when it comes to social events. Especially dances. I never know quite what to do or say. I get frazzled, and then stupid things come tumbling out of my mouth."

"How long have you been driving?"

"Just a year," said Kate. "How am I doing?" She looked over at Anne, and her car began to drift toward the edge of the pavement.

"Keep your eyes on the road," said Anne with repressed panic, jabbing a finger toward the road ahead and clutching the edge of her seat.

"Oops, sorry," she said, easing back into the middle of her lane. "Anyway, glad you're here."

Anne wished she could have shared that sentiment, but she was a sucker for begging and pleading by people she liked, and she liked Kate, as socially awkward as she was. So, when she called the second time that evening, Anne gave way to her unrelenting appeals and uncorked desperation. Anne agreed to accompany Kate. As a consolation, though, she convinced herself that she might have a bit of fun and maybe, with a little luck, even learn something that might help her complete the job she was hired to do.

It was a ten-minute drive from the small community of Halkirk to the dance near the town of Montague. The number of vehicles peppering the parking lot suggested they had arrived at the correct location. Kate had called it the "community centre," but it was located in no particular community that Anne could perceive.

The building itself was a large old wood-frame structure that at some time could have served as hardware store, school, warehouse, or even a small manufacturing facility.

Music seeped through the old walls of the community centre and spilled into the parking lot as Anne and Kate walked toward the broad veranda out front. A large poster on a notice board proclaimed the appearance of the *Eastern Bandits*, a four-piece combo that played a mix of country and rock tunes. As the women reached the portico to the community centre, an overhanging light shone down on them. Anne noticed that Kate had shed the plainness she had cloaked herself in at the factory. She now looked rather pretty, thought Anne. At the same time, Anne felt suddenly quite out of place.

Anne slipped through the doorway and into the hall. A rack of amplifiers pumped out lively music. The place was crowded, and the hubbub inside was overwhelming. There was a five-dollar cover charge. Anne paid for both of them. Kate's lips moved, but Anne could hear neither Kate's protest at Anne's generosity, nor the thank you that followed. The band closed their set with Toby Keith's "I Love This Bar," backed up by a number of drunken regulars adding their own discordant howls. Then the band laid down their instruments and slipped out a side door for a cool draft of air, cigarettes, beer, and whisky.

Long ago Anne had acquired the practice of becoming very

aware of her surroundings wherever she travelled. Perhaps it was a skill she'd acquired from years on a soccer field as a teen or her work as an insurance investigator or as a detective with Darby Investigations. Perhaps it was innate curiosity or simply a prudent habit for a single woman to keep safe. In any event, to do so had become second nature.

They had passed the service bar as they entered. Now it swarmed with patrons buying refills before the band mounted the stage for another set. A couple of dozen customers pressed against the rail, vying for the attention of harried bartenders and waitresses. Beyond the bar a bank of slot machines entertained customers, held rapt by the cheery jingles and promises of a win on the next pull of a mechanical handle. A collection of sixteen tables filled the mid-section. All were occupied. Small groups gathered along the wall or between tables. The chatter was jovial, the laughing alcohol-fed, the mood one of coy flirtations and less-guarded sobriety. The bandstand stood stark and empty but for three guitars and a drum kit glittering in the undimmed spotlight. An atmosphere of damp heat and light perspiration hung about the place, and a dissonant mix of perfume and aftershave wound its way through the crowd of partiers.

Kate returned from the bar with two glasses. She handed one to Anne.

"Are you sure you don't want a real drink?" she said. "You can let loose if you want to. After all, I'm driving, right?"

"I'm fine," said Anne. "I like the band... I mean what I've heard so far."

"They're great... draw a big crowd whenever they play here. Not too much of that droney old-time country stuff. More upbeat. Contemporary."

While they chatted, Anne's eyes methodically scanned the crowd. Bernie White, the factory foreman, was the first familiar face she spotted. During the break he had slipped into an empty seat in front of a hungry gaming machine. He pumped a fistful of coins into the slot. He looked up once, saw Anne, and waved casually.

Most of the party crowd's age ranged between mid-twenties and forty. Anne was at the high end of that spectrum but, in the dim light, she appeared no older than thirty. Even in natural light, there was little to betray her age beyond a few wrinkles in the corners of her eyes and the absence of that rosy youthful blush in her cheeks. For this good fortune she was thankful, though she realized it was due to good genes more so than any patented cosmetic or Eastern spiritual regime. Much to her daughter Jacqueline's consternation, though, Anne sometimes still passed as Jacqueline's older sister.

They headed toward a small table deep inside the crowded room and, just as they reached it, Anne felt a jolt. Someone had collided with her from behind.

"Oh, god, I'm sorry," he said. A bit of Anne's drink had sloshed over the side of her glass and spilled on her wrist and dribbled onto the floor. Anne looked up.

The man standing in front of her was handsome. Tall, broad, glistening teeth, square jaw, an inviting smile.

"Didn't see you there. Sorry. Can I buy you a replacement? Get you something to dry your hand?" Kate had already pulled a tissue from her pocket and handed it to Anne.

"No. I'm fine. Thanks, anyway."

"Later then?" he said, turned and moved on through the crowd, looking back once.

"Who's he?" The question just slipped out of her mouth, and she winced at the eagerness that coloured it.

"That's Hec Dunne. It's another way of saying 'trouble.'"

"Oh," said Anne.

**

Several women nestled against the bar across the room. One of them was Cookie Doherty.

"Whatcha lookin' at?" Cookie asked, nudging CeeCee. Cookie was a tall and lanky woman with a bumpy figure. Her head was large and her features quite small, leaving a face *poorly populated with pretty furniture*, a local wit once said.

CeeCee Dunne had been keeping a close eye on her husband. CeeCee had good reason to watch him, but Cookie felt ignored. She had been midway through a muttered condemnation of one of the waitresses.

"That gang over there," said CeeCee.

"Who... where?"

"Over there," she said. Her voice carried an undercurrent of annoyance. "There," she said again. "The gudgeon's here."

Cookie looked puzzled. CeeCee smirked.

"The gudgeon... that Anne Brown one... over there with mate-less Kate. Hec was just talking to them. What's he talking with them for?"

***

While gazing around at the crowd, Anne spotted something odd, a woman staring at her. Anne didn't recognize her at first and couldn't account for her scowl, but eventually Anne realized the woman was CeeCee, the disgruntled co-worker who had belittled her on the production line. Stripped of shapeless factory clothes and dressed for a good time, CeeCee looked different, but her glare suggested unresolved bitterness. Anne pondered the temperament behind the scowl and wondered if that hostile appearance would fuel hostile actions. Anne also wondered whether her decision to come to the dance had been a worse mistake than she could have predicted.

Anne and Kate moved farther into the community centre, closer to the bandstand. Anne sat with her back to the bar purposefully to avoid direct eye contact with CeeCee or her friends, something she suspected might provoke an awkward scene.

After the band had begun another set, Anne was able to put CeeCee out of her mind. Kate and Anne freshened their Coke and ice drinks. They settled into the music, light conversation, and laughs, but Anne flinched when she felt an unexpected damp hand on her shoulder.

A young man stood behind her. He asked her to dance. When Anne looked back at the table, she saw Kate looking very alone and rather fidgety. Anne felt bad for Kate, and she sat out the next few dances to keep her company. They chatted. Then someone asked Kate up on the dance floor.

Another damp tap on Anne's shoulder. This time it was a pig farmer from Cardigan. Anne felt sure she'd caught an unpleasant whiff of farmyard from his shoes. His dancing style was rough and bouncy, and he managed to tread on her foot more than once. Anne elected to sit out the next one, but she scarcely had returned to her seat before another man asked her to dance. His name was Arnold. Arnold was a roofer from New Perth. He was a pleasant fellow, young, short on talk, awkward with women, over-schooled in politeness. They walked to the dance floor, now crowded with a dozen other couples. He danced timidly, a half beat behind the music. Casually, Anne mentioned her daughter, Jacqueline, now in high school. There was an awkward silence at the end of the song, and Arnold walked her back to her chair. She thanked him but, before he faded away, she said, "And this is Kate Chapman. She's a good friend. Perhaps you know each other from school. You're both almost the same age. Where's the ladies' room?"

Kate pointed. Anne left quickly, hoping that one of them would pick up the thread of conversation she had left dangling there.

Anne walked back toward the bar. The ladies' room was down a corridor to the left. She saw a short lineup at the door. Anne was in no hurry, so, when she glanced around and saw Bernie White still at the gaming machine, she strolled over to him.

"Hey, Bernie. How are you this evening?"

"Just fine," he said without taking his eyes from the screen. "You?"

"Great. Thought I'd take a look at the local nightlife. Meet a few people."

Bernie grunted an acknowledgement.

"You winning... or losing?"

Bernie pointed to a tally on the screen.

"That's more than I had when I started. So I guess I'm winning."

"You'll be a loser before you leave," said a playful voice behind

Anne. She felt a large muscular arm drape around her shoulder and give her an affectionate squeeze.

Anne smelled liquor on his breath and pulled away, far enough to see who was behind her. She saw wavy brown hair and a formidable build. He was handsome, self-confident to the point of vanity, and charming. At the same time, Anne could not help but view Hec Dunne now with as much disdain as awe.

Bernie, not to be outdone by the wisecrack, fired back, "Hec, I could lose everything but my shirt in the next hour... and still be better off than you ever dreamed of."

Hec laughed. "Wanna bet?" he said.

"Go away, Hec. You've got bad karma. You'll throw my game off."

"I didn't come over here to talk to you. Me and the little lady here are just havin' a polite talk, aren't we, hon'? In fact, I sense that we've got plenty in common. Why don't we have a talk about that?"

Anne looked up into his eyes. They were beautiful, bright, alert, moist brown eyes. She undraped his arm from her shoulder. She had remembered Kate's warning that he was trouble.

"Good line, Hec. I bet it works magic around here... but... I'm not from around here."

The wait for the ladies' room had dwindled, and Anne headed that way without looking back. Anne remained inside and hoped that Hec would lose interest or that his train of thought would jump the rails with another drink. Anne loitered there until she heard a few anxious raps on the door.

She peered cautiously up the corridor. The coast was clear of trouble.

12.

CeeCee left the community centre while the Eastern Bandits took their third break. It had been steamy inside, and the cool early summer breeze was invigorating. It cleared her head and steadied her on her feet. She felt almost sober, but that was not necessarily a good feeling tonight.

She spotted old Newton Grant loitering in the shadows and leaning up against his pickup truck. Spit and Squeak were smoking inside the cab.

"Fig," she said, "whatcha got?"

"Pints and jars."

"A pint then. How much?"

"Fifteen, tax included," he said with a smirk.

CeeCee's fingers lost themselves in her purse, fumbled, and surfaced again with a couple of crumpled bills.

After she re-entered the community centre, CeeCee vanished into the ladies' room and primped in front of a mirror. She had drifted a good distance from the naïve pretty girl she had been as a youth. She had grown more and more wild, and wild things often attract others for the basest of reasons. Much of the time, she could run a straight course. Others times she strayed into unfamiliar waters. Hec Dunne was one of those "other times." Pregnancy had followed, producing a boy, cut from the same cloth as his father. The second was a girl, an apple not fallen too far from her side of the tree. CeeCee felt guilty that she didn't like the girl. She tried, but the girl was too much like herself, another mirror she had to look at. Another life heading down the same dead ends that fate had fashioned for her.

CeeCee was heavier now, after two pregnancies, after boom-and-bust diets, after a husband still sowing oats in neighbouring fields. Her once lovely, firm skin had turned blotchy. More makeup diffused the flaws. She grimaced at seeing the dark roots of her hair. She'd have to fix that, she thought. And the blonde curls were losing their hold in the hot, sticky interior of the community centre.

She looked in the mirror again, felt sad, and pulled the un-labelled pint bottle from her purse. She put it to her lips and swallowed. The liquor burned. Her face twisted from its sharp bite. Then she felt a warm current trickle through her body and seep into her limbs. It dulled her feelings and enlivened her imagination.

***

"She's at it again," said Cookie just as CeeCee returned to the bar. Cookie had saved her bar stool. "She's at it again," said Cookie a second time, a bit louder.

"What the hell are you raggin' on about?" said CeeCee.

"The... gudgeon. She's been puttin' the move on Hec. Right over there," Cookie pointed. "He had his arm around her. She's a bold one, isn't she?"

"I don't see him," said CeeCee.

"I don't know where he is now, but they were getting chummy right over there in the corner near the gaming machines. See. Right there by Bernie. He saw it all, too. Ask him if you don't believe me," she said and turned sulkily toward her drink on the bar. "Just trying to help. That's all I was tryin' to do," she muttered.

"Bernie! You seen Hec," CeeCee hollered.

Bernie just nodded.

"Who was with him?"

"Don't recall. I got my own business to mind."

"Who was with him?"

Intimidation and anger salted CeeCee's words like a fresh wound. Bernie caught the nuance. He didn't want a row with her. It'd probably dampen his luck. Besides, he had successfully sidestepped most employee entanglements in the past. He didn't want to change things now.

"Coulda been anybody. Don't recall for sure. Didn't pay much attention."

"That little weasel is trying to cover for Hec," she said to Cookie. "Where's the gudgeon?"

Cookie pointed again to a table where Anne and Kate were seated. The women could barely be seen behind the growing crowd that had gathered in between. CeeCee's anger smouldered. She imagined Hec and Anne planning some sordid deception. She imagined them together at some rendezvous, maybe tomorrow or maybe even tonight.

"That bitch is going to get what she deserves. She can't pull that stuff with me."

CeeCee roughly pushed away from her bar stool. Her forearm nudged a customer's glass of beer. It tumbled, its foamy contents spilling wildly across the counter, her elbow jabbing Cookie's side in the recoil.

Cookie was too overwhelmed by CeeCee's sudden fierceness to stop her, but she managed to grab her before she made too much headway and resolutely guided her down the corridor toward the ladies' room, scolding her along the way.

The ruckus at the counter of the bar attracted little attention. The band had been loud, the music throbbing, and the added harmonies of would-be singers in the hall had become a source of hilarity and the object of mockery from the audience. The waitress was quick with a mop-up, and she treated the beerless customer to a refill.

***

Anne glanced at her watch for the fourth time. She did it furtively. Anne had had her fill of country music and barroom drama, and she kept looking over her shoulder for CeeCee or Hec, people she hoped to avoid.

The truth of the matter was that recently Anne's thoughts always gravitated toward her new "romantic interest." The word "boyfriend" could not yet form itself in her mind. It was as if she couldn't believe that such a state of being was possible for her.

She hadn't known him very long, of course, and that worried her. She wanted an end to the emptiness she'd felt ever since her husband's tragic death so many years ago. She needed it, more so now than ever before. She nudged Kate.

"Maybe we should go soon. I'm getting kind of tired... and it's so hot in here. What do you think?"

"Next break?" said Kate, looking at her watch.

"That sounds good.

"In that case, maybe I'll take a break until the break. It'll be cooler outside. I'm almost soaked through."

"I'll join you in a bit. I think Arnold's hovering."

"Good luck."

Anne pushed through the veranda door and strode onto the porch. The cool air and a light southerly breeze felt wonderful, and her thoughts drifted to where he and she had walked hand in hand along Charlottetown streets and through city parks not too many days ago. She gave her imagination free rein to transport her there again and recreate the path down which their intimate talks had taken them. She reached into the heart of that experience again. It warmed her. She felt a ripple of apprehension and a thrill of excitement.

The veranda of the community centre was empty now. A half moon hung in the southern sky. It had been bright and vivid earlier, but a wave of damp air had muted it. Now it bore a haze, and it had acquired a mysterious quality. Anne wondered whether the moon was waxing or waning, and that led her to question whether, in her own life, the affection she recently felt would grow stronger... or fade slowly away, and for a moment Anne could feel his arms gently encircle her waist.

Only they weren't *his* arms. And it jarred her from her reverie.

"Hey, babe, beautiful night, isn't it?"

Anne turned and stared once again into the eyes of Hector Dunne. Hec's eyes had lost their former glimmer. Now they were bleary and slow to respond.

"Let go," Anne said in surprise. But Hec did not let go. Instead, the arms encircling her waist were pulling her closer. His stance was unsteady, and she caught stale alcohol on his breath. His arms caressed her sides, and his hands explored the curve below her waist and then drifted with an assuredness up under her arms toward her breasts.

Anne felt a rush of panic and pushed him sharply back. Hec looked surprised and offended.

"Now why would you do that? It was just a little bit of fun," he said.

The entrance door clanged open. CeeCee burst across the threshold. She looked quickly about, and her watery eyes landed on Hec and Anne, still too close to one another for idle conversation.

"Hec Dunne, what the hell are you doin' out here... with her?"

"Not a thing, hon'. She was comin' out and I was comin' in. We just kinda ran into each other."

"You think I believe that, you lyin' two-faced sonofabitch?"

CeeCee strode angrily but somewhat shakily toward him. Anne stepped back a few steps so that Hec was between her and CeeCee. Then, when CeeCee had backed Hec against the porch banister with a prodding finger, Anne swept by them both and pushed into the crowded foyer of the community centre. She passed by clusters of partiers chatting and drinking at the threshold to the events room, and stopped at the table where she'd been seated.

"It's time to go," said Anne. Kate looked up at a sober and determined face. "Now," said Anne with an urgency that moved Kate up. She grabbed her purse and followed Anne toward the door. Once again Anne faced a wall of people close to the bar. Between two clusters she caught a glimpse of CeeCee, who had not yet spotted them.

"The ladies' room. Now!" said Anne, and they retreated in that direction. The room was vacant. They locked themselves inside, and Anne explained her predicament to Kate, whose face little by little assumed a troubled expression.

13.

Even after Anne had left the veranda, CeeCee continued to punish Hec with venom and rage. She struck his chest and shoulder and pushed him against the railing. Hec raised his arms to dull her attempts to pummel him, and offered platitudes and excuses which sounded plausible enough, but not enough to deplete the stores of anger, past experience, and suspicion that CeeCee carried with her.

Hec had been through this before. Several times. His marriage had not turned out as he had expected. CeeCee had been untamed and headstrong as a young girl and, at the time, Hec had found that quality rather alluring, and he looked upon CeeCee as a challenge. For Hec it became a personal challenge, like a cowboy's need to break a horse or a fisherman's ambition to land a record catch.

Hec learned too late, however, that there is always another wild horse in the offing and another record catch just beyond his grasp. He realized that CeeCee was a trophy gathering dust. And his marriage dissolved into a drudgery of commonplace duties and responsibilities: thankless tasks, unmanageable children, elusive goals, and a woman dissatisfied with the course of her own life.

Hec freed himself from CeeCee's assault and fled the veranda before anyone stumbled upon the spectacle of CeeCee beating on him. He didn't fear CeeCee so much as becoming the butt of public ridicule. After all, he needed to keep some semblance of respect.

CeeCee let him go. She'd deal with him tomorrow while his head still throbbed from tonight's drinking. Meantime, she had unfinished business. She headed inside.

***

A few minutes later, Kate poked her head outside the door to the ladies' room. Satisfied with what she'd seen so far, she walked farther along the corridor toward the bar. Still no CeeCee. Then Kate saw her heading into the events room. CeeCee appeared to be looking for someone. Probably Anne, thought Kate, and she realized that this could be their window of opportunity, but, by the time she had summoned Anne, CeeCee had doubled back.

Kate and Anne reached the gaming machines near the bar just as CeeCee targeted them. Abandoning civility, CeeCee pushed and shoved a path through the crowd.

"That bitch," she shouted. "I'll throttle the guts out of 'er."

CeeCee bumped and plunged to get through. Drinks sloshed from jarred elbows, customers were cut off, jostled, and knocked against one another as CeeCee barged her way toward Anne. Anne watched her boorish charge with concern and alarm. She had never been in a barroom brawl. Nor had she ever seen one involving women. And there was something so surreal about the phenomenon that she couldn't conceive of it until CeeCee actually reached her and pushed Anne with such force that she toppled, fell, and skidded across the floor into a corner near the last machine. The gamblers at the machines abandoned their seats and scattered. Anne saw the glimmer of rage in CeeCee's eyes. CeeCee's friends made a feeble attempt to hold her back, but CeeCee pushed them roughly away.

Anne recovered, rose quickly to her feet, and took stock. She was cornered. A solid wall of gawking customers had gathered to watch a fight, and that left no gap to reach the door. CeeCee stood in front of her. She looked like she meant business, and Anne suspected she would be no pushover. She was taller and heavier. She had a sturdy frame, and Anne knew that she was an able and strong woman, a woman who worked hard.

Anne couldn't let CeeCee catch her off guard again and, if CeeCee charged wildly and grappled with her or caught her in a bear hug, she would be helpless to protect herself. So Anne's best hope was to fend her off as best she could and catch her by surprise.

CeeCee, more confident now, prepared to attack again. Anne assumed a stable fighter's stance, as if she were about to pummel the heavy bag at a gym. CeeCee rushed forward, her arms outstretched. Just before impact, though, Anne ducked and sidestepped. CeeCee flew past. Her momentum carried her, stumbling, into the alcove wall.

Anne spun around and followed CeeCee toward the wall. Anne reached CeeCee just as she began to recover for a second attack. By then, Anne had prepared herself for whatever the outcome would be.

CeeCee was partway to her feet and half turned around when she saw Anne standing just an arm's length in front of her. CeeCee's mouth gaped when Anne's fist struck her. Two quick right jabs struck CeeCee's nose. A left cross knocked her off balance, and she fell to the ground.

As CeeCee stood again, blood streamed down her nose and stained her beige skirt. The crowd closed around her in a tighter semi-circle. CeeCee's tears mixed with the blood and a dribble of saliva. Cookie held out a handkerchief, careful to avoid blood on her own clothes. Anne and Kate quietly slipped through the ring of spectators and disappeared.

14.

Anne and Kate bolted toward the car. Kate put it in gear, the wheels spun, and the rear end skidded across the gravel roadway as she pulled away from the community centre. It was enough commotion to draw comment from Spit and Squeak still peddling moonshine from Fig's truck nearby. Fig just lent a cold eye to their flight.

"Sorry," said Kate about her reckless driving.

Kate's face was pale and her speech nearly breathless as she drove.

"That's the most exciting evening I've ever had… ever," she said.

"Something for your diary, then," said Anne.

"I don't have a diary," said Kate, "but I think I may start one. That was so fun. I mean exciting."

"It's exciting if you're watching maybe… not so much fun if you're in the middle of it," said Anne.

Anne's heart was still pounding, and the pain in her knuckles and fingers was just beginning. She massaged her hands. They'd be sore tomorrow, she thought. Swollen, too. She had taken self-defence classes before, and she'd even sparred a few rounds with another woman. But she'd never struck anyone or anything with bare knuckles. No, it wasn't fun, she thought, and hoped she hadn't broken anything.

"You should've seen Bernie's face," said Kate, and looked quickly at Anne. "At first he looked amused. Later he looked stunned. I think he expected scratching and hair pulling and girls rolling around on the floor... that kind of fight. But when you put her down, he said, 'Must've been some engineering school she went to.' He laughed and shook his head, but then he got this weird look on his face. Must've been worried about what will happen at work on Monday. What do you think?"

"I think I'll let Monday work itself out. Don't stop at the boarding house, Kate. Pull into Mossey's. I'll pick up my car first."

Kate pulled over. With no lights nearby to illuminate it, Mossey's Garage looked even more like an abandoned building.

"By the way," said Anne, "those old guys in the parking lot. They looked familiar. Who are they?"

"Oh, yeah, the short guy is called Spit. The skinny one is Squeak."

"I remember now. What about the bigger fellow?"

"That would be Fig. They hang around together... local bootleggers... and they work on the wharf during lobster season."

15.

Anne looked at her watch. It was a little after one a.m. A good time to go to work, she thought. Maybe even get a little physio. It was a ten-minute drive to the wharf at Little Rose Harbour, and that's where she headed. As expected, the parking lot was empty. The wharf was vacant. At times, the odd fisherman had been known to drive down in the wee hours to check mooring lines, drink away troubles, watch the lap of the tide, or bathe in the amber lights illuminating the wharf and its buildings.

Anne walked down the boat slip. Tide was high. She knelt down at the water's edge and extended her aching hands deeply into the salt water. The water was cold with the fresh tide. The chill of the water might bring the swelling down. She could have done the same at the boarding house, but cracking open trays of ice from the refrigerator might wake someone, and Anne wasn't prepared for explanations and justifications at this hour of night. She was happy enough to be alone for a while and to allow her knot of thoughts to loosen and unravel unimpeded in the calm of a balmy summer evening. She sorely needed some clarity.

Anne removed her hands from the water and flexed her fingers. Everything moved. Nothing was broken. There may have been inflammation in her left fist, but it was hard to tell in the dull glow of the pole lamps.

Anne put her hands back into the water and listened to the sounds of the harbour: the groans of bow and stern lines, the occasional hum of a bilge pump, the playful lap of ripples against concrete, and the buzz of wharf lights. But other sounds soon joined the chorus: a truck engine, idling indistinctly, muffled voices, the creak of a tailgate. Then the soft grind of a rusty door, and Anne heard no more of the truck.

Anne flexed her hands a few more times. No serious damage, she decided. Then she made her way up the boat ramp to the wharf. She had expected to see the truck she had heard somewhere nearby, but it was nowhere to be seen. Perhaps it had crept away again, she thought, but then something pricked her ears. She listened closer and caught muted sounds, a shuffling, and hushed voices.

The sounds came from the other side of the factory's processing plant, somewhere along a narrow corridor of storage containers, warehouses, repair sheds, and vehicle storage garages. Anne walked slowly in that direction and peered up the corridor. It was dark, but she saw the outline of a pickup truck near one of the warehouses at the far end. She saw movement, at least one person, but little else. And it was a peculiar time to be working, even for a fisherman.

Anne didn't want to expose herself unnecessarily, and she would have been spotted if she continued up the lane between the buildings, so she backtracked to the wharf and made her way toward the end of the pier under cover of a lengthy factory building. Halfway along, Anne turned toward one of the boats tied up to the wharf. She went down a ladder onto the deck of a fishing boat. She hurriedly searched the wheelhouse for something useful. There was little variety. In the end, she settled on a roll of electrical tape, some twine, and a box cutter, and, after noticing it lying on the washboard, she snatched a two-metre boathook that crewmen used to snag lobster buoys.

Anne reached the end of the lobster factory. The end of the pier was nearby. Beyond it, the bay spread out in a vast grey mass, broken only by the red and green flash of buoys marking the channel.

Anne moved cautiously around the end of the building and peered around the corner. She spotted two men. Both wore jeans and ball caps covered by hoods. Both were small and slender.

One man stood alongside the truck. The other passed or tossed boxes down through an open loading door on a second-floor loft. Already the truck was half-filled, quite an accomplishment for such a short time, thought Anne.

Anne studied the men's movements and routine for a few minutes. The man at the truck had his back to her. His hood had fallen back, revealing long dark hair. His attention focused on his partner in the loft and signs of movement or lights appearing near the entrance to the lane.

The truck itself covered Anne's advance and, in the shadowy unlit corridor, Anne managed to reach the right rear wheel without being noticed. A few light, rather cumbersome boxes filled the loft door now.

Anne readied the long shaft of the boathook. The man on the truck bed reached up and took the parcel being passed down. As he did, Anne snagged his hood with the boathook and jerked it. The man stumbled backward, the box falling on top of him. His shoulder struck the side of the truck bed, and he cried out. Anne closed in, grasped two fingers on his outstretched left hand, and twisted firmly. The man shrieked in pain again.

"On your belly," she said. The throb in his hand lessened as he rotated onto his stomach and, without letting go of her grip, Anne slipped over the side of the truck into the bed, and pinned both arms behind him. Her teeth found the loose end on the electrical tape, and she bound his wrists together.

Anne grabbed for the box cutter in her pocket and exposed the sharp edge. Anne looked quickly over her shoulder again. The man's accomplice remained frozen at the loft door six feet above her. He hadn't moved. He seemed stunned. So she turned attention back to her prisoner and rolled him onto his back. She stared closely at him. Then she studied the thief still framed in the door of the loft.

Anne felt a wave of disappointment envelop her when she realized that the men she had captured were just two scrawny young boys.

16.

"You! Get your skinny butt down here. Now!"

He disappeared. She heard shoes clomping down a dark ladder. Then she added for effect, "Let's go! I don't have all night. Move it." Almost as the words left her mouth, he appeared in the door-frame. He looked frightened, pathetic. Anne knew he was, and also knew that stark fear was the best tonic for him right now.

Anne waved him forward. She spun him around and taped his hands behind his back.

"Okay, both of you, take a seat on one of the boxes you stole. Face the back of the truck."

Anne took out her cellphone camera and took a position behind the tailgate.

"Smile now. Police will want a shot of you two at the scene of your heist." She clicked and checked the quality of the picture. The older boy looked like a deer in the headlights. The younger one was about to cry.

"I just forwarded this picture to my office. I'll add it to my collection. Next one will go to the RCMP. Are you ready for me to do that?"

Both shook their heads.

"Sure about that?"

Both nodded.

"Then maybe we can work something out. I want some information. First, what are your names? Ages, too."

"Norman... Norman Sennett, sixteen," said the older one.

"Rufus Dunne, fourteen," said the other.

"Who're your parents, Norman?"

"My dad's Mackey. Mom's gone."

"And you?"

"Hector and Charlene," said the other.

Shit! More Hec and CeeCee drama, she thought. That's all I need.

"Good," she said. "Now for the big question. The one that'll keep you out of jail if you tell the truth. Who do you sell this stuff to?"

Each boy looked at the other for a safe passage through a dark hole they had just fallen into. Neither had an answer.

"Don't worry. I can fix it so he won't find out who told on him."

Rufus looked dumbfounded. Norman looked terrified but blurted it out.

"Edgar MacAulay is his name. He's older."

"And how long have you been stealing for Edgar?"

"A year or so," said Rufus.

"Maybe less," said Norman, and Rufus nodded.

"Who taught you the ropes?"

"Edgar."

"How long have you been stealing from the factory?"

"Two or three weeks is all."

"Did he arrange for you to steal from other places, too?"

Both nodded.

"Edgar said he'd find out if we ever told," said Norman.

"He said he'd kill us if we told," said Rufus, "and bury us in the middle of the woods."

"That will never happen."

"Are you going to tell our parents?" asked Rufus. He looked about to cry again.

"I need to ask a few more questions before I decide about that," she said. Her tone had become less sharp and more motherly.

Anne pressed the boys for more information about Edgar MacAulay and learned that he was not only a fence but a drug dealer as well. Edgar was just nineteen, but he had already spent time at a youth facility.

The information Anne got from the boys seemed plausible, and she was confident they had levelled with her. Then, after her interview, she made them tote all the goods they'd stolen back up into the loft from where they'd taken them.

Satisfied, she left the boys with a cover story to appease Edgar MacAulay: they were to tell him they had tried to steal the merchandise, but a truck full of teens drove down, started drinking, and weren't likely to leave, so they couldn't pull it off.

Furthermore, Anne warned them to stay away from MacAulay. She also told them that she may want to speak to them in another day or two and, if so, she'd contact them by cellphone. Finally, if they followed her instructions, the police would never be contacted, their parents would never learn of their thefts, and the damning picture of their capture would never be seen again.

17.

It was after two a.m. when Rufus and Norman drove off. Anne thought about leaving for the boarding house, but her mind still raced from her last surge of adrenalin. And her hands still hurt from her fight with CeeCee. It would take a bit more time before her nerves settled enough to lay her head upon a pillow and sleep.

But, for the present, it was peaceful here, alone, on the water-front, in the middle of the night. It was relaxing, feeling void of small-town drama and free from obligation. So she walked about. But she was still unable to set aside her investigative instincts, and she pulled on each door handle she passed and tugged on every lock hasp.

Along the way Anne noticed a faint light in a second-floor office of the factory complex. Anne hadn't noticed it when she arrived. The pole lamps along the wharf burned brighter and must have obscured its glow. Anne tried the door to the build-ing, but it was locked. There would have been no one inside, and there was no doubt the building and its contents were secure. So, an employee forgetting to switch off a lamp was insignificant.

However, curiosity compelled her to probe further.

She had been given master keys to the property. She dug into her pocket, drew out a ring of them, let herself in, and quietly mounted stairs to the second-floor complex of offices.

At the top of the landing a corridor led about thirty feet ahead. Several doors were open. The first one was reception. It connected with the offices of the secretary and bookkeeper. She passed a meeting room, several washrooms, two locked rooms that she didn't open, and another large room that appeared to be a lounging area. At the far end of the corridor was a half-open door in which a dim light burned.

Anne gave the door a gentle nudge. The hinges responded with a disturbingly loud moan and framed in the opening was the figure of a man slumped back in a chair. His head tipped back as if broken. His feet splayed out in front of him. Both of his hands extended and dangled over the armrests like a dead man's.

However, this man wasn't dead. The methodical grind of his snoring testified to his continued existence. He was in his mid to late sixties. He was short, with a sturdy build, a pleasant face, and rough-looking hands. He was balding and any remaining hair had been shaved away, leaving a perfectly round head.

A ledger lay on the desk in front of him. It was a logbook for the night watchman. The dim illumination of a lamp revealed that the records for his nightly rounds had already been entered. So had most future ones. A small clock on the desk, set to go off at five, would ring him awake. His shift, based on previous days' entries, ended at six in the morning.

The log also indicated that his name was Luc LaVie.

Anne let LaVie slumber on. The "stepped-up security" that Jean claimed to have put in place had serious flaws, and Bernie had "neglected" to mention a security guard in his brief orientation, but she decided not to reveal what she knew right now. Keeping some information to herself might prove more useful later. She returned to her car, drove to the Manor, and drifted into a troubled sleep.

18.

Sunday

"It's too late for breakfast, but there's coffee in the urn if you've a mind for some… after your night out," said Jane Finnerty. She had hollered from the kitchen. Then her voice trailed off into mostly inaudible mutterings about *late hours* and *gallivanting*.

Anne ignored her but poured a large cup of coffee with extra cream and sugar and retired to the sitting room. It was empty, but it was a bright room with dark furniture, and the Sunday morning light was strong and cheerful. It warmed her and comforted her at the same time.

The coffee kicked in. She grew livelier, and she slowly emerged from the jumble of thoughts that had woken up with her. By the time she drained her cup, she had sorted her day into a workable agenda: breakfast at some café in Montague, head for Charlottetown, a pit stop at her office, lunch with her daughter, and a meeting with her client. Then maybe there'd still be time to touch base with a few friends before returning to Halkirk and work.

Anne left the sitting room, returned to her own room, gathered a few things into a sports bag, and passed through the foyer toward the front door. She heard the clatter and clang of tableware and pans in the kitchen. She called out: "Miss Finnerty, I'm leaving now. I probably won't be back until tomorrow afternoon. Business in town."

Jane Finnerty did not reply.

***

A proper plate of scrambled eggs, marmalade and toast, and another hot coffee at a Montague restaurant put her world properly in perspective. Then she drove into Charlottetown, capital of Prince Edward Island. She found the central city area rather empty of traffic, even for a Sunday, and pulled into a parking space quite near her office on Victoria Row.

The black lettering on her second-floor door read *Darby Security and Investigations*. It had been her uncle's business after his retirement from police work in Ontario and PEI. Anne moved there from Ottawa where she had worked as an insurance investigator. Her Uncle Bill's death had been sudden and unexpected, and it left Anne picking up the pieces of her own life, too. In the end, she decided to take over her uncle's business under her birth name, Wilhelmina "Billy" Darby. It was a career decision she did not regret.

Anne pushed open the door. There was some resistance from the small gathering of sales sheets, letters, and newspapers that had been dropped through the mail slot in the door. Anne gathered up the handful of them and walked through a small reception room into her large, comfortably furnished office.

An immense oak desk faced the door and backed against a large window with a view of the fashionable Victoria Row below and the Confederation Centre of the Arts across the street. A large, impregnable antique safe stood to one side. It stored an assortment of firearms that had belonged to her uncle. It also held her more sensitive files and reports that couldn't be as safely secured in the several filing cabinets nearby. Anne sat behind her desk and shuffled through mail. To her right were a sofa and several plush leather chairs, a coffee table, and a separate stand for a coffee percolator, a pitcher, and several glasses and cups.

A large square section of wall displayed photos of her uncle. Plaques and framed, yellowing news accounts chronicled his career as a police officer. Next to these was Anne's Bachelor of

Arts diploma from the University of Ottawa, much of which she had earned part-time as a working mother. Her private investigator's credentials and several professional course certificates were on display. So were several citations, one from the PEI Minister of Justice, the other from a senior RCMP superintendent thanking her for assistance with an unspecified investigation.

Anne checked her office phone for messages, made a few notes, and left, locking the office behind her.

The Blue Peter was a restaurant a few doors up on Victoria Row. The Blue Peter was Anne's favourite spot, and was owned and operated by a long-time friend, Mary Anne McAdam. Anne slid into the booth farthest inside, facing the door. Mary Anne was at the register with an employee. She and Anne exchanged waves and Mary Anne came over.

"Hey," said Anne.

"Back at ya. You look like hell. What ya been doing?"

"Thanks a lot. Just got back from the spa. Rough crowd there on Sunday morning," said Anne with a wink.

"No kidding. So what ya really been doing?"

"Believe it or not, my first barroom brawl."

"Seriously?"

Anne nodded. "You should see the other guy... I mean gal."

"Women only fight over one thing..."

"Yeah, I know. No fault of mine, though. He was drunk and started hitting on me. I told him to shove off, but he's a slow learner."

"Good-looking?"

Anne nodded. "Very."

"The territorial imperative," said Mary Anne tersely, as if that summed up the entire discussion.

Anne looked up, knit her brow skeptically, and said, "You been reading *Cosmo* again?"

"It's cheaper than grad school... and more practical, too. Sunday special or the menu?"

"Menu. I had a late breakfast. Haven't worked up an appetite yet. How's Jacqueline doing?"

Mary Anne, who had just stood to leave, sat back down again. "Jacqui's not a normal girl, is she?"

A cloud of concern swept across Anne's face. "Why? What's she done?"

"I'm not sure I can handle her any longer. Friday night... Saturday night... what does a normal kid do? Parties... dances... stalks cute guys. What does she do? Studies for final exams... works on some end-of-school project or other... and pokes around for a summer job. It's just not right, Anne. You should have a talk with her. I'll send the waitress over," she said and stood up to leave.

Anne's concern dissolved into a proud smile, and, as Mary Anne walked off, Anne called after her: "Thanks for looking after her the last couple of days." Mary Anne's arm waved back in silent acknowledgement.

Anne's mind drifted from the warmth of her friendship with Mary Anne and her delight with her daughter to a half-formed vision of the new man in her life. That vision had not fully materialized before the arrival of her waitress who slipped the menu in front of her.

"Here's the menu, Miss, but there's also a brunch..."

Anne looked up.

"...special... Mom?"

"Jacqui? What are you doing?"

"I'm working. I told you I'd be looking for summer work. Don't you remember? After all, school's out in a few weeks."

"I mean, what're you doing... here?"

"One of Mary Anne's waitresses got sick, and she asked me if I'd like to see what it was like for a shift or two. I get paid a salary... plus tips."

Anne stared at Mary Anne across the room. Mary Anne pretended to be busy, but then she looked back. She wore a mischievous smirk and shrugged her shoulders as if this were something she had little control over.

"So how did this all come about?"

"Basically, I told her I was looking for summer work. I knew she was short-handed, and I offered to fill in. Then I bugged her until she finally caved. It was pretty easy really."

"So how's it going?"

"Good. It's not rocket science, but it's fun meeting people, and it'll look good on my resume. So... are you back already?"

Anne shook her head. "No, it'll be a few more days anyway."

"So I can stay here with Aunt Mary Anne?"

Anne nodded.

"And can I keep the job if I want to?"

Anne nodded again. In her mind she felt she should say something like, *But you'll have to keep your grades up*, or *Only if you're on your best behaviour*, but she didn't. She couldn't. Jacqui had never been a slacker or gone through a rebellious streak like so many other teens, at least not yet.

"You better get back to work then. Time is money, they say."

"Oh... when are you going back?"

"Not sure yet. Tonight... tomorrow some time... depends on my meeting with the client this afternoon. Why?"

"I have rehearsals this evening for the recital. Thought you might like to watch."

"The Shakespeare thing?"

"Actually, it's a revue of sorts. You know, singing, dancing, comedy, drama. A potpourri. That kind of thing. I recite a Hamlet soliloquy. You could give me some feedback—if you weren't too busy."

"Wouldn't miss it."

19.

The Charlottetown office for M. Gauthier & Son was located downtown, rather close to fashionable new waterfront developments. It had been carved out of an older two-storey residence that had been refitted for office space. A law office and an accountant occupied the top floor. A financial advisor had set up business on part of the ground floor. The other half of that level was taken up by M. Gauthier, et al.

The small reception area that faced Water Street led into a comfortable and cozy business room. Beyond that were a full bath and a connecting corridor to a private suite providing temporary local living quarters for Jean Gauthier while he sorted his Prince Edward Island business interests.

Anne arrived for the client visit around two. She knocked and tried the entry door. It was open.

"Mr. Gauthier?" Anne looked around but saw no one. She called again a bit louder. "Mr. Gauthier."

Jean Gauthier appeared soundlessly, almost magically, from the recesses of his private quarters. Anne was momentarily startled.

Jean was medium height, a head taller than Anne. He carried an athletic build. His hair was black and wavy.

"It's wonderful to see you again, Anne Brown... or is it Billy Darby?" He strode toward her as if to shake hands. His smile hovered on the brink of mischievousness. His demeanour was relaxed and confident.

"You get the two-for-one special today: Anne Brown *and* Billy Darby."

"Charm... and business," he said.

His arms encircled Anne. He drew her close. He caught a vague scent of perfume as he bent down and kissed her.

Anne's fingers trembled. Then she heard a faint click and footsteps in the hallway. She stepped back quickly just as a figure pushed through the door to the office.

"Papa..." said Jean.

"Not too late, am I? Or perhaps too early," he said wryly.

"No, no. Ms. Brown—Anne—just arrived a moment ago. Anne, this is my father, Michel Gauthier."

"We spoke briefly on the phone yesterday," said Anne, "but it's a pleasure meeting you in person. Shall we begin?"

Jean pointed toward an arrangement of chairs.

"I like her already," said Michel. "Gets right to the point."

For a man Anne guessed to be in his late sixties, Michel carried himself well, but he moved a bit stiffly across the room. Michel stood about as tall as his son. He had a full head of white hair, neatly cropped. His complexion was ruddy, his features fine and well shaped, and Anne surmised he would have been quite handsome in his youth. As Anne began to guide them through her narrative of the last few days, she could not help but notice his eyes. They were alert and responsive and, from her experience, indicative that Michel Gauthier had a sharp mind.

Anne's account was orderly, detailed, and unadorned with emotion or opinion. She described her meeting with Bernie White, her undercover activities as an industrial engineer, the resentment of some employees, the flattened tires, and the dust-up at the community dance. Both Michel and Jean leaned forward in their chairs as Anne described the capture of the young thieves and, at the end of her exposition, Anne just stopped, leaned back, and waited for questions.

"So are you convinced you've gotten to the bottom of the troubles at the factory? Young vandals?" said Michel.

"Not at all. The boys began a short time ago. The thefts at your facility date back a few years, probably more."

"What will happen to the boys?" asked Jean.

"I've got them over a barrel right now. They'll cooperate, give up some more information, but I don't think they'll be a problem in the future. They admitted to theft but not to vandalism, and they had no reason to damage property. Edgar MacAulay, now he's a different story. There may be a motive there. So I'll be checking him out in the next day or two."

Both men nodded.

"Also, there's a weakness in the security set-up. Luc LaVie, the night watchman, was asleep during the break-in."

"Replace him," Michel said to Jean.

"I'd rather you didn't do that, at least for now. He may be complicit in the thefts, he may not. But he's been around the plant for quite a few years, and I think he may still be a useful source of information. I'd like to check him out before you get rid of him."

"Are you still planning to investigate undercover?" asked Michel.

"I will as long as I can. It's easier to get information when you're part of the community. I'm not there yet, but I'm getting there. The grapevine was a bit overcharged yesterday with news of a dead baby uncovered at Sullivan's Point... Bernie White still doesn't know about me?" she asked.

"What dead baby?" said Michel.

"Just outside a pioneer cemetery a couple miles away. Been there quite some time, they say. Bernie still doesn't know about me?" said Anne again.

"We haven't informed him, if that's what you mean," said Jean.

"Good. I'd like to keep it that way. Everyone knows who the village idiots are, but people are not always quick to name them. My identity will come out eventually, but if I can keep a low profile for another week or two and gain a few confidences, I'll be satisfied. I can't help thinking, though, that the thefts and vandalism at Little Rose Harbour have deeper roots."

"What do you mean?" asked Michel.

"I've asked around. The vandalism and thefts Jean mentioned seem to predate your ownership of the company. It might help if I knew how M. Gauthier & Son got involved with this factory in the first place."

"Well, it wasn't my idea," said Michel. His hand gripped the armrest of the chair, and his inflection voiced irritation. Jean shifted uncomfortably and glanced quickly to Anne and back to his father.

Michel gave himself a moment. Then he took a deep breath, loosened his grip on the chair, smiled benevolently, and began again. "I started in the fishery over forty years ago in Nova Scotia. I saved my money, reinvested it, and in time I built up my own fish-processing facility. It grew. Eventually, I bought four others and expanded into shipping and marketing fishing supplies. Now we have quite an enterprise in Nova Scotia, and one day soon Jean will have it all. But Jean has an independent streak—which grudgingly I have to admire—that led him to strike out on his own... in spite of the fact that even now Jean has control over many of the management decisions at M. Gauthier & Son."

"What Papa is trying to say is that I bought two flagging lobster plants on PEI against his wishes. I wanted to expand on PEI. Papa didn't. He preferred the idea of moving into European exports."

"So you run two plants on PEI," said Anne.

Jean nodded. "One near Egmont Bay. The other at Little Rose Harbour."

"Did you buy them at the same time?"

"No. The Egmont Bay facility was last fall. Little Rose Harbour was shortly after that."

"And are there problems at the factory in Egmont?"

"No."

"Purchased from the same owners?"

"No. I bought the Little Rose Harbour plant from Big Sea Products, a holding company that was divesting some assets. Actually, Papa bought it on my behalf."

"One of a few business mistakes I've made and really regretted."

"Why did you buy it, then?" Anne asked Michel.

"Big Sea Products wouldn't negotiate with Jean. I don't know why. Maybe they didn't think he had enough capital behind him.

They weren't interested in talking to me either, but I know some first-class negotiators, and they were able to close the deal, and it wasn't cheap either."

"So why did you agree?"

"Bottom line? It turned some profit. And it was close to our Nova Scotia distribution centre. At least that made sense. And Jean... I think he would have found a way to make it happen even if I hadn't stepped in."

"Was Big Sea Products just flipping the business?"

"No, they'd operated it for at least ten years. Bernie would know more about that. They bought it from him."

"Bernie... Bernie White?" said Anne.

Jean nodded and looked at her curiously.

"I see," she said.

20.

It had been wonderful to see Jean again, and Anne bathed in the memory of that brief meeting and their single kiss. She had known him only a short time, just a few weeks, and it hadn't been a client-investigator relationship, not at first, anyway. They had met at church, not for a religious ceremony, but for a concert. St. Mary's Roman Catholic Church in Indian River had been decommissioned years before, but the church itself was renowned for its acoustics and had become a favourite venue for musicians and singers. Anne had planned to go to a jazz event with Mary Anne but, at the last minute, Mary Anne had to cancel. An emergency at the restaurant, she had said. And, not wanting to waste her ticket, Anne had gone alone.

Anne had acquired a late appreciation for jazz after she had met Dit Malone. Dit was a close friend of Anne's. He had been a semi-pro hockey star until a swimming accident left him paralyzed. After the accident, he discovered a love for electronics, and thrived at it, eventually starting his own company, which, among other things, developed specialized electronic equipment for law-enforcement groups in several countries. Dit had played in the brass section of his high school band. He loved jazz and introduced Anne to that genre. Dit had especially liked Ornette Coleman, but Anne found his style too frenetic and inaccessible. She preferred Miles Davis and Louis Armstrong.

Funny how fate works, she thought. Mary Anne cancels. She reluctantly goes to the concert alone. A handsome, personable guy sits next to her, also alone. They chat, they find things in common, and, completely out of character, Anne invites him to join her for coffee after the concert.

Anne is somewhat embarrassed when he turns her down. He apologizes. He has another commitment. Another time, he says. Anne senses a wife in the background, but sees no ring on his finger. Best to forget him, she thinks.

Two days later, though, he shows up at her office. They duck out for coffee, though not at The Blue Peter. No point in getting Mary Anne's matchmaking machinery running overtime. He gives Anne a Chet Baker CD by way of apologizing. The fact that Anne is six years older than he doesn't deter his interest. He also confirms his bachelor status, something that Anne double-checks after he leaves.

So much and so little had happened since then. The attraction between them kindled. Then Jean found the need for the services of a private detective and hired Anne Brown of Darby Investigations to do the job. That's when Anne tapped the brakes on their personal relationship. Don't mix business with friends, Uncle Bill had warned her, and she took that advice seriously.

Anne slipped into her car outside the office of M. Gauthier & Son and drove across town toward her home, but she detoured a few blocks away and, instead, took a slow ride through Victoria Park, along the roadway bordering Charlottetown Harbour on one side and the Lieutenant Governor's residence on the other. It was a lovely afternoon, sunny and warm, and she needed a few moments to herself. So she pulled over onto a scenic lookout and stopped.

She rolled down the windows and pushed the CD into a slot on the dashboard. Chet Baker's trumpet was plaintive and hopeful. His vocals spoke with muted joy:

> *I dim all the lights and I sink in my chair.*
> *The smoke from my cigarette climbs through the air.*
> *The walls of my room fade away in the blue,*
> *And I'm deep in a dream of you.*

In addition to Uncle Bill's advice, something innate in her makeup had always driven Anne to put responsibility ahead of desire and, in the end, that attitude gave her the objectivity to think clearly, make sound decisions, and retain respect for herself. To carry on a personal relationship with a client might cloud her judgment, and she wouldn't let that happen. She couldn't.

***

After Anne left, Jean and Michel walked to a small avant-garde spot a half block away for coffee. Michel had not commented on Anne's interim report, and Jean noticed his reluctance. He took it for polite reserve but it annoyed him nonetheless. Finally, he could no longer suppress his curiosity.

"What was your take on Anne Brown?" he asked.

Michel pondered the question longer than Jean had expected. He felt a level of concern rise up within him, but he stifled the urge to defend her.

Finally Michel broke the silence: "I like her. She's level-headed, efficient, and part pit bull." Then gravity clouded his face: "But she's made too many enemies too soon. She can't just slip under the radar like you had hoped. She'll likely get hurt, and we don't want that to happen, do we?" Michel looked up. His face was stonily cold. His tone was authoritative. He said, "She's got to go. Get rid of her. Agreed?"

His father's bluntness drove every thought and response from Jean's head.

Finally, Jean slowly nodded. "I'll give her a day or two. Then I'll take care of it."

21.

Anne spent a quiet Sunday afternoon at home alone. She phoned her friend Ben Solomon. There was no answer. It was too lovely a day to be indoors, Anne concluded. He and his wife probably had taken a drive into the country. She considered the same herself. Then, suddenly, Anne felt quite weary. It had been a busy, rowdy, and trying Saturday night, and she hadn't fully recovered from it.

She lay down on the sofa to relax and rest her eyes for a moment. Her mind emptied of everything but food, and a succession of tasty dishes paraded through her head like fashion models on a catwalk. She hoped to settle on one special entrée that Jacqui would love for supper. Lasagna, tossed salad, and toasted Italian bread was the last repast she envisioned before falling asleep. She awoke ninety minutes later with a persistent ringing in her ears. It was the telephone.

"Hello," she said, realizing almost immediately that she sounded as goofy and dazed as a midlife suburban mom on Valium.

"Good afternoon, would you have Anne Brown phone me when she returns?"

"Jeez, Ben, you just woke me up. You been taking smart-aleck lessons since I've been away?"

"No, I come by it naturally. You called?"

"Just thought I'd touch base, say hello. I'm here for the day, back into the trenches tomorrow."

"Sounds like you need a vacation already."

"One day of real work and one night of real play, and now I'm almost ready to pack it in and reserve a room at Hillside Manor. Shuffleboard and gin rummy are sounding pretty good today."

"You'll snap back. Hang in there. Sarah and I were at The Blue Peter earlier. Mary Anne said you were in town, and we thought we'd have you and Jacqui over for dinner. Nothing fancy. Just lasagna and the usual fixings."

"Sounds perfect."

✳✳✳

The Solomons, Ben and Sarah, lived in a quiet cul-de-sac in the Charlottetown suburb of Parkdale. Their house was two blocks from a fine golf course that neither Ben nor Sarah had ever played and a ten-minute drive to his office-with-a-view in the complex of government buildings near Victoria Park.

Ben's acquaintance with Anne dated back six years. His friendship with Bill Darby, Anne's uncle, stretched back to the 1970s when both men had been cops in Ottawa. After retirement, Billy Darby returned to his birthplace on PEI and set up a private detective agency. Ben came east years later after being offered an attractive salary increase and advancement to detective sergeant with the Charlottetown Police. After that, an especially sensitive case he worked on with Anne led to his appointment to a newly created, high-profile provincial government post. The new job came with the cumbersome title of Provincial Special Investigator and Liaison for Intergovernmental Law Enforcement Operations. Ben felt embarrassed at such an unwieldy label and secretly feared it sounded too similar to gag lines in a TV farce. To offset that comparison, he simply referred to himself as the Provincial Special Investigator.

Jacqui gravitated toward the Solomons' kitchen and lent Sarah a hand. Ben steered Anne toward the living room and poured out several glasses of red wine.

"Sarah? Do you want wine now or later?"

"Later, please," she hollered back.

"Need help?" said Anne.

"Nope. Got all the help I need right here, thanks."

Ben passed Anne a large glass half-filled with Merlot. "Anne, you sounded stressed when I phoned earlier," he said.

"Tired mostly," she said and launched into a Reader's Digest condensation of her adventures in eastern PEI.

"Reminds me of Saturday nights in Sudbury or Hull," he said, adding with a wink, "Ahhh... the good old days."

"You know what you can do with your 'good old days,' don't you?"

"Of course, Sarah reminds me all the time. But, seriously, how's the investigation going?"

"Too early to tell. Still following the breadcrumbs."

"Any leads?"

"Maybe. I've got a name. Edgar MacAulay."

"Want me to run his name?"

"Well, it would save me a little legwork."

"Not a problem. Call me tomorrow."

"Everything's done," said Sarah rushing into the room with a steaming casserole dish in her hand and Jacqui hard on her heels with the salad. "Sit in," she said, pointing to the table in the adjacent dining room.

"Looks yummy," said Jacqui.

***

After supper everyone looked sated. Sarah's offer of early strawberries and ice cream for dessert renewed the gleam in most eyes. The exception was Ben. He slipped the spatula into the casserole dish for a second large serving of lasagna.

Everyone helped clear the table of dishes. Then they retired to the living room. Ben sank into his favourite chair, which those who knew him avoided, lest his glare of disapproval pointed out their error in judgment. The rest of the guests settled in other spots.

"So... what are you doing next year, Jacqui?" Ben asked.

"I got accepted at the university here, as well as at Dalhousie, but I really haven't decided yet."

"And your major?"

"Haven't decided that either. I'm good at sports and English, and Mrs. Beale thinks I have real talent in drama."

"Omigosh!" said Anne. "You have the rehearsal tonight." She looked at her watch and added, "We'll have to go now."

"We really don't need to, Mom. It's not required. Besides Mrs. Beale said my delivery was just what she was hoping for."

"Well, I was hoping to hear it myself."

"There's no need. You'll be there for the real performance. Besides, you looked so worn out this afternoon. Thought you could use a little downtime."

"Well... how about you doing a private performance here?" asked Sarah.

"She doesn't have the script here, Sarah," said Ben, half-hidden in the plush of his comfy recliner.

Sarah looked at Jacqui.

"I don't need a script, Uncle Ben. I'm a professional." She stood, cocked her head theatrically, slid her fingers through her hair with a sardonic grin, and strode to her marks on the ersatz stage in the Solomon living room.

22.

Monday

Anne headed back to the village early. She had no loose ends to contend with in Charlottetown. Ben would run Edgar MacAulay's name through the system for a criminal history. She'd met up with some of her friends. She'd seen Jean and let him know that, when she was on the job, she must act professionally. Business and pleasure don't mix, she'd said. He'd agreed, but Anne wasn't convinced.

And she'd had a pleasant time with Jacqui, too. She had matured so much in the last year, and it had caught Anne off guard. A teenager one minute, a young woman the next. Perhaps even leaving home and going to university in Halifax. Anne couldn't imagine coming home to an empty house. Of course, there'd be weekends and holidays. Halifax was only a three-hour drive. Still...

Anne's attention turned to the road and traffic. Several lanes of vehicles stalled bumper to bumper on the inbound lane at the Hillsborough Bridge. Vehicles had backed up for several miles. At ten to seven, though, Anne's road ahead, outbound, was clear, not a car in sight.

Anne's thoughts shifted to the evening with Ben and Sarah. Jacqui's reading of Hamlet's soliloquy from Act I was stunning.

Of course, Anne had read *Hamlet* in school a long time before, and she could still recall the opening phrases from several monologues: *To be or not to be* and *what a rogue and peasant slave am I*. But Anne had no recollection of the first soliloquy at all. She must have glossed over it, discounted it for some reason, and, when she asked why she had chosen to recite that one, Jacqui said that it showed Hamlet on the brink of emotional desperation, and it gave her a better opportunity to display her acting skills. She was right, and she did.

It was nine o'clock when Anne's car pulled up outside of Halkirk Manor. The sun shone. The morning was gaining warmth. The sky had puffy white clouds. The blue had a crispness that reminded her of autumn. She was done with the production line hands-on work. That had been mostly window dressing for her cover. Now she could move about as she wanted.

First, though, a quick wash-up and a review of her notes.

Not surprisingly, the foyer and the main-floor rooms were quiet and empty. Enid would be cooking lobster at the plant, Jack Pine would be hauling traps aboard Hec Dunne's vessel, *Hell to Pay,* and Tom Bean would be tinkering in his basement workshop. And Jane Finnerty? Who knows where she might be lurking, thought Anne, pleased to believe the woman was harvesting gossip somewhere in the village.

Anne gripped her little overnight bag and padded across the worn red and grey carpet that ran from threshold to staircase. Her knuckles were still sore and her grip still tender from the punches she'd thrown at CeeCee. She visualized the hit again. It had felt solid and oddly surreal. As Anne trod up the stairs to her room, she hoped she hadn't broken CeeCee's nose. Her lesson to that woman should have been enough to set her straight. And Anne herself came to realize that she may have gained some ground in the process. She may have made an enemy of CeeCee but, when someone makes an enemy in one corner, allies flock from another.

The door to Anne's room was ajar when she reached the second-floor landing.

She stood there quietly for a moment, stared suspiciously at it, then continued stealthily toward the opening. She pushed gently until the outline of Jane Finnerty appeared in the doorframe. Her back faced Anne, and her fingers shuffled through several of Anne's papers.

Silently, Anne swung her overnight bag back and gently tossed it forward. The bag dropped onto the bed a few inches from Jane's elbow.

Jane tried to suppress a yelp and whirled about to see Anne standing behind her. "What are you doing here? You said you wouldn't be back until afternoon?"

"My question is: what are *you* doing here... in my room?"

"Cleaning up, of course. That's part of my job. Making the bed and cleaning up after guests." Jane's tone was accusatory and defiant.

"I made the bed before I left."

"It wasn't made properly," she said, a feeble note creeping into her voice.

"What are you doing with my papers in your hands? Snooping?"

"You think you're so smart, but you're not." Jane waited for Anne's retort, but she offered none, and, in the looming silence, Jane continued, "I know what you're up to. You call me a snoop, but you're the biggest one of all. You're here under false pretenses, and when I'm through with you, you won't be able to show your face in public. You're a fraud, and everyone will know you're a fraud." Jane issued a grunt of emphasis and headed toward the door.

"Put those papers back," said Anne, sticking her arm out to block Jane's departure.

Jane stopped and stared at Anne for a moment.

"I suppose you'd strike me, too, wouldn't ya?"

Anne glared firmly at her, but said nothing. Jane turned back and threw the pages onto the bed.

"I don't need these. I can remember a thing or two," she said. With her forefinger, Jane tapped her temple knowingly and started to leave again.

"I haven't finished with you yet, Ms. Finnerty."

"Well, I have nothing further to say to you, Ms. Brown... or is it *Darby*?"

Anne continued to block her exit with a granite stare.

"The way I see it, Jane, is that before the morning's over, you'll tell me things I need to know from your vast storehouse of local gossip, and I'll forget for the time being what I know about you."

"I'd rather rot in hell, than tell you anything."

"Rot in hell, rot in a jail cell. Not much difference, is there? Or maybe you'll get lucky. Maybe the judge will only give you a month or so. No one around here would take much notice of that, would they? Then again, there'd be the fine. And the back taxes. Though that would be hard to come up with when the Province revokes your license to operate a hotel."

"What are you talking about?" Jane's face grew a shade pale.

"I'm talking about the little fraud you've got going at Halkirk Manor. Shall we go downstairs to the sitting room? I could use a fresh coffee. You make wonderful coffee, Jane. Besides, you probably could use a moment to reconsider your next move."

***

While Jane brewed a fresh pot of coffee, Anne settled into a comfortable chair in the sitting room and gathered her own thoughts together. When Jane returned, Anne unhurriedly sipped coffee and nibbled on a cookie from a separate serving dish. Then she quietly said, "It must be hard making a living out here... a single woman and all."

Anne let her words drift unadorned for a few seconds into the warmth of the sunny room on a fine summer day. Eventually, Jane looked up without expression and nodded faintly.

"I can sympathize with that. I'm a widow and a mom, no family, no man around to lend a hand. I know it's hard," she said. "So I can see why someone may need to cut corners a bit here... a bit there... you know... to take the pressure off..."

Jane's posture grew less rigid the longer Anne rambled. Her shoulders lost their bony tenseness. Her hands smoothed out her dress unconsciously. Only her eyes betrayed decades of caution-ary reflexes and suspicion.

Anne chatted on idly for several minutes about the trials of bringing up her own child and the difficulties of gaining respect as a female private investigator, some of which was true and some of which she fabricated to set a tone of amity and empathy.

"Like I said, everyone cuts the odd corner to take the pressure off. So I can understand the need to run a business on a cash basis and keep a double ledger of guests and lodgers. I can appreciate keeping the tax people somewhat in the dark regarding your actual revenue. It's a normal reaction to circumstances. And we all know that it's the rich thieves like Conrad Black that should be taken to task, not plain people like us trying to make a go of it. That's my opinion. I say let the cops chase real crooks, let the rest of us do what we do to survive. You have to make a living, I have to make a living."

Anne relaxed and said no more. She glanced once at her watch. Jane poured herself a second cup of coffee and reached for a cookie. She took one bite, chewed it as slowly and finely as if it were a rich imported delicacy, and stared through the gauzy curtains at a car winding through the tiny village.

"Maybe we can work something out then," Jane said.

"I was hoping we could, Jane."

Anne started by explaining what Jane had already deduced from her limited paperwork on the case: her concern over ongoing and unusually frequent vandalism and theft over the years at the Little Rose Harbour facility, and Anne started the tap flowing by mentioning a name: Edgar MacAulay and his family.

"A pissant," said Jane dismissing him out of hand. Then Jane went on to explain some dynamics of rural relationships. "He has no depth, no history. His father and mum came from Truro, Nova Scotia, about eight years ago. That's hardly time at all to build up a hate in a family or against them. His parents never stood out one way or the other. They worked, went to church by times, never cheated anybody so as they noticed it. If they had, then old Joe MacAulay would have got a thumpin' here or there, but I don't recall that ever happening. And Edgar, the boy, is just a spoilt kid, angry because he's not rich enough to be lazy for the rest of his life. He'll get his own righteous thumpin' soon enough. It might set him straight... might not."

"So you think that vandalism at the factory has a longer story to it?"

"It's been going on for some time. It could be some fisherman that was shorted at the weigh station ten years ago. It could be some old girl who worked at the factory and wasn't hired back the next year and held a grudge. She laments her misfortune for six or eight years, and maybe a father or husband or son decides to right her wrong. Some ill will goes back generations even. And folklore becomes gospel, regardless of facts. So where do you want to begin? I can tell you the stories, dearie, but I can't tell you the truth."

"Why don't we start with the story of the factory?"

Jane settled back in her chair and appeared to conjure up and sort out a jumble of memories. Then she leaned forward as if to share some confidentiality and began to speak.

"Well, according to my parents, the factory started out as a fishermen's co-op during the Great Depression. The locals started it as leverage against the big canneries which held the prices for lobster so low—a few cents a pound—that it wasn't enough to live on even then, and a lot of fishers were forced to leave home in the fall and head off to the lumber camps in New Brunswick or Maine. Interest in the co-op fell off in the fifties and sixties. For one thing, it became harder to compete with big companies. And there were internal squabbles as well. Eventually it was forced to close. Bernie White came along in 1980. He had some big ideas and a bit of cash set aside. He bought what was left of the plant and made a go of it until the cod fishery fell apart ten years later. Then he sold it to Big Sea Products, but they kept him on as manager."

"What's the story on Bernie? Was he liked?"

"As good as any other businessman around. He was fair enough, but he didn't part with a penny he didn't have to when he owned the business or even when he managed it. I know this because I worked on the production line when I was younger. He was a smart businessman then. Still is, I suppose. And he had his generous moments, too. He wasn't all business."

"How so?"

"It was a life without frills even in those days. Money was hard-come-by, and from time to time some fishermen might need an advance loan against their spring income. They might want an advance to replace fishing gear or some such. He helped them out if he could. It was good for them and, in the long run, it was good for his business. Most paid him back as soon as they could manage it. The odd one, though, just got drunk with the loan money and had nothing to show for it in the end. I recall one fella that sobered up long enough to ask for a sizable loan but, once he got it, he fell off the wagon, went on a bender, and drank it all away. Trouble was, he had used his family homestead as collateral. And he lost it."

"Sounds like he might have a grudge. Right?"

"Wrong. The thing was, Bernie never seized the land or evicted him. He just let him live there. There were no more loans for him, though. And his drinking didn't slow down much for quite a while. I suppose that's twenty years back."

"So Bernie White is a pretty good guy in your opinion."

"That's what I think anyway."

"So tell me about Big Sea Products. What kind of an outfit were they?"

"Don't know much about them. They kept Bernie on as manager. Not much seemed to change."

"Why did he sell and not leave?"

"You'd have to ask him, I guess."

"What about his personal life? Family?"

"His wife took off years ago. She wasn't from here. A city girl. Didn't much care for the smell of fish on his clothes or the long hours he worked."

"Never remarried?"

Jane smirked. "Didn't need to with the parade of young women that comes through that plant every year."

"Any problems that arose from his... dalliances? Jealous husbands, spurned lovers?"

"None that come to mind."

Jane continued on for another half hour. She recounted two families that hadn't reconciled a petty grievance for several decades—a great-grandfather had traded a cow for a half-acre patch to square off a field, but the deed was never recorded. She pored through more subtle disputes between fractured religious groups, as well as more heated ones—quarrels over fishing grounds, civic wrangling, political rivalries and shenanigans, and pranks gone awry.

That half hour ran into another. Anne found Jane's storytelling skills fascinating, and Jane proudly showcased a trove of secrets she had amassed. Her detail was noteworthy, her delivery memorable, and, by moments, her eyes glittered. In time, Anne's head was awash with names, places, dates, and incidents, most of which would have little bearing on her investigation but gave her new insights into small-town life.

Anne motioned for Jane to stop. Her monologue ended, and she looked up quizzically and expectantly. She seemed disappointed.

"A deal's a deal," said Anne.

Jane seemed satisfied with the trade-off. She leaned back in her chair as if to relax. Then her figure slowly stiffened. Her eyes grew cold again. She cleared the coffee table and returned to the kitchen.

23.

The label on her nametag read "Alvie." She slipped a plate in front of Anne who sat in a booth, the only customer at the only café in the village.

Alvie was the solitary waitress on duty. She was an attractive girl, barely twenty. Her brown hair glistened, even in the dim light from the window. Her complexion was clear, her features finely etched, and her manner more confident than one might expect from a woman so young.

She and the cook worked the place by themselves until about one o'clock in the afternoon. Then business picked up. Disoriented tourists would stop, seek directions, and stay for a snack, or idle locals would appear for their own lunch or a chat over coffee. Two other waitresses replaced Alvie's shift. The big crowd descended after four to avoid labouring over their own stoves or after working a long, steamy shift at the Little Rose factory.

"Alvie. That's an uncommon name. I've never heard it before."

"It's short for Alvina, another rarely heard name these days. Named after my mother."

"Alvina? Would you be Jack Pine's daughter?"

Alvina nodded cautiously.

"Nice man. I'm staying at Halkirk Manor. That's where I met him. He spoke of you."

"Not all lilacs and roses, I would guess."

"He wasn't hard on you. He knows how it goes. Young people explore, old people worry."

Alvina listened politely, but her eyes drifted toward an empty corner of the café like those of a cat, indifferent and aloof. Then she returned to the kitchen.

***

It was a few minutes after twelve when Anne's car pulled into the parking lot of M. Gauthier & Son at Little Rose Harbour. She checked her watch, pulled out her cellphone, and made a call. Rufus Dunne was slow to answer. It went to voice mail. Anne redialed. He answered the second time. His voice was hushed and a bit shaky.

"You don't have to say anything, Rufus. Just listen. I want to meet you and Norman at the wharf after school today. I have a few more questions."

There was a moment of silence on the other end of the call. Then a wavering voice said, "Norman doesn't think he can make it."

"Is Norman there?"

Anne couldn't hear a reply, but she could sense the nod of Rufus's head.

"Tell Norman that if he doesn't show up with you, then I'll have no choice."

Then she disconnected.

Anne didn't explain what her choice would be. Anne wasn't entirely sure herself. She expected, however, that their own imaginations would conjure up the worst possible outcome for themselves and, fearing that, both boys would follow her instructions.

***

Three women sat on a low concrete abutment near the edge of the wharf a short distance from the factory. They nibbled bits and pieces from lunch boxes and laughed and chatted between morsels. They drank cans of cold soda or sipped on Thermos coffee.

Kate was the first to see Anne striding in their direction, and she jumped up excitedly.

"Anne! You're here. We thought you quit and went back to town." She sounded relieved.

"Not a chance. I haven't finished yet."

"Can't let people like CeeCee push you around," said Enid. "She might give you a wider berth from now on."

"That's what I'm hoping for."

Anne caught a glimpse of colour moving in the distance behind Enid. The bumpy figure and empty face belonged to Cookie. She disappeared into the darkness of the doorway leading to the employees' lunchroom. Anne imagined venom already dripping from her tongue, in her eagerness to tell CeeCee the news of her return.

Enid had caught Anne's change in expression and turned in time to see Cookie scamper like a spider into the dark hole.

"Don't mind her. You'll find you have more allies around here than you might think. Those two need a comeuppance."

"I really appreciate your support, girls, but I'm not here to teach life lessons. I just want to finish a job." Anne chatted with the women a little longer.

"Enid, what can you tell me about the office staff? I don't really know them well."

"Well, don't know how much I can add to what you know already. Bernie's the boss. Pretty good one so far as I know. What ya see is what ya get with him. And whatever else rattles around in his head usually stays there. Barby and Tammy? Some call 'em Tweedle-dee and Tweedle-dummer. Local gossip tickles their tongues, but they're not so mean as Dearie. Morgan… She's…" A few minutes later the buzzer sounded for the end of lunch break, and everyone hurried for the door to the factory.

24.

Anne loitered a few minutes. She felt the warmth of the sun and a soft breeze flowing into the bay. It was a good feeling and a pleasant balance with the scent of salt and seaweed, the rumble of engines, the jabber of foamy water in the wake of boats, and the lament of eager seagulls looking for their own share of the day's catch.

Anne took a few more deep breaths, clutched her handbag, and made for the door. With a renewed vigour and resolve, she vaulted up the stairs to the office complex.

Morgan Sark, the receptionist, sat at her desk. A large glass window framed her against a striking panorama of the harbour. Enid had described Morgan as an efficient, middle-aged woman, who had been orphaned at ten and married off by foster parents at fifteen. She'd been abandoned by two wastrel husbands and was single again. Enid had seemed to admire Morgan. In spite of misfortunes that would have crushed others, she maintained an optimistic appearance. Still, Anne wondered if that was a shield to guard her from her past. *The past has been known to hunt you down*, Enid once said, reflecting on her own early life to Anne.

Morgan offered a bright smile and a cheery greeting that Anne felt was genuine.

"Is Bernie in?" Anne said.

Morgan glanced toward an adjoining door. "Door's ajar. That means there are no deep, dark secrets hanging in the air... and he's not dozing. Just go right in."

Anne rapped lightly out of courtesy and pushed open the door to Bernie's office.

"Have I interrupted?"

"No, not at all. Actually, I was expecting you bright and early. I was becoming concerned."

"My work for your boss takes me other places than here."

Bernie laughed. Then it turned into a smirk. "Figured you might have stopped to pick up the trophy."

"What trophy?"

"I think they call it 'Free-style Brawling Finals,' pink-fist division."

"Very funny, Bernie. I could've got killed."

"Could have, but you did pretty damned good, if you ask me."

"Got lucky."

"Seemed like more than luck… for an engineer."

"I minored in Phys. Ed."

"You did?"

"Of course not. But when you're cornered, there's only one way out. My uncle taught me that."

"I'll remember that if I ever get you into a corner."

"That'll never happen, Bernie. Not in your wildest dreams."

"Just kiddin' around. So what's up for today in your research?"

"Well, I did a time analysis of the production line Friday. I've still got those numbers to crunch. I'll be looking at product movement, snags in the supply line, storage, shipping to distributors, and a bunch of other objectives. If you want details, check with Mr. Gauthier."

"All right. Enough. You're giving me a headache already. And I take it you're not going to do all that today."

"No, of course not. The basics will take days. Everything will take a couple weeks, maybe a month."

"So you're going to be hanging around here for… maybe a month."

"Here, and elsewhere. Could be… dunno… depends how far the Gauthiers want to go. Oh, I almost forgot. I'll be looking at inventory loss, too. That can affect the bottom line as well."

"Inventory loss? Whatcha mean?"

"You know... theft, vandalism, skimming, employees with a sticky-fingers affliction."

"Ya don't say. Well, there's no more of that happening here than anywhere else... but you might want to talk to Luc LaVie. He's our security guy. He reported a break-in over the weekend."

"Thanks. Will do." *Wasn't that a timely remembrance*, she thought.

25.

Anne had walked down the corridor past the empty third room to the fourth office. Two women were sitting there, each with a coffee, immersed in casual conversation. This space belonged to Tammy Wallace, office manager. With her was Barbie Beaton, the company bookkeeper.

"Good afternoon, ladies. I'm Anne Brown. I believe you're Barbie... and Tammy... if I remember right. I've met so many employees the last few days, it's hard to keep names straight."

Tammy stood, walked over, and shook her hand. It was a firm, confident, one-pump handshake. She pulled up another chair to the desk.

"Have a seat. Coffee?"

"Thanks, and yes, coffee, if you have some. Cream and sugar."

Barbie remained in her chair, tossed a nod in Anne's direction, and offered up a guarded but cordial smile.

Tammy had her own percolator, the decanter half-filled, on a side table. She was a tall, rather stiff woman, but she had a pleasant face and demeanour. She wore khaki slacks and a blue Oxford shirt with button-down collar. She kept a blue ballpoint pen and notebook in her breast pocket. She poured Anne a fresh cup. Then she sank back into the chair behind her desk.

Both Barbie and Tammy looked toward Anne and took a sip of coffee. Both smiled again. Anne felt an awkward pause.

"I hope I'm not interrupting something. I could come back later."

"Sorry. We weren't expecting you back... thought you packed it in," said Tammy. Then she and Barbie burst out laughing. "So now we just need to stall another moment or so to think up a better lie—like we were just now preparing a business forecast or an inventory update—to hide the fact that we were just gossiping."

Anne relaxed with their candour.

"Well, if it weren't for gossip, coming to work wouldn't be worth the trip, would it?" said Anne and joined their giggling. "So what's the big topic today?"

"There's two. You... and Fig Grant," said Tammy. Anne felt herself tense up again.

"Three, actually. You, CeeCee, and Fig," said Barbie.

"You're at the top of the chart. CeeCee's number two, and Fig was bumped to number three," said Tammy. Both women fell into volleys of unmanageable laughter.

Anne felt her face redden. Then a wash of embarrassment swept over her. Her lips suddenly went dry. She grasped her coffee mug with two hands to take a prolonged sip, hide her face, and conceal her humiliation for a second or two more. At that, the girls howled even louder, and watched Anne shrink deeper into her chair.

"Okay, okay, you nailed me," said Anne good-naturedly. "But it wasn't my fault."

"That's what my son used to say when I caught him with his hand in a bag of mischief," said Barbie. More laughter followed, but it quickly faded into seriousness. "I know what you're saying, though. CeeCee can be a bitch. Anyway, you're a pop star for the next few days."

"But watch CeeCee," Tammy warned. "She can be vengeful... especially when her pride is damaged."

"I'll keep an eye open. What about this Fig character? I hear his name bandied about the odd time."

"Did you hear about the baby that was found dead? It was on his family's old homestead. The Grant place."

"I did. What a frightful thing. Does anyone know who it belonged to or what happened?"

"The RCMP aren't saying much. They never do, but the workman who found it told my cousin that he dug it up with his machine next to the old cemetery there. There wasn't much left of it, he said. He guessed it had been there for an awful long time."

"Outside the cemetery?"

"That's what he said. Next to an old tree they'd cut down."

"What kind of work are they doing out there?" said Anne.

"They're clearing land for a summer home," said Barbie. "A big fancy one, I hear."

"Maybe it'll be a permanent home," said Tammy.

"Yeah, maybe so," said Barbie. "Lucky her, if it is."

"Whatcha mean?" said Anne.

"My sister, Carrie, saw the new owner of the place with some girl at a restaurant in Charlottetown a while back. They looked pretty lovey-dovey to Carrie. She's pretty good at putting two and two together."

"So, who's the new owner of the place?" said Anne, curious now.

"The new owner," Barbie repeated.

Anne looked confused.

"The new owner," Barbie said again. Now both Barbie and Anne looked confused.

Tammy recognized the misunderstanding between the two girls. She chuckled a bit. Then she broke the impasse. "The new owner of the factory is Mr. Gauthier. He's also new owner of the Grant homestead."

"Jean Gauthier? Or Michel?"

"Jean," said Tammy with a withering frown. "Why would an old man want a big new house in the middle of nowhere?"

Anne felt a small panic swell up from the realization that someone in the community had seen her and Jean together. Before long everyone would learn of their relationship and that would compromise her cover, as well as her investigation.

She glanced quickly at her watch, jumped up, and said, "Gotta go. Thanks for the coffee."

26.

Anne turned left as she made her hasty goodbye in Sarah's office. A few feet ahead, the corridor split left and right. The left corridor led to the staff lounge. The door was half-open and the room empty. A steep staircase led down to where the fish processing was taking place. A small storeroom and a closet for cleaning supplies occupied the right wing. At the junction of the two wings was the security office she had visited Saturday night.

Anne thought this might be an opportunity to have a close, uninterrupted look at the security log—the current one and maybe even a few older ones—especially since no one would have cause to disturb her for several hours.

She poked her head in. The room was empty. She entered and closed the door behind her. In spite of this being her second visit to the security office, Anne was surprised by what she had missed. The wall behind the guard's desk was one glass panel from waist height to ceiling, and it spread out nearly as wide as the room itself. What before had seemed like a dingy, closed-in office now felt bright and spacious. What generated that impression was the view from the window. Anne moved toward it. It revealed nothing of the harbour or the surrounding grounds, but most of the factory floor itself and dozens of employees so intent on their job that none seemed inclined to look up.

Anne stepped back from the window. She preferred that no one on the factory floor see her peering down. Some would take it as snooping in its nastiest sense, and that would breed more mistrust, speculation, and gossip.

Lights from the ceiling of the processing room below amply lit the security office as well. So there was no need to flick on the light. Anne settled into a chair. The logbook was centred on the desk. She opened it to the entries for Saturday night.

Anne ran her finger down the list. They averaged an entry for every half hour of the guard's shift. The recorded times were irregular, and they varied from inside routine checks to outside patrols. Her finger stopped at about the same time as she had come across Rufus and Norman. That entry indicated Mr. LaVie was patrolling the exterior facilities of the wharf and factory property at the same time that she had detained the boys.

Most of the records were falsified, but it was evident that LaVie had made at least a few security checks. He noted that just before dawn he had found a broken lock on the warehouse but nothing appeared to be missing. In reality, though, none of his reports could be taken seriously.

The sound of footsteps trudging down the corridor caught Anne's attention. When she guessed that they were passing Tammy's office, she settled back in the chair, and waited for the knob to turn or footsteps to continue along one of the wings.

The doorknob rattled, the door opened, and Luc LaVie jumped at the sight of Anne sitting quietly in his chair.

"Omigod," he said. "You give me a awful start." Luc stood there not quite knowing what to say or do.

Anne relished the surprise she had inspired. She also made a mental note: French name, French accent, and diction as well. Anne stood as he came into the room.

Luc LaVie was shorter than she had estimated when she watched him snore through her Saturday night observation of him. Still, he was four inches or so taller than she. As she remembered, his head was shaved. Now, it was apparent that the close-cut remains were white. Luc was probably in his sixties, though he still looked hale and sturdy.

"I'm Anne Brown."

"And I am Luc LaVie."

"I didn't meet you at the orientation on Friday, but I've been hired by the owners to study the operation here and make recommendations on improving efficiency. Mr. Gauthier has given me free run of the place."

"Efficiency..." he said.

"Part of that involves looking at how to save money."

"...save money... yes," he repeated.

"Sometimes money is lost through break-ins, sometimes by employees taking things home. My job is to look at what's happening in those areas. And that's why I'm here looking at the security log and why I'd like to speak with you about what happens around here. You must've seen a lot of things while you've worked here."

"Yes... a lot, I think so."

"Good. So let's start with Saturday night. Maybe you could tell me what happened then."

"Well, it was quiet mostly. Not much is going on. Not that I see anyways when I do my rounds, but maybe around four-thirty I see the lock is broke off. It was on the place where they keep supplies to sell the fishermen. I look inside but see nothing is disturbed. And I put it in my report."

"Why do you think the lock was broken?"

"Maybe I scare them away when I start my patrol."

"Are there many break-ins here?"

"Not so many, I guess. Sometimes things get taken. Most of the time it's kids who do damage... break things... hard to catch them at night in the dark. Sometimes they steal from the boat."

"And how long have you worked here as a guard?"

"This year only and last year. Just the six or eight month when the plant is working. I do carpentry the rest of time."

"By the way, where are the old security logs? I didn't notice any others on the shelf."

"I don't know. I never see them either. Maybe they put them in the file somewhere. Maybe there are none."

"Thank you, Luc. I appreciate your alertness, and I'll mention your diligence to the boss."

"...diligence... yes... thank you."

"By the way, do you remember when the pipes burst in the spring?"

"I was here."

"You were a security guard?"

"No, no, I don't work that until April. Bernie call me to help him. So I come and help."

"Do you have any idea what might have happened? Vandalism? Some mistake? Anything?"

"I don't know. Door was lock. Pump was on. Water coming from every place."

"The pump was on?"

"Yes, I hear the motor when I come here."

"Isn't it necessary to turn off the pump before you drain pipes?"

"Yes, but it was on. I know that."

"Can you show me the pumphouse now?"

Luc seemed eager. He led Anne along the corridor, out and down the stairs. Anne trailed behind him. They rounded the corner at the end of the factory. A small wooden structure was attached to it. It was solidly built. Luc keyed the padlock and swung the door back.

Inside, Luc pointed out pipe leading to the casing around the well. Smaller-dimension pipe carried water from the pump through the rear of the pumphouse into the factory's supply lines. A comfortable opening led from the pumphouse directly into the factory. Luc pointed out the electrical switch on the pump and a few of the nearby drain cocks.

"So let me get this straight. To winterize the plant somebody must turn off the pump switch and open the drain cocks to drain the pipes. That's it, right?"

"Flush th' toilets, too. Drain th' holding tanks. I help Bernie do that."

"So to flood the place and destroy the plumbing, the drain cocks have to be closed, and the pump switch has to be flipped on by someone."

"Yes."

"But there was no sign of break-in."

"Yes."

"Keys?"

"Only Bernie has keys then."

Anne stared at Luc skeptically.

"So how does somebody get in if it's not Bernie?"

Luc replied with a vacant, embarrassed expression.

Anne escorted Luc back to his office and plied him with more questions along the way. Something about the pumphouse bothered her.

"Why is the pumphouse outside the factory?"

"Years ago th' old well goes bad with sea water. So they drill a new one. A deeper one. They have to drill outside the building. So they dig close by and build th' shed around it."

"Who built it?"

"I did, and it's strong as anything. Same as other fisherman building on th' wharf. I build them, too, many years ago."

"Thanks so much, Luc."

He smiled eagerly. He reminded her of a spaniel her parents had when she was a child in Ottawa.

"Oh... and by the way, Luc, I hope I don't find your office door open and confidential logbooks and files open for viewing again. I would have to pass that info on to the boss."

Anne smiled back.

27.

Anne felt no obligation to pass on any details regarding Luc LaVie's diligence or lack of it—at least not this early in the investigation. No sense making enemies where they aren't needed. He may be an incompetent watchman, but he may still provide useful information. Besides, Luc's responses were quick and spontaneous, and that suggested complete candour.

Anne glanced at the wall clock. It was nearing four o'clock, and she realized that Rufus and Norman would be waiting for her on the wharf. She hurried noisily down the steps and out the door. The sun was bright and strong. She shaded her eyes and scanned the wharf, the collection of factory buildings, and outbuildings and sheds. But the boys were nowhere to be seen.

Anne turned around in exasperation. She felt annoyance welling up inside her, and tried to imagine what weakness in her subtle threat to them or deviance in their puerile thought process had led them to dismiss her and bugger off.

Then she looked up. Both of them were walking leisurely up the road from Halkirk, each sipping a can of pop, and chatting. Anne felt vindicated at their arrival, but remained annoyed at their relaxed attitude. She hailed them with a raised arm and motioned them toward her.

A large grey pickup truck rumbled past them and sailed up the road toward Halkirk. A couple of seagulls swooped over the empty truck bed for remnants of food, landed on the road, and pecked at a discarded paper wrapper. An empty forklift squealed along, its forks jangling noisily at every imperfection in the pavement.

Anne wanted a private, undisturbed conversation with Rufus and Norman. So she ushered them away from the wharf and factory toward the cluster of outbuildings alongside the processing plant. She found a quiet, little-travelled spot and led them between two sheds.

"Rufus, Norman, we're going to have a little chat here. I need some more information. After you give me straight answers, then we likely won't need to speak again, and those photos of your Saturday night exploit will be buried in my archives and won't see daylight again. Okay?"

Both boys nodded, Norman's head moving less earnestly.

"I need details about Edgar MacAulay," she said. A flicker of dread animated Rufus's eyes. A protective twist of Norman's torso had sparked an instinct to run. Anne perceived the reactions. But both boys remained.

"Giving info about Edgar is scary, but he'll never know who gave up the details. Understand? Actually, there's a good chance he won't have a clue that anything was passed on. Trust me. I have no intention of embarrassing you or making trouble. Okay?"

Anne took out a notebook and pencil. She began with innocuous questions like what his house looked like inside, the layout of rooms, where he spent most of his time, his personal habits, and whether or not he lived alone. Then she asked for names of his buddies and girlfriends.

As the boys settled into the routine, Anne ventured into uncomfortable territory, questions the boys knew were risky to answer, but their pump had already been primed, and, now that they had committed to the process and begun to spill information, they felt that there was no way to extract themselves and stop.

Yes, there was a shotgun next to Edgar's front door.

No, they didn't know if he kept it loaded.

Yes, Edgar kept a stash of drugs in the house.

No, they didn't know where exactly, but it was somewhere upstairs.

No, they weren't users or sellers.

Anne carried on with even tougher questions.

Who were Edgar's business associates?

What security precautions did he take to protect his house and goods?

Where did he keep the stolen goods? If not at the house, where?

Is he a violent person?

The boys began to look weary. They knew the gravity of the questions and the answers, but, if they were in for a dime, they were in for a dollar as well. They had no choice.

Anne felt sorry for Rufus and Norman. She watched them slowly wither under her examination. In fact, they seemed to shrink into the ground.

"Tell no one about today. No one. Right?"

Anne gave them a final pep talk after she put her notebook back into her pocket. She hoped it gave them reassurance. Then she sent them on their way.

28.

Anne felt somewhat guilty about badgering kids for information, especially information which, if the source became known, would dump a mountain of trouble on them, but it had to be done. Besides, the boys were on a road to self-destruction, and Anne believed that nothing could turn that around but putting distance between them and MacAulay.

Her interview of Rufus and Norman had resulted in quite a few notes. She paged through them as she made her way back toward the factory and the wharf. The sun was strong and glared against her notebook. She had enough information, she thought, for her next move, and that would come soon. A couple of phone calls away, at most.

She pocketed the notebook, reached for her cellphone, and looked up. A figure loomed in front of her. It was CeeCee Dunne. Anne's feet skidded to a stop on the loose gravel and dirt on the pavement.

CeeCee stood squarely ahead like an impassable wall. She had finished her shift and wore street clothes. Her mouth was grim, her lips tight lines. Heavy makeup applied that morning had faded in the heat and steam of the busy factory floor and revealed the blotch of a bruised eye and the swelling of her nose. Her thick blonde hair had grown unruly after her day's work. Her pretty veneer had vanished and been replaced by what Anne perceived as the face of a woman unhinged, unpredictable.

Anne took a silent moment to slip the cellphone into her pocket and take two discreet steps back. Anne's hands were free for whatever might come, and Anne kept close watch on CeeCee's, which hung at her side, elbows bent and fingers flexing as if preparing to snatch and crush something.

"You were talking to my boy. Don't try to deny it. Somebody seen ya and told me," said CeeCee, "and I seen ya myself from the upstairs window there."

Anne started to speak, but CeeCee interjected. "Don't try to deny it."

CeeCee's voice was sharp and loud and carried far enough to draw a small, curious gathering of off-shift factory women and men gabbing next to a few cars along the wharf. Enid, Cookie, and two or three others formed a loose gathering nearby. A handful of local men and the crew from a Georgetown vessel stood a little farther afield, grinned and joked, and waited for some fireworks to light up a tiresome afternoon.

"Don't try to deny it," CeeCee said a second time, but with more malice.

"I'm not going to deny anything, CeeCee. Sure, I was talking to them, but it was just chitchat. Nothing else. Besides, how would I know it was your kid?"

"I don't believe that for a minute."

"It's true. The boys were strolling up the road here. I was heading for my car. I said hello. They said a few words back, and we chatted for a bit. That's all there was to it. Nothing to be concerned with."

"I don't believe you."

Enid stepped forward and placed herself between Anne and CeeCee.

"Okay, girls, why don't we call it a draw? You're not going to settle things by brawling on the wharf, are ya? If somebody calls the police, then you'll both be paying fines before the magistrate, not to mention paragraphs of nasty publicity in the *Eastern Graphic*. Nobody wins no matter what you two are trying to accomplish."

Enid was twenty years older than CeeCee. She was good-natured and even-tempered, but she was also strong, rough to look at, and heavily framed.

"She's lying," said CeeCee to Enid. "She was talking to Rufus and Norman, and she was writing in a notebook. Nobody writes chitchat in a notebook."

"Tell you what, CeeCee, why don't you just go home and talk to Rufus first. See what he has to say."

"Maybe I will. Maybe I'll just do that," she said glaring at Anne.

"Are we good then?" Enid said, looking first at Anne and back at CeeCee.

Anne nodded. CeeCee eased her combative posture, but held onto her fierce expression a bit longer.

"Good enough for now, but I'm going home, and I'm going to drag the truth out of those boys, and..." CeeCee's voice dropped into a raspy whisper as she leaned forward toward Anne. "When I do, I'll be back, and we'll settle this once and for all, and you can bet that this time I'll be dead sober, and you'll have nobody to run interference for you. Got that, gudgeon?"

CeeCee and her supporters disappeared among the banks of cars and pickups in the parking lot. The curious vanished into quieter corners of Little Rose Harbour. Motors revved and wheels spun on the gravelly patches. Dust kicked up into the dry air. Anger fled down the road to Halkirk, the roar of engines slipped under the lap of waves on the rising tide, and the gulls soared silently, and watchfully, overhead.

"There goes trouble one more time," said Enid. "I really think that woman has a screw loose. Something's not right up there. I suggest you stay clear of her, but I don't know how you'll manage that."

When Anne's cellphone rang, Enid waved goodbye and walked off. The phone call was from Ben Solomon.

"Good news, I hope," said Anne.

"Well, one person's good news is usually someone else's bad," said Ben.

"Let's have it then."

"Edgar MacAulay. Age nineteen. Born April 8th in Truro Memorial Hospital to Reginald and Beatrice MacAulay. Quit school in grade ten. Arrests for shoplifting, break and enter, and vandalism. Breach of conditions twice. Cannabis possession once. These were handled in youth court through restorative justice guidelines. Then he hit the jackpot. Convicted of arson at seventeen. The arson victim was a known petty drug dealer. MacAulay spent a year in a closed facility. He was released a year ago."

"Thanks, Ben."

"Good news or bad?"

"A dead end, I'm afraid."

"That makes it good news."

"How do you figure?"

"Well in my textbook, every time a lead falls apart, you move one step closer to the right one. One less distraction."

"Yeah, maybe you're right, Ben, but I've got one more nail to drive into this coffin, before I move on."

Anne hung up, searched for another phone number, and made a second call.

One more nail, she thought, just before her call was answered.

"Hi, this is Billy Darby of Darby Investigations and Security. I'd like to give some information regarding drug possession, theft, and firearms violations to an investigator at the local detachment. I know it's kind of late in the day, but some of the information may be time-sensitive."

29.

Anne couldn't complete her conference with the RCMP and make it back to Halkirk Manor in time for Ms. Finnerty's "six o'clock sharp" serving of supper. So she stopped at the Golden Dragon restaurant in Montague before continuing home. She slid into a booth near a large countertop aquarium.

Anne ordered the number three dinner: an egg roll, sweet and sour pork, and chicken fried rice. Her clash with CeeCee had sparked an appetite. Anne ate voraciously and watched enormous goldfish swimming circles in a large aquarium. They seemed to be watching her. Anne felt suddenly vulnerable.

Anne learned that her nickname at the factory was "gudgeon," the term for a small baitfish, and it raised her ire. Anne had always been self-conscious of her height, or the lack of it, and, throughout her life she had overcompensated for it, in spite of denials to herself that she had. During most of her adult years she had been able to bury it in a remote corner of her mind. Her new nickname made her feel like a kid in grade school again. She hated it, but there was little she could do about it. To whine or snap back at the label would accomplish nothing, and it would inevitably lead to behind-the-back denigrations, the same way that "Dearie" had become to Jane Finnerty.

Size mattered, but there was more to it than just that. It began with Anne's mother, Hazel Darby, who had lost her first child. The years of childlessness that followed left Mrs. Darby empty and unfulfilled. Then her unexpected pregnancy and the birth of Anne led Mrs. Darby to think of little Anne as the "child that survived," a phrase reflecting constant fear for young Anne's well-being and heightened vigilance for her daughter's safety, an obsession that frustrated Anne for much of her childhood.

Eventually, Hazel Darby lost her grip on Anne's reins. Most of the credit for that could be attributed to the subtleties of her Uncle Bill Darby, then an Ottawa police officer, who lived with them at the time. He became an advocate for young Anne, and a buffer between girl and mother.

There were side effects however. After having been held back for so long, Anne discovered a need to excel—to study more, play tougher, work harder, and reach higher than her mates at school, and, later, her colleagues at work. In the end, that attitude became a habit in her life.

Anne pulled into a small driveway alongside Halkirk Manor. It was too early for dusk, but the incoming cloud cover gave that feel to the evening, and, in the dimming light, Anne caught the frame of a large man descending the stairs from the rear pantry door. Anne couldn't name him, but his bearing was familiar, and she felt she had seen him before.

Anne walked around to the front door and entered. Enid was just heading for a sit on the front veranda. Tom and Jack were chatting in the reading room. Jane was probably in the kitchen cleaning up the dishes.

Two children burst from the dining room. They headed for the door and brushed by her as they did. They were followed by loud chastisements in French. A man and a woman hurried past Anne, muttering apologies and pursuing their children.

Anne wasn't ready for the empty quiet of her room, and she was reluctant to meet up with Jane just yet. Instead, she detoured into the reading room, greeted Tom and Jack, grabbed a cup from a tray, poured a fresh coffee, and retreated to the veranda.

"Thought maybe you beat it for town," said Enid with a small grin.

"Not a bad suggestion, but I had some business to clear up. Thanks for the intervention, by the way."

Enid just shrugged.

"Wasn't much to it. Most people don't want to fight. CeeCee's no different. My being there was just an excuse to allow nothing to happen... and still save face."

"She seemed determined enough at the time."

"She's got a lot on her plate. Husband with roaming eyes..."

"...and hands..."

"...a couple of kids who are worrisome... a bit of a drinkin' problem... and an arm a bit too short to grab respectability. What was that nonsense about you and her kid she was spouting off about?"

"I did talk to him. Just polite conversation... not much more," said Anne.

Enid looked toward Anne. The older woman's eyes expressed a measure of doubt.

"You know, I likely won't be handy the next time you two cross paths."

Anne nodded. Then she changed topic. "Who was the man coming out the back door when I drove up?"

"Didn't see him," said Enid.

"A big man, probably a local. There wasn't much light. No car or truck. And he headed the other direction. A big man," Anne repeated. "Short hair, grey maybe."

Enid sat thoughtfully for a moment. "Big ears?" she said.

"Yeah, big ears, too."

"Could be Fig Grant."

"Is he a friend of Jane?"

"You might say that. They had a thing going a long, long time ago, so the rumour mills said. Of course, that was before Jane became respectable."

"Looks like it may be rekindled."

"I'd doubt that. More likely he's delivering shine to a few fellas in the village, maybe a jar to Dearie as well."

"I saw him and a few other fellas outside the community centre the other night. Looked like they were selling stuff out of the back of a truck."

"Did they look like Mutt and Jeff?" asked Enid.

Anne looked puzzled.

"Mutt and Jeff. Comic-strip characters. Before your time, I guess. One tall and scrawny, the other short and stout. Both always getting jammed up in some harebrained scheme," said Enid. "Pretty funny, actually."

The confusion on Anne's face cleared. "Yeah," she said, "a tall, skinny guy and a short, sturdy sort."

"That would be Spit and Squeak. Sampson Pitt and Wesley Peake. Add 'Fig,' Newton Grant, into the mix and you have the *Three Amigos*, only not quite so humorous."

Anne recalled Jane Finnerty's mention of Spit and Squeak in her exposition of local tomfoolery. She also recalled Dearie's omission of any negative reference toward Fig Grant. Such a reluctance may have been accidental, but, in view of her relationship with the man, it might well have been on purpose.

30.

"So what's the story on Fig? I seem to recall that name popping up in some other circumstance recently."

Enid settled back in her wicker-back chair and stared into dimming grey-violet clouds. One hand slowly massaged the other as if they were pulling half-forgotten or half-buried memories from remote corners of her childhood.

"You know, it's kind of strange looking back to those times. Then, for a kid, the whole world seemed bright and cheerful and full of good things to come. That's how it was for me—for a little while anyway. Then my parents died. They were good people... good but poor, y'understand. Dad got cut bad in a chainsaw accident and bled to death. Mom wasted away with work and then got cancer. She died. After that, I got packed off to live with Aunt Belle and Uncle Fred. I grew rougher there, and my expectations got narrower..."

Enid took in a long, slow breath. It slipped out again with a slight quiver of remembrance. Then she continued: "But I'm not complaining. I got by. I did all right, y'know."

Her eyes peered into memory for a moment before going forward. "Others didn't fare so well, though. Fig Grant was one of them. He had it tough."

"How so?" asked Anne.

"His father was a hard man... a brute of a man. Pardon me for saying so. I don't usually speak ill of the dead—or the living—but if he had been born a dog, he would have been put down without hesitation or regret. I was still a little kid when I knew him. I didn't like the look of him then, and Daddy was skittish of him, too. I could tell that, but I never knew why."

"Did you know Fig then?"

"I'd see him. He was older, of course. A nice-looking boy… quiet… strong. But old Declan worked him like a horse. He'd pull him out of school whenever he wanted help around the house— cutting logs and splitting firewood, setting nets for fish or snares for rabbits or fox or whatever else he could squeeze a dollar out of. In spring he'd pull Fig out of school altogether and take him aboard as crew to haul lobster traps. School board didn't like much it much, but people let people be back then. I don't think Fig ever got past grade six because of it."

"Sounds rough, but some kids can put bad childhoods behind them. Was Fig that kind of boy?"

The summer evening held its warmth even as the sun slipped beneath the horizon. The sky darkened. A light breeze drifted through the village, but it was a warm and humid draft. Enid moved uneasily in her chair, looked disdainfully at her empty coffee cup, and pushed it away.

"You must be getting bored with these old wives' tales. Gossip and rubbish from a hundred years ago, it seems. And not pleasant things to recall," she said. Then she shifted to a different subject. "I don't hear the boys chattering away in the reading room. Jack must have hit the sack. He boards Hec's boat around four. It'll be an early night for him. And Tom… he's usually not far behind. Maybe you're ready to call it a night, too. You've had more than an exciting moment or two to rest up from today."

Anne was surprised and disappointed that Enid wanted to discontinue her half-finished recollection. She pushed her to continue. Enid was hesitant, but Anne urged her to finish.

"Sad recollections make me thirsty," said Enid. She reached into the handbag that settled near her feet and pulled out a pint of rum. "Join me?" she said and added, "It's dark enough now that the righteous in the village won't see enough to take offense, not that I give a care."

Enid poured a measure of rum into her coffee cup and added an equally generous measure into Anne's extended cup. Enid lingered in silence for several minutes until she felt the burn of the rum smoulder in her belly, seep through her chest and arms, and transcend some old reluctance. Then she continued her story.

"Well, old Declan finally died... I call him old, but he wasn't much over forty at the time. Some accident aboard his fishing vessel. Don't recall the details. Fig was fifteen, sixteen at the time. Responsibility for the family fell on him after that. Miriam, his mother, wasn't very old either, but she had no skills to speak of. There was a girl there, too. Fig's sister, a pretty little thing. Her name was Mary, I believe."

"Sounds like things improved... with Declan gone."

"I believe there's bad-luck families," said Enid, "and this was one of them. Sure, Fig took over his father's fleet the following year and seemed to be doing well enough with it. A few other fishermen kept an eye on him, too, so's he wouldn't get into too much trouble with his gear and could get into some decent fishing grounds. He got through his first season all right. But just when a person thinks everything will work out, it collapses. His mother, Miriam, lasted just a year after Declan. Influenza took her. His sister, Mary, was maybe five years old."

"Goodness, who looked after her then? Fig would have been too young for it."

"Maybe so... but he became the parent after that. No other kin around, ya see."

"I can't imagine what that would have been like."

"He worked hard. He did his best. He provided for her, kept her in school. She had friends, too, as I recall. A popular girl. Cordial. The pretty ones usually are, of course. Fig seemed real proud of her..."

"Pride often comes from a job well done. I think I can understand that. I'm delighted whenever I look at Jacqueline, my daughter. I'm so happy with what she's become."

Enid nodded agreeably but said, "Or maybe he was proud because she didn't take after Declan or Miriam."

"So it all worked out?" said Anne.

Enid took the last sip of rum from her cup. She splashed in a bit more from her flask and downed that in one swallow.

"Time for bed," she said to Anne and stood to leave. "How old's Jacqueline?"

"Eighteen."

"Eighteen? That's a good age. They've got their heads almost together by then..."

Anne smiled in agreement.

"...but Mary Grant... she was but fifteen when she drowned, poor thing."

31.

Tuesday

When she arose the next morning, Anne felt exhausted. She knew she'd dreamed, but she had no recollection of sleep. The contradiction of a troubled night.

Her dream, of course, was a hodgepodge of the real, the imagined, the possible, and the preposterous. She dreamt that she and Jean were living in his new mansion on Sullivan's Point. Life was wonderful: their relationship firm, their station in the community respectable, their future limitless. Then came the angry knock on the door and the arrival of Declan Grant, his wife Miriam, Fig, and little Mary. The Grants bickered and fought and elbowed their way inside. The children fled to remote corners and cowered.

Jean ordered them to leave, but Declan attacked him, saying it was his land and his house. He tossed Jean and Anne out the door. Police were called, and Declan argued his point in Gaelic with a shotgun balanced in the crook of his arm. Although the officers couldn't understand his gibberish, some oddity convinced authorities to accept Declan's claim, and Jean's objections were discounted. Anne tried reasoning with the police as well. She begged them to protect the children still cowering in the corner, but her efforts were ignored, too.

The police forced Jean and Anne to leave the property. As they fled, two pairs of children's eyes peered helplessly through the sheer curtains in an upstairs window. Jean and Anne trudged the several miles to Halkirk and caught a taxi for Charlottetown, knowing that their dream had been crushed, the children lost, and they could never return there again.

In the vague light of Tuesday morning, Anne felt affront and injustice and embarrassment at the goings-on in her dream. She felt angry, too: anger at the police for ineffectiveness, anger at Jean for not standing tall, anger at herself for not landing on some way to extract the children from their bizarre captivity. When she realized that she was angry at the phantoms of a weird nightmare, she began to feel foolish, and she would have laughed at herself if the last embers of fury were not still smouldering in her heart.

Even later, Anne felt that this was not the kind of nightmare she could laugh off. Perhaps that was why Enid had preferred not to to dredge up old stories. Perhaps more pain than Enid would admit still resonated in her darker recesses.

Anne felt renewed after her shower in spite of the slowly fading quantity of hot water. Her mind had sharpened, her body had gained vigour, and her spirit had dispelled the most sordid remnants of her dream. It was seven o'clock when she made it down to the dining room for breakfast. Jack Pine was already three hours at sea with a packed lunch that Jane had prepared for him in lieu of breakfast. Enid had finished eating and was upstairs dressing for work at the factory. Tom busied himself with dabbing peanut butter on toast and jotting down notes regarding a quicker method of rebaiting lobster traps.

Anne quickly finished off her boiled egg, toast with marmalade, and strong coffee, and pointed her car in the direction of Little Rose Harbour. She was halfway there when she pulled over onto the shoulder, doubled back to an access road, and headed instead in the direction of Sullivan's Point. The road wasn't paved all the way, and she wasn't entirely sure where she was going, but the fresh tire marks of heavy trucks emerging from a dirt road suggested her way.

A few hundred yards farther along the trail, she arrived at Sullivan's Point, the former home of the Grant family and the construction site of Jean Gauthier's new PEI home. It was a bit too early for the work gangs to arrive, but that was what Anne had hoped for.

The real Sullivan's Point was not a replica of the one in her nightmare. Instead, it was quite beautiful, she thought. Rugged, but beautiful. Wildness with a sense of isolation. Qualities difficult to find almost anywhere.

Police tape marred the effect somewhat. It encircled the pioneer cemetery and a significant space beyond, but not enough to slow construction on the site. The spot for the house had been cleared and excavated, and forms had been erected for the foundation. Five acres of scrub had been cleared and levelled. Landscaping probably would begin after concrete had been poured and the house erected. Clusters of trees lined the shore. They would ensure privacy and still provide a remarkable view of the bay and its approaches.

The water was glassy, the wind calm, the sun still low and soft, the sky clear. Anne was left with a feeling of wonder and peacefulness that contradicted the madness of last night's dream. The only breach in the serenity was the grumble of a small engine in an old fishing vessel. Its wake cut a ripple of vees into the mirrored water. It was a small boat, perhaps a twenty-seven-footer, an open deck with a small cuddy forward, and it plodded slowly and steadily toward Little Rose Harbour.

32.

A small fishing vessel turned its bow into Little Rose Harbour, swung around, and nestled against an empty berth not far from the Queens County Packers truck and weigh station. The boat's deck was empty of traps or fish trays. There was no hired man aboard to haul gear, measure the carapace, or band the claws. It was not a working lobster vessel.

Fig Grant tied up, mounted the wharf, and took his place at the weigh station with Spit and Squeak. It was nearing nine o'clock, a bit early, but one or two of the quicker inshore vessels might make it in, and the wind was freshening. Weather reports had forecast strong easterlies, and those warnings might encourage a few others to head ashore, too.

"Wh-what's the news?" asked Spit, staring out the channel. Fig noticed that Spit's brow was even more wrinkled and worried than usual, and his greeting was glum.

"Somethin' got your drawers jammed up?" said Fig.

"I g-got a feelin'," he said.

"What d'ya mean?"

"Police. Seems to be m-more of them around. T-talkin' to you. C-cruisin' down here more than usual, and they hit mm-MacAulay's place last night. Took him in. Searched the property," said Spit.

Squeak nodded his head in agreement and scratched the remnants of his corn-silk hair.

"Frank Lavers saw a string of them rippin' past their place just as he was dressing for fishin'. No lights, no sirens," said Squeak. "It gave him a kind of queer feelin', he said."

"Well," said Fig, "I'll tell you somethin' that'll give you a good feelin'. That barrel of mash is ready to run off. We can go at it this evening."

"Maybe w-w-we should hold off on it 'til things settle down," said Spit. He looked expectantly at Fig and then at Squeak.

"Look, you're worryin' about nothin', Spit. They couldn't spot the still... not even from the air. The brush is too thick. There's no road and no trail worn in. And if they came that way, we'd hear them... and if they came by boat, we'd hear them or see them comin' that way, too. And if them easterlies build up a bit, there won't be traceable smoke from the still."

"I'm okay with it," said Squeak. "My Gail would've had a contrary opinion, though."

"She always had a contrary opinion," said Fig. "So they nail us, find the still, seize the shine, and take us in. So what? It's not like we're growin' dope for school kids or stealin' from neighbours, is it? And what'll happen if the police do sniff us out? Break up the still and fine us. So what? We pay the fine, put together new equipment, and find a new place to cook."

"I guess," said Spit.

***

Anne took the steps at M. Gauthier & Son's Little Rose factory two at a time. At the top of the stairs, she threw a wave and a smile to Morgan and strode past her down the corridor toward the office of Tammy Wallace. As before, Barbie Beaton was sipping coffee with her.

"A cup?" invited Tammy.

Anne nodded. "Cream and sugar."

"I make it the first time. After that, you're on your own," said Tammy pointing to the percolator.

Anne grabbed an empty cup and coffee and plopped into a chair.

"What are the headlines today?"

"The Daily Gossip is fickle. You're old hat today."

"I'm disappointed," said Anne.

"So am I. I had hope for your continued success. You had potential. Storm clouds were gathering late in the afternoon, I heard. A bit of thunder but no fireworks. You would have made headlines on a slow news day, but it just didn't happen."

"Who beat me out today?"

"You wouldn't have heard of him. Edgar MacAulay's his name."

Anne assumed a mildly puzzled look and shrugged.

"A local character. A young fella that works hard at petty crime and aspires to greater glory in his chosen field."

"What'd he do?"

"Not quite sure, but RCMP raided his house early this morning and took him away. Grapevine says he's into drug peddling and stealing stuff."

"Some people will do anything to grab a headline," said Barbie. "Present company excluded, of course."

"I appreciate the character reference," said Anne. "I'll work harder at it tomorrow. By the way, you're looking especially dapper today. What's the special occasion?" Anne pointed to the blue and scarlet tie Tammy wore with her button-down Oxford shirt.

"Why, thank you for noticing. Just something I threw on at the last moment..."

"Special occasion?"

"Actually, yes, kind of. The boss showed up this morning. I keep a tie in the drawer for surprise visits from him... or the Prime Minister... or any royals who show up for a quickie tour of our humble employ. As if..."

"The boss?"

"Uh-huh."

"Mr. Gauthier?"

"Well, I know it's not Bruce Springsteen."

***

The churn of exhaust fans, the clank of machinery, and the

distorted chatter of factory workers merged into one mountainous din. CeeCee levelled a dour look everywhere, and everyone kept as clear of her as they would a growling, slinking dog. Everyone, that is, except Cookie Doherty.

Cookie felt immune to the meanness CeeCee could and did unleash toward those who disturbed her turf. Cookie saw herself as CeeCee's protector, the eyes and ears that brought her news of import and words of warning. Cookie may have been a panderer, but she was no fool. She knew that someday CeeCee might find fault and turn on her, and, for that possibility, she played a few cards close to her chest, just in case she had to protect herself.

CeeCee had been especially quiet this morning. Cookie noted this mood, but she had been unable to assign a cause.

"Something bothering you today, CeeCee."

"I'm fine, just fine," she said.

"You don't seem fine. You've got that evil eye thing going. Looks like you're going to explode or something."

CeeCee ignored her, grabbed another lobster. Her gloved hands snapped it into three sections with no more sensitivity than a weasel at the throat of a pheasant chick.

After that, Cookie kept quiet long enough for her previous comments to slip from CeeCee's mind. Then she changed the conversation toward something she believed safer, CeeCee's running feud with Anne Brown.

"Saw Jimmy Doyle this morning. He was at the wharf yesterday when you two were at it. Jimmy said he couldn't understand why you let Anne get away with it."

Cookie glanced sideways at CeeCee's eyes. Something registered there, but she couldn't guess what. She pressed on.

"A couple other girls wondered, too. They were surprised."

"Who cares?" said CeeCee. "I don't give a rat's ass what they think."

"Just sayin'," said Cookie dismissing her own observation as inconsequential. Cookie grew puzzled.

"Just sayin'," she said again. "One girl thought you might be afraid of her. I don't, but that's what she said. I told her you weren't. Thought you should know. That's all."

"Now I know."

"Couldn't even imagine you afraid of that little Anne Brown turd. Can't even imagine it! A gudgeon like her."

CeeCee cracked the hard shell of another lobster with a viciousness that made Cookie recoil slightly. She could almost feel her own neck breaking.

"Will you shut the fuck up about Anne Brown?" she shouted. "Just shut the fuck up!"

CeeCee grabbed the lobster sections she had just broken apart and hurled them down table into a plastic tray. She used enough force to jolt the tray when the shells struck it. Lobster juice sprayed the air and splattered several women working nearby. They let go a storm of vulgarities that rose above the ordinary racket, and two other workers returned CeeCee's hostility with a barrage of trash and offal.

A melee would have broken out except for the quick intervention of a supervisor with a menacing look and sharp threats.

***

"What the devil are you doing here?"

Anne was furious when she pushed through the door to Jean Gauthier's office at M. Gauthier & Son at Little Rose Harbour. Jean had never seen her angry before. He returned her temper with an amused smile.

"Please have a seat, Ms. Brown. No need for a hard sell so early on in our negotiations. I'm confident we can come to an agreement about your concern."

"It's not funny," said Anne.

"It most certainly is. Not quite slapstick… but definitely in the neighbourhood of romantic comedy."

Words like "that's not funny either" popped into Anne's mind, and those words would have made it to her tongue, were it not likely they'd confirm Jean's comedy reference.

Anne shut the door, calmed herself, and sat down in the chair in front of his desk. It proved too large for her. Almost immediately she felt as if she were back in the vice-principal's office for some petty infraction at her Ottawa high school.

"Now," he said, "where would you like to begin?"

"Why don't we start with 'why are you here?'" She had composed her temper and hastily assumed a professional deportment. Jean was out of line, she thought. He had agreed to give her space to do her job. Now he had grown lax and unthinking and weak. He would undermine her. So she felt entirely satisfied with the tough stand she was taking.

"I'm here because I was in the neighbourhood."

"Not a believable reason."

"Sometimes the truth is not always conveniently believable... but I stand by it. There were, however, contributing factors. I admit that."

"Like..."

"In no particular order... I got tired of tripping over my father's reminders of why I should never have got involved in business on PEI... I feel obligated to keep an eye on both businesses I own on the Island... I haven't dropped into Little Rose Harbour in a week... and... I adore my new associate, an industrial engineer... perhaps you've met her... charming woman... charming."

"Compelling reasons, but I haven't heard a valid one yet."

"Well if you're looking for something tediously official: how about an invite from the police?"

"To come here?"

"No, not here exactly. Their detachment in Montague. They needed me to identify some stolen goods seized in a raid. Edgar MacAulay is held there pending charges. Thank you for that, by the way. They raided his house last night. Some of the gear was stolen months ago. It still had the shipping invoices attached, and they needed verification that they were stolen, not purchased."

"And that brought you here."

"Like I said, I was in the neighbourhood. Ten minutes away."

Anne felt herself slowly softening. Jean's humour and boldness and unabashed affection for her were disarming. The scowl she had levelled at him grew unstable and twitched into embarrassment and a timid smile. Her narrowed eyes grew warmer and forgiving.

"So why are you really here?"

"I told you. Don't you believe me?"

"I think there's more to it than that. Put all the cards on the table."

"You're pretty sharp, aren't you?"

"It's what you're paying me for. Right?"

"Okay, there is a little more to it. I'd heard that there was a bit of a confrontation yesterday."

Jean paused for Anne to interject, but she remained stoic and silent. He went on, "I thought the presence of an owner here might keep the lid on whatever was brewing under the surface. Everyone would be on their best behaviour."

"I get it," said Anne, "but I don't need help, and I don't want any. It's part of the job, and I can take care of myself. Thank you very much, but no thanks."

Anne's voice had grown more forceful but remained low and tightly controlled. The impact on Jean was perceptible. He realized he had overstepped a boundary and hoped she would not become angry again.

"Who's the Good Samaritan you've had watching me?"

"I don't have anyone watching you. It's just that somebody who was concerned about your welfare offered the information."

"Who?"

"I'd rather not say."

"Who?" she demanded. "I'd rather not work this job if I don't know exactly what's going on. And don't worry about me calling him or her out and causing a scene. This isn't high school. I just want to know who's doing what that concerns me and my investigation. Okay?"

"Okay. I'll tell you. It was Bernie. He's really worried you'll get hurt."

"You said the other day that he didn't know I was a private investigator. Does that still hold true, or does he know?"

"He doesn't know anything."

"You're sure."

"Absolutely."

"Okay. Fine. Let's keep it that way."

Silence hung in the air of Jean's office. It felt oppressive. It also felt sad. Seconds tumbled like minutes. Neither Jean nor Anne said anything more lest the consequences collapse into an unbrigeable obstacle between them. But when their eyes met, the affection of one pair met its match in the other.

"Friends?" asked Jean, reaching out and touching her hand

"Friends," she said.

"More than friends?"

"I hope so."

They stepped toward each other, Anne almost teary-eyed at the near end of their relationship, his arms opening for a warm embrace.

"But not here," she said.

A sharp rap on the door and the sound of a hand clutching the doorknob decisively ended his advance. They were facing each other with foolish looks on their faces as the door opened.

"Sorry," said Bernie White. "Didn't know you had a visitor. Your father called. He said he's heading for the Egmont plant and that, if he has time, he might drop in here for a quick visit."

"Thanks, Bernie."

The bewildered look on Jean's face persisted well after Bernie closed his office door and returned to his own office up the hall.

"What's the matter?" said Anne.

"Oh nothing, really," he said.

"That's good, isn't it? Your father taking an interest in your business."

"It's not like him. He's always been opposed to operating on PEI. And he's never visited here."

"Maybe he's finally coming around."

"Can't see it. He's stubborn... and proud. If it's not his development plan, then it's not a good one."

"But when he sees that both plants are profitable and efficient, won't he have more confidence in you... loosen the reins on managing everything himself?"

"Maybe. Maybe not."

"I imagine it must be tough for him to let go after so many years. A self-starter, a hands-on businessman. He probably sees himself being put out to pasture. And that's sad."

"Yeah, that's a possibility, but I can't help thinking that his sudden interest is just a ploy to find fault with the PEI expansion and convince me to sell it all off."

"It's not the right time to worry about that. It's just speculation. Everything will settle out soon enough. I'm sure of it."

"Well, you've got two days to make that happen."

"What do you mean?"

"Just that. Papa's worried about your safety. He thinks it's getting too risky. He wants you off the case. And he wants to dump the Little Rose Harbour facility... to get clear of it."

"Don't you have any say in the matter?" Anne's tone grew solemn and distant. "It's your business, isn't it?"

"Nothing is simple when you're dealing with family. Anyway, I got you two more days. That's the best I could do."

Without a word Anne turned and walked out of Jean's office. She felt blindsided. Betrayed even. In the past she had always avoided investigations with friends or relatives. She knew that objectivity erodes under those circumstances.

In reality, though, she couldn't blame this on any bad choice she'd made.

33.

Anne felt herself sinking into an investigative quagmire. She suspected that some old grievance was at the heart of this case, but she had no idea what it was, or what had nurtured it.

Most grudges emerged from a personal injury and, like cancer, could grow slowly or burgeon with speedy vengeance. Almost everyone has done some wrong or craved redress for some grievance, Anne thought. Sometimes the damage may have been egregious enough to attract a small band of sympathizers to rally round the victim. Politics, religion, land ownership, fishing territory, or personal wrongs could be flashpoints. And what may be just cause for one may be insignificant to another. Consequently, any grievance could incite revenge if embers of the offense were fanned long enough. In the end, Anne's mind staggered at the field of suspects, too plentiful to address, and the causes, too arbitrary to discern. And, now, she had been limited to two days to figure it out.

In fact, Anne couldn't even identify the victim. The company appeared to be so, but any individual who represents the company could also be the target. Jean, as a new owner. Bernie, as a former owner. And there were owners or managers before him. It could be somebody still harbouring ill will against the defunct co-op, the original fish canner, or Big Sea Products, a more recent operator of the Little Rose Harbour facility.

It's also possible that another company is behind it: a competitor trying to drive down profit and scoop up the factory at a bargain price—perhaps a thwarted buyer.

Anne's mind began to sink beneath the growing sea of possibilities. Anne's instincts often returned to strategies in soccer games she'd played: the goal is always ahead, but lateral moves or passes to the rear can open an unexpected door forward.

Anne felt a need to widen her perspective, to take in a bigger picture of the factory at Little Rose Harbour. She'd get that in Charlottetown, she thought, with a little digging into provincial government records, and that's where she drove late that morning.

The records Anne wanted were in the Shaw Building, one of several provincial government office buildings. After explaining what she needed, a clerk escorted her to a cubicle and showed her how to locate information she was looking for via a local computer terminal. Her forty-minute search and two return visits for help from the clerk resulted in several pages of notes on the factory's ownership history.

The old fishermen's co-op had ceased operation in the 1970s. Anne scribbled names of its former shareholders. The co-op's building and stock had gone up for public auction in 1980. Bernie White had won that bid and formed a company called Little Rose Cannery, which operated under his sole proprietorship until 1994. In that year, the cannery was purchased by George Livingstone, agent for Big Sea Products. M. Gauthier & Son purchased the business from Big Sea two years ago. The only common thread in the chain of ownership or management was Bernie White.

Anne conducted a web search for George Livingstone and turned up nothing except some footballer and a war hero, both long dead.

Once again Anne beckoned the clerk for help regarding business records, this time regarding George Livingstone. Those efforts were fruitless as well. Relevant taxes had been paid by Big Sea Products. But there was no personal information on Livingstone and surprisingly little information about the company. The clerk called her supervisor who suggested that Livingstone may be an assumed name, a business pseudonym—something unusual, but still legal.

The supervisor sat down at the computer station and began her own search. It revealed George Livingstone as sole proprietor of Big Sea Products. No other company officers were identified.

"What do you make of it?" asked Anne.

"It's looking like Big Sea Products is a shell company," said the supervisor.

"Is that legal?"

"The term 'shell company' sounds illegal because it's so secretive. Canadians don't like secrets when it comes to businesses—or politics—but the fact is that it's perfectly legal, and quite common, in Canada and the US... so long as no hanky-panky is going on."

"What's the purpose of this secrecy?"

"Sometimes one business doesn't want another company to know what it's up to. It protects some strategy or other."

"So how can I identify George Livingstone, and who the real owner of Big Sea Products is?"

"Know anybody in the CIA... or CSIS?" she said and laughed, and, when Anne didn't respond to her humour, she quickly added that taxation officials and any lawyers involved in the purchase were also bound by privacy laws.

Anne found her way to the lobby and perched on a bench in the foyer. The security guard gave her a casual glance as she took out her cellphone and tapped a number.

"Ben, remember that scene in *Lawrence of Arabia* when Peter O'Toole is exhausted, almost dying of thirst with his boy servant in the desert?"

"The quicksand scene?"

"Yeah, that's the one. I'm in town, and I've just escaped the PEI business archives. Need coffee. Growing desperate. Terribly dehydrated. Don't think I can last much longer."

"Lucky me. I'm at the oasis downstairs. The cafeteria. I see a half-full... no, half-empty pot of fresh black coffee. Can't promise relief, though. It may be a mirage."

Anne skipped down the stairs to the lower level of the Shaw Building and walked a long corridor to the cafeteria where Ben Solomon was munching a cheeseburger and fries. A bottle of pop stood next to his plate. A cup of coffee and a cranberry and walnut muffin occupied the empty table space across from him.

"Thanks," she said, nibbling at the muffin. "What do you know about people using false names?"

"Not much, I'm afraid. Why? Give me some information here."

"One of the doors in the case I'm working has a fake name on it."

"And?"

"I want to find out what's hiding on the other side of that door. Doesn't it make you suspicious?"

"It makes me curious, not necessarily suspicious... And who's asking for this info?"

"Me."

"Nobody else?"

Anne shook her head.

"Tell me then, is 'me' Anne Brown, working mother and widow, or is 'me' Billy Darby, talented and mildly hard-boiled private investigator? Should I be suspicious of you?"

"Don't be silly. You know why I have two names, a single name and a married name."

"But you use both names, don't you? For business purposes. You used your nickname Billy as a substitute for Wilhelmina so that it mimicked your Uncle Bill's name. For business purposes. Nothing wrong with that. Lots of people do it. Most of Hollywood. Plus phonies like Mark Twain, O. Henry, Bob Dylan, et cetera, et cetera."

"Okay, enough of the analysis. How do I find out someone's real identity who doesn't want it known?"

"You'll need a warrant."

"How do I get a warrant?"

"You need evidence the person is using the name to commit a crime or avoid prosecution. So... what's your evidence?"

"Are you going to cripple me with technicalities?"

"'Fraid so."

Anne turned quiet, munched a bit more of her muffin, and sipped quietly from her cup. Ben didn't like quiet, especially when it came from Anne. He enjoyed her energy and pugnacious spirit. Now, she looked more like a deflated balloon.

"Well, on the positive side, I did prevent you from dying of thirst and wasting away from hunger," said Ben.

"And I do thank you for that, Ben. Any sage advice?"

"Well, if you can't find a hole through the middle, try an end run."

Anne wasn't sure if that advice fit her problem or not. She wasn't even sure if her problem was a problem at all. *Maybe he was right,* she thought. *Maybe it was just a curiosity trying to puff up its real value. And what did he mean by an end run?*

34.

By the time Anne reached the Jones Building, a stone's throw from the Shaw Building, Anne had managed to process Ben's end-run metaphor from a football reference into its soccer equivalent of a wall pass. Anne's next visit, to the PEI Land Registry, didn't qualify as an "end run," though. It wasn't a lead or a hunch or a theory or intuition. It was just an odd, compelling curiosity about the Grant homestead. A "sidestep," perhaps.

She wanted to know the history of Sullivan's Point. Discovery of a child's corpse there had morbidly set it in mind. Jean's purchase of it added a semi-personal link. Enid's tale of Fig Grant's insufferable upbringing there underscored it. And its setting for her nightmare had disturbed her. Then something peculiar had happened. During her visit there the beauty of the site had swept all of her previous distaste away. It had also awakened her imagination to the possibility that it could become a part of her future.

The business segment of her visit to government records in the Shaw building had seemed tedious, indirect, and unpredictable in spite of all the help from staff. She had felt out of her depth and had no more control of the goings-on than playing a pinball machine or navigating a dream. The land office at the Jones building, on the other hand, was different. Determining sequence of ownership was clear. Once a parcel of land had been identified, the record of the site unfolded quickly.

Ownership of the Grant farm in the records dated from 1892 and passed from Pius to James to Declan and finally to Newton in 1964. In 1988 a lien was placed against the property. The lien holder was Bernard White's company. Big Sea Products acquired the lien when they bought the factory from Bernie, and they bought the farm when the provincial government put it up for public sale in 1995 for unpaid land taxes. Twenty years later M. Gauthier & Son assumed title to the farm when it acquired the assets of Big Sea Products. Just a few months ago, Jean Gauthier purchased the land from M. Gauthier & Son.

Anne found the details interesting. She hadn't been expecting to find anything relevant to her investigation, but the loss of a family homestead may be worth looking at more closely as a motive for payback. So Fig Grant, or Newton, or whatever he was called, was looking like the next person she should interview.

Anne nudged that idea along as she headed toward her car. She had parked on the street in front of the Shaw Building. A one-hour parking sign stood near her car. Anne saw a slip of paper fluttering under the wiper blade on the windshield. She looked at her watch. She had been gone for an hour and forty minutes.

Damn it, she said, and the words echoed several more times in her head before fading under the snapping sound of paper, yanked from its secure spot under the wiper. Her exasperation faded into a creepy unease. Block letters on the note read "LAST WARNING. DON'T RETURN."

35.

As she headed east toward Little Rose Harbour, Anne's thoughts fixed on CeeCee Dunne. Somehow, a blunt threat in note form on a car parked in Charlottetown didn't fit CeeCee's personality. She had struck Anne as one who acted on impulse, whether alcohol-fuelled or provoked. CeeCee wouldn't plan a payback. She was an in-your-face responder. This would have taken too much planning for her, Anne decided, and, as a result, that weird, troubling feeling returned.

Anne raised and pondered a number of plausible reasons for the threat, but nothing stood out, and, when she arrived back at Little Rose Harbour and the M. Gauthier & Son sign loomed from the side of the processing plant, she decided to focus on her original plan, a chat with Fig Grant.

The Queens County Packers truck was dockside along with vehicles of half a dozen other buyers. Anne walked to the truck, but Fig was not there. Squeak was aboard. His long lanky figure splayed out on an upturned lobster tray set against an inside wall of the truck body. He looked half asleep, but he roused. He said he didn't know where Fig was, and he didn't know where Spit had gone. He looked and sounded a bit confused.

Anne gazed about the harbour. No Fig Grant anywhere. So Anne looked elsewhere.

For a while, Anne allowed herself to relax, emptied her mind and wandered with no particular purpose, much as she did when stumped by a difficult crossword puzzle.

Eventually, her contemplation took her up a long wharf lined with fishing shacks, each identical in construction. She remembered Luc LaVie saying he had built or supervised the building of all of them years before. Each had a wooden door and a hatch above for a small storage loft. Each had been painted. Each fisherman owner kept up his own repairs and maintenance.

The afternoon was pleasant. It was warm. A thin veil of cloud subdued the glare of sun. A scent of old fish and dried kelp and salt touched the air. Activity along the waterfront had dwindled. A few trucks crept along. A few forklifts whined. Seagulls kept silent watch upon the peaks of fish shacks and lined up with almost military precision and interval, each patiently facing the harbour below.

Luc's fish sheds had been well built. Nothing had been skimped on construction materials. Many had been recently repainted and reroofed. Others were eyesores: cracked or splintered boards, scars from trucks that had backed into them. Doors sagging with damaged hinges, and others swinging limply with faulty hasps.

Anne was uncertain how the idea came to her. Perhaps some detail from the dilapidated bait sheds caught her eye and imagination, but it was there nonetheless, and she strode excitedly to the pumphouse attached to the factory wall. She ran her hand over the metal strap hinge holding the door in place. Then she fetched several Robertson-head screwdrivers from the trunk of her car and returned to the pumphouse.

She tried the screwdriver on the door side of the hinge and twisted. It didn't give way. No matter how firmly she tried, it held fast. Then Anne tried the frame side of the hinge. The screw was well set in but, with rather little effort, it loosened and withdrew. A second screw loosened with even less effort. The matching screws on the bottom hinge backed off easily, too.

Anne finished the job by removing the last screws on the frame. The hinge side of the door sagged, but parted easily. Anne dragged it open, the lock and hasp still holding it up.

Now it became clear how someone could enter the factory secretly and destroy the plumbing without a key from Bernie. For a moment or two Anne revelled in her discovery, but then she realized she was no still no closer to knowing who had made the illegal entry, or when it had taken place.

36.

It took only minutes for the wharf to come to life again. Three offshore vessels had rounded the cape and headed toward Little Rose Harbour. A few more hands appeared near open loading doors at the factory. A couple of pickups rattled down the wharf road. Heads popped out the back of visiting buyers' trucks. A forklift buzzed and sprang to life. It clanked and bounced and whined along the uneven asphalt.

Anne saw Spit's head gaze toward the harbour entrance, conclude that it wasn't one of their own sellers, and return to his quiet roost inside, but not before he waved away a signal to someone near the open loading door of one of the factory's receiving stations. Anne caught the direction of his signal and headed that way. Inside the cool shade at the opening, she found Fig Grant chatting with a few idle factory workers.

The chatting stopped when they saw Anne's petite figure framed in the doorway. Cigarette smoke hung like a luminescent cloud in the stillness.

"Can I help you?" asked one.

"Looking for Fig Grant," said Anne. "Are you him?" she asked, staring in Fig's direction.

"That I am," he said. His eyes twinkled. He suppressed a laugh. The men nearby giggled and smirked and muttered a few asides, which Fig waved off and Anne couldn't make out. "What can I do for you?"

"If you've got a minute, I have a few questions."

"I guess I have a few to spare. What d' ya want to know?"

"I work for the Gauthiers as a production engineer."

"I know all about it. But I don't work for the Gauthiers. So how does this have anything to do with me?"

Anne felt uncomfortable as she became part of a sideshow for factory labourers on a break. And she didn't want to quiz Fig amid a backdrop of snickers and lewd insinuations. So she cocked her head toward the sunlit opening. Fig followed her. He looked only mildly curious about her inquiry.

"So what d'ya want?"

"At this stage in my work I'm looking to reduce the waste, property loss, and vandalism that might affect the profitability of the company."

"Again, what d'ya want from me?"

"You've been around here for a long time. You must have heard things... seen things... that might help. You must have some ideas, right?"

"I try to mind my own business. That policy's always worked good for me."

"Have you ever had business dealings with the factory?"

"Not much."

"Ever sold to them... worked for them?"

"A bit, years ago."

"Why did you stop?"

"Everybody knows why. I was a drunk back then. It took a toll. Look, why don't you come to the point? You're working your way to somewhere, and I'm beginning to tire of the dance. So get to it."

A short stack of lobster trays dropped onto the deck of a nearby boat. Anne flinched and looked over. Her hand rose reflexively to shade the glare of sun off the water.

"Your family homestead. That's what I'm getting at. Big Sea Products bought it for unpaid back taxes. It must have been difficult to see that land go for a few bucks. Maybe it was enough to hold a grudge... maybe do something about it... get even somehow."

"You're beginning to sound more like a cop than some kind of engineer, and I'm tired of listening."

"Do I look like a cop? Use your head. The company has been losing thousands over the years to high inventory losses and vandalism. It seems to me that someone has it in for the company. I want to know who that might be."

"What company are you talking about?"

"Let's start with the current owners. Jean Gauthier just bull-dozed the old homestead. That's got to mean something. That's got to hurt. All those memories."

Fig laughed.

"Most of those memories were hellish. And the land never grew nothin'. My memories of that place are long dead and buried—as they should be—and as for Gauthier, we spoke about it. He knew the history. I told him there's no hard feelings on my part. It was my own damn fault. We laughed about it. He even gave me a bit of money to help make up for it. And he didn't have to do that."

"What about Big Sea Products, the company that seized your land to begin with?"

"Now they were pricks. I'll grant you that."

"Bernie was manager then, wasn't he?"

"Bernïe kinda looked after me, if yer thinkin' about bad-mouthing him. The deed was in his company's name, but he let me live there until Big Sea took over. Things were different after that. Big corporations, ya know."

"So you have reasons to get back at them, wouldn't you say?"

"I suppose I would. Then again I suppose other people 'round here have good reasons, too."

A forklift turned off the main road, rounded the corner, and clattered toward the head of the wharf. It carried a load of wooden pallets, piled high and bouncing precariously with each bump it hit.

"I'd like to hear more about them, too."

"Keep asking questions around here, and you'll figure it out for yourself... or maybe you'll get a thumpin' for bein' too nosy." Fig grinned as if he were telling a joke. Anne wasn't amused.

Anne squinted and shaded her eyes. The forklift whined shrilly.

"I'm part pit bull," said Anne. Her words sounded firm and self-confident, but Anne felt quite differently. She felt vulnerable standing in front of Fig. He was an old man, but he was large and exuded strength and ability. She knew that he could break her in two and toss her into the bay with no more effort than it would take to put the run to a surly cat.

Then without warning, Fig's big hands sprang out. Anne froze in space and time. Her mind hadn't quickened enough to generate a flicker of fear. His hands clamped her shoulders like vices. Anne felt her body lift. She dangled mid-air. Fig swung her ferociously. Her head snapped, her eyes blurred, and she felt like a large, stuffed toy doll as he hurled her through air, back into the dark shade of the receiving station, where her limp body struck the cluster of slack-jawed men who worked there.

Just before Anne fell to the ground, the receiving station grew dark as a cloud blackened the sun. A chaos of noise filled her ears: the discord of metal clashing metal, a strident laboured whine, the screech of twisting steel, the dissonant grind of destruction, the rumble of an avalanche, the acrid smell of rubber, and the groan of sagging beams.

37.

Anne struggled to find herself and understand what had just happened. Slow-witted confusion enveloped her. She felt pain and numbness, and she struggled to find the source. Slowly, she moved one limb at a time. Nothing broken, she thought. Everything worked. Then the pain centred itself. Her shoulder ached from an impact on the concrete floor, and her forearm burned from a raw scrape.

Anne rolled over onto her stomach, pulled herself up, and stumbled toward the light at the entrance. A mound of heavy wooden pallets sprawled across the entry and blocked her way. She climbed over them and stumbled down the other side.

Anne shaded her eyes enough to make out the blades of a forklift, which had impaled the half-opened door at the entrance. Already, a crowd had begun to gather. One fisherman had stilled the scream of the forklift's engine and put an end to the incessant spin and burn of its tires. Others started a search inside for anyone who might have been injured. Some lent a hand to clearing debris. An idle few mulled over the calamity and speculated about the incident.

Anne scanned the crowd for Fig. She found him sitting alone on the pavement outside the building.

"You okay?" she asked.

He nodded. His right hand gripped his left arm. Blood seeped between his fingers.

"You?" he asked, looking up.

"I'm good," she said, "but you should have someone look at that."

"Workin' on it."

"And thanks... for what you did back there. I could have been killed. And in a forklift accident of all things. That possibility wouldn't have made my top hundred best guesses. Actually it wouldn't have made any list."

"Accident? That was no accident."

"What do ya mean?"

"I figure your nosiness has already poked somebody pretty bad."

"Here ya go, then," said Jack Pine. "Got the fixin's right here," he added, opening the first aid kit he'd taken from Hec Dunne's boat and squatting next to Fig.

"And how's Anne doin'?" asked Jack.

"I'm okay."

"Good, then. Fig, a bit of a bleedin' will clean the wound, but I'll squirt antiseptic just in case."

Jack fixed a sterile patch over the cut. "Hold this," he said, passing Anne the end of a gauze strip. He took several firm turns around his arm, fastened it with tape, and proclaimed, "Good as new."

✳✳✳✳

Bernie had heard unusual sounds of commotion from his office and, when he looked out the window, he saw fishermen rushing somewhere. He knew something was amiss and sprinted from the office across the lot to the wharf. He was out of breath and panting when he arrived, but, after seeing the crowd and the damage, Bernie White's anger turned to rage, and, when he saw the forklift driver standing nearby, he lost control.

"What the hell did you do?" said Bernie. He grabbed the driver by his throat and drove him against the forklift. The driver was pinned. He struggled to speak, but Bernie's grip was so tight he could only voice a pitiful babble. His eyes bulged, and his feet thrashed about for a footing. "What the hell did you do? What the hell did you do?" Bernie repeated with each squawk.

Anne left Jack Pine and Fig when she heard the uproar. She saw Bernie's fist hover in the air. The driver blinked stupidly. A trace of spittle leaked from corners of his mouth.

Anne shouted. "Bernie. Bernie. Get a grip."

Bernie's fist lost purpose and faltered. He seemed uncertain for a moment. Then his grasp on the driver's neck loosened, and Bernie stepped back.

"You're fired. Get out. Get your things and get out now."

The driver stumbled through the tight circle of bystanders and found solace with a few friends who led him away. The remaining spectators slowly dispersed.

"Idiot driver... moron... fucking imbecile ..."

"Okay, you're starting to repeat yourself now, Bernie. Enough."

Finally, he stopped and stood still and just stared at the fork of the machine piercing the corrugated steel siding.

"Another few inches, and it would have cleared the door frame and gone inside."

"...and maybe killed me and Fig, too."

"You were there? Mr. Gauthier said you weren't coming back. You were going to finish your work back in Charlottetown or Halifax or something."

"He got the dates wrong. You were pretty brutal with that driver. Is he a new guy?"

"He was here last year. He should have known better."

"Some fellow in the crowd said he wasn't the driver... said someone had taken it when he was on break. Said he chased it down here."

"He never told me anything like that."

"Did you ask him what happened?"

"Why should I? It's his responsibility. He'd probably try to squirm his way out of it somehow."

"So how do we explain *this*? Doesn't look normal to me," she said.

Anne pointed to a length of twine, one end tied to the rim of the steering wheel, the other hanging loose. Anne climbed aboard the forklift. A short length fastened to a hook under the driver's seat. When Anne extended both ends toward each other, they met up.

"If I had to guess, I'd say that someone tied off the steering wheel to keep it on track. And this," she said, "might work nicely to keep the accelerator jammed to the floor." With some effort Anne dragged up a heavy block of wood from the floor of the cab.

"If the forklift wheel struck a rough spot, the jolt could snap the twine and send the machine a bit off course," mused Bernie.

"You got the idea now," said Anne. But one big question remained unresolved: who was the target: she or Fig?

38.

Vic Condon was huddled with a few friends in a fish shed when Anne found him.

"I remember hearing your voice," he said, "when Bernie was about to throttle me. Thanks."

"Bernie's got a short fuse... not that that's an excuse. Anyway, there's some evidence now that someone else probably took your forklift and did the damage. So you're just about in the clear, and I'll do my best to see that you get your job back. Okay?"

"I need a job, but I don't know if I can work for that jackass." His words ground out through a raspy throat.

"Well, that's up to you, but I can fix things up."

"How?"

"I'll convince him that you've got him over a barrel... that you're thinking about calling the Mounties and lodging an assault charge. I'm sure I can talk him into an apology, and, if not a better job, then a raise in pay. I do need some info, though, and you can help me with that."

Vic Condon nodded and Anne went on. "How did you happen to leave your forklift unattended?"

"A runner from the office said I had a call on the line, said it was important. I thought it might be my wife. She's pregnant and near term. So I went in. But there was no one on the line. I called home, but there was no answer there either. I thought maybe she was taken to hospital. I made a few other calls. Then, I look. The machine is gone."

***

Anne left Vic to commiserate with his friends and ponder Anne's offer, and she headed to the factory's office. Morgan, the receptionist, verified Vic Condon's account of the mystery phone call, but she didn't recognize the caller's voice. She recalled little except that he was male and that his words were few and direct.

"I found one thing peculiar, though," said Morgan. "The caller asked to speak with 'the forklift driver,' rather than ask for him by name."

From there, Anne returned to where Condon had left the forklift. Anne worried about the time. It was getting late, nearing suppertime, and the number of people near the wharf was sparse. In spite of that, she was hopeful she could find someone who remembered seeing the forklift, and, better yet, who took it.

One of the few still hanging about was Squeak. Squeak had a gawky appearance, tall and angular. He sat on a large overturned fish tub near a little-used derrick at the edge of the pier. He seemed deep in thought and stared toward the icehouse.

The icehouse cast a hypnotic effect on many who lingered nearby it. The hum of the refrigeration unit conjured images of Eastern temples and orange-clad monks. The tinkle of ice sliding down metal chutes relit memories of wind chimes lulling idlers into a summer trance. It's likely that Squeak had fallen under its spell because, as Anne drew near, Squeak neither saw her approach, nor heard her, and he gave a nervous jump when he caught the scrape of her shoes on the grit along the west wharf.

"You look on edge, Squeak. Nerves shot?"

"Nope. Just enjoying the quiet. Never heard you sneak up. And I'm just about to go to supper." He stood up and ambled a few steps away as if intending to take his leave.

"Before you go, though, I have a question. Were you here about an hour ago?"

Ice rattled softly; a motor hummed dutifully. Squeak stared

at the icehouse door and found an answer.

"I believe I was chattin' with Spit, waiting for a few late boats," he said.

"But I was talking to Fig about then and didn't see you about," said Anne.

"Then perhaps I wasn't. Can't remember exactly." Squeak avoided looking at Anne. He swallowed uneasily. Anne couldn't determine whether he suffered from guilt or timidity.

"It was just before the forklift accident. Vic Condon parked his machine up there," said Anne, pointing. "When he came out, it was gone. Someone took it. Any idea who might have done that?"

"I didn't see anything. No one 'round here pays any mind to forklifts. They buzz about... common as horseflies."

"Can you drive a forklift?" said Anne.

"I can drive anything with wheels and a gearbox. So can most anyone else around the wharf. Fig nearly got run down, too, ya know. And we've been friends for over forty years. So if I knew who done it, I'd tell ya. Think it's about suppertime now."

Squeak turned and began a slow walk toward the head of the west wharf.

"You're headed the wrong direction for supper," said Anne.

Without looking back, Squeak said, "I left some fishin' gear up the other end."

"Well, that's the long and short of it, if I do say so m'self," said a familiar voice.

Anne hadn't seen Jack Pine's approach, but his affable chatter was always pleasant. Jack grinned at the overworked joke about height that he had adopted long ago as part of his own patter. Anne detested wisecracks about short people, so she ignored him. Jack waited for her smile at his witticism. When she didn't smile, Jack persisted.

"Come on then. A smile is such a *little* thing to give up. Come on, you can do it. Even a teensy lip wiggle will do, girl. Don't know if there's any truth to it, but they say that a good smile costs three-seventy-five up in Toronto. Would ya take a cheque fer one then?"

Anne's attempt at a stony face dissolved into a self-conscious smirk.

"This one's on the house. Best I can do," said Anne. "But I'll hunt around. Maybe I can dig up a better one. See you at Dearie's for dinner."

"Look forward to it, missy. A few chores to do here first," he said, flourishing the first aid kit.

"So do I," she said with a wave and headed back toward the factory.

Jack climbed down into *Hell to Pay*, Hec Dunne's boat. The tide had fallen. Now the cabin had fallen below the rim of the wharf. Jack snapped the emergency kit back onto the wall in the wheelhouse and puttered about in the forward compartment.

Squeak, seeing no one on the wharf behind him, returned to his roost near the icehouse, but, when he heard the banging about in *Hell to Pay,* he hollered down to Jack, "You still here, Jack? I thought you was goin'. It's suppertime, ain't it? Dearie'll throw a fit if ya come in late, won't she?"

"Might... might not." Jack didn't need to stick his head out from the boat cabin below. His voice was big and loud enough to carry topside. "And what are you so interested in my suppertime for? I had a mother to tell me what's what when I was a little fella. I don't need another one to do the same thing now, especially one that looks like a—Har! Har!—a dried-up old beanstalk. And if it's suppertime, what the hell are you still doin' here?"

Squeak missed the tail end of Jack's critique because he was already at the heavy door of the icehouse. He knocked lightly, but heard nothing. He knocked again a bit harder. Still nothing. Squeak had a sort-of plan. It was hastily cobbled together in his head, and it now hovered among three options: hammering harder but drawing Jack's unwanted attention, cracking the door open to give warning, or abandoning his post completely to the vagaries of fate. Squeak had always found it difficult to distinguish between degrees of calamity. So he ran off in the hope of temporary relief and safety in the passage of time and distance.

39.

After Jack Pine and Hec Dunne had landed their catch that afternoon, Jack had put off his boat chores until later. Now, he put his back into it before he headed to Dearie's for supper.

Old Squeak had been right. Dearie would raise an eyebrow and mutter a criticism or two. She'd huff and glare. She'd sulk and grunt. As Jack scrubbed the working deck with a swab, he thought about Dearie, and he thought about his ex-wife, Margo.

Then it dawned on him: "God a'mighty, my trials at the Manor are no easier than m'sufferin' wid Margo'd been back in Pickle Bay."

Jack scrubbed quicker and with more zest to get the job done and go "home." He flushed the deck with seawater, the slurry draining through scuppers and dribbling into the harbour. It tinkled as it fell. The sound mixed with the tinkle of the icehouse chimes. Jack smiled to himself. Then the bilge pump cut in with an agonizing moan. It ground out a few litres of water, just enough to put an end to any pleasure still lingering in his head.

Jack took one last look around and, satisfied with his cleanup, he clambered onto the washboard and hoisted himself step by step up the steel ladder alongside the wharf.

Jack's head and shoulders rose above the rim of the wharf as the door to the icehouse opened. Out of it came a rush of noise from the fan and refrigeration motor. And out of it came Hec Dunne. His face was flushed, his trousers sagged, and his shirt was partly tucked. He squinted into the brighter light of day. He carried a heavy wool blanket. When the eyes of both men met, though, it was as if a movie had frozen to a sudden stop at one frame. Both became motionless.

Then Hec's eyes registered surprise and awkwardness. Jack's eyes registered confusion at first, and, as his eyes drifted to his hastily dressed daughter, Alvina, standing in the shadows just behind Hec, Jack felt something welling up inside. It grew like a rogue wave, suddenly and powerfully, and carried with it the rancour of betrayal and the mindlessness of vengeance, and swept sanity and decorum away.

Jack mounted the remaining steps of the ladder with an agility that alarmed Hec.

"Jack, just take a minute..." but by that time Jack had reached Hec with his fist. It was a grazing blow to his face, and it raised a scream from Alvina.

"Dad! Don't... Please!"

Jack didn't hear or didn't care. Hec turned, sidestepped, and attempted to grapple Jack and bring him to the ground. Hec was younger and stronger, but Jack had fury on his side and craftiness learned the hard way in scraps in Newfoundland outports and tussles in the waterfront dives of St. John's.

"Jack, this is no way to settle things... and I never took advantage of her. She's a grown woman," he said as he circled, waiting for Jack to come to his senses or make a misstep to his advantage.

"Hec Dunne, you're a womanizer and a miserable little prick, and when I'm through with you I'm goin' to cut it off and use it for fish bait."

Hec suddenly rushed forward and hit Jack hard enough with his shoulder to drive him back toward the boat. Jack's feet came out from under him. His head struck the edge of the wharf. It had been a long time since Jack had seen stars after a head bang.

Hec dove and landed on top of him. He pummeled Jack's face. Blood trickled from his nose.

"Hec! Stop it! You're going to hurt him! Stop it!" Alvina cried.

Jack's hands were large, his grip strong, and his intent grave.

He stretched up his arms and deflected Hec's flailing jabs. Hec couldn't land a solid blow. Jack's fingers grasped blindly and found Hec's throat.

Fright scored Alvina's face. Her feet froze to the pavement. Her arm stretched ahead weakly as if force of will would magically end a tragedy playing out before her.

The madness of vengeance gripped Jack. He was enraged at Hec's betrayal, frustrated at his own blindness, ashamed of his failings as a parent, and let down by Alvina's recklessness. He gripped harder.

"Dad! Don't kill him! Dad! Don't kill him."

Hec had stopped his flailing. His face became puffy. His eyes drained of spirit. He grew silent, and a trace of spittle foamed between his lips.

"Please, Dad! Please!"

Across the parking lot and halfway up the hill, Alvina saw the spindly figure of Squeak running toward them, but Alvina knew he wouldn't arrive in time to help.

She retreated to the icehouse. When she returned, Jack Pine saw stars flash in his head for the second time that day. Alvina had swung a rusty shovel and struck the back of her father's skull. It stunned him, and he lost his stranglehold on Hec's throat.

"That's enough. Both of you. It's all done. Finished."

Jack had rolled instinctively away from Hec. He stared in surprise at his daughter and then with caution at Hec.

Both men seemed spent. Jack panted heavily and felt the heaviness of his aging body. He didn't know how much energy remained.

As the two fishermen now stood facing each other, Jack caught a glint in Hec's eye.

"It ain't over until your old man says it is... and also says he's going to mind his own business from now on."

"On a cold day in hell I will! You'll stay away from my daughter, and that's that."

"Stop it! Stop it now. Now!" Alvina's pleas slipped away with no more import than the squawk of a passing seagull.

Hec smiled confidently. Both men circled. Alvina was awk-wardly caught between the two of them.

"Let it go, boys. Ya don't want to draw the law down here, do ya? That wouldn't be good for either one of ya," said Squeak scuffing to a halt as the bitterness flared.

"Go home, Squeak. You're no help here," said Hec. "I'll make short work of this old man. And I'll need a new hired man for tomorrow, too. Maybe you can round somebody up for me."

"That's enough from both of you!" said Alvina.

Jack and Hec continued to circle, each one cautious, each one waiting for the other to slip up.

Jack was the first to do so. With his back to the wharf and a lowering sun bright in his eyes, Jack tripped over a fault in the concrete. His eyes dropped.

Hec bolted forward, shoving Alvina to one side, but not before her ice shovel whacked his knee. He muttered painfully as he hurtled, off balance, past her. Jack had fallen, but, at the last moment, he rolled out of Hec's path. Hec's momentum carried him too far ahead. He tripped on the toe rail at the lip of the wharf.

His eyes widened, his jaw dropped, his arms snatched at air, and he plunged toward the water below. Hec felt only a jolt and heard a thump as his shoulder struck the stern of his boat. A gasp of surprise sucked seawater into his throat. He gagged and choked until it cleared. The emerging pain from a fractured shoulder humbled his cravings for retribution.

Both Squeak and Jack made their way down the ladder and boarded *Hell to Pay*. They pulled him from the water. Hec cursed the resurging throb in his shoulder. The men laid him across the stern deck. Jack retrieved a blanket from the cabin. Squeak covered him, and Alvina called an ambulance.

40.

Late Afternoon, Charlottetown

Jean Gauthier shuffled a few papers he'd been examining and shoved them into a desk drawer in his Charlottetown suite when he heard his father arrive.

"Bernie said you had planned to come out to the Little Rose factory in the afternoon. What happened?" said Jean.

"I got stuck at the Egmont facility longer than I expected. J.R., the manager, wanted to take me out in one of his fishing boats and show me the inshore lobster grounds," said Michel. "It delayed me, but I had a pleasant time."

"You wouldn't have been dressed for that work," said Jean, pointing to his sport jacket and dress shoes. His father laughed.

"No, but I keep a few things in the car in case I decide to try trout fishing. Plus, J.R. gave me a heavy jersey, and he had a spare set of oil clothes in case the weather turned."

"Been a long while since you were out on the water. How was it?"

"Like riding a bike. Took a little while to get my sea legs back, but it was good. Sorry I didn't make it out. Tomorrow for sure. Did you tell her?"

Jean nodded.

"How'd she take it?"

"Not well. Not well at all. Her feelings are hurt. She felt she was just starting to dig into the case, and she hadn't been given a chance to work it. I gave her two days."

"When I fire somebody, they're gone that day. You know that. You can't leave former workers hanging around. They turn sour pretty quick."

"But…"

"There's no 'buts' about it. That's the way business is done. If someone's been a good employee, give them an extra week's wages or something, but get them off the premises."

"It's not that simple, Papa."

"It is if you're not involved with her."

"Who?"

"No need to play dumb with me. I'm not an old fool."

Jean added nothing more. Michel continued, "Don't get me wrong. I do like her… and, when this is all over, maybe you can get together." Michel Gauthier smiled knowingly and rested his hand on his son's shoulder. "One more thing while we're on the subject. Never hire friends—especially girlfriends—or relatives. Enough about business for today."

Jean seemed lost in thought. He had no reply to utter. No questions to ask. He simply nodded and turned away.

"Look," said Michel, "why don't we do something together tonight? Go to a movie maybe. There's a French film revival at City Cinema this week. *Le Plaisir*. A comedy. What do you say?"

41.

Late Afternoon, Little Rose Harbour

Anne mounted the stairs to the office. She hoped that Morgan or Bernie would still be there to update her on other witnesses to the afternoon's incident. But the place was quiet. The door to Morgan's office was ajar, but Morgan had left for the day. Anne scanned the top of Morgan's desk, but she saw no relevant messages.

Most employee vehicles had left the parking lot. An assortment of noises filtered up from the factory floor below: a racket of scrubbing brushes and flushing water to disinfect the cutting tables. She thought she heard something from Bernie's office. His door was closed. Anne knocked politely, but there was no response. She rapped harder, but the quiet persisted.

She had locked her bag and a light jacket in the security office earlier in the day, so went to retrieve them before she left. She lingered there momentarily and stared through the big window down onto the processing floor. Two women, the end-of-shift cleanup crew, were finishing but still too busy to notice Anne watching them.

Then Anne heard the door close behind her. Caught unawares, she gave out a small gasp and whirled around. CeeCee Dunne had shut the door, and now she stood facing her. Anne suddenly felt like a squirrel caught in a live trap, and she doubted that CeeCee had ever been fond of catch-and-release practices.

"I know what happened. So I don't want to hear the usual bullshit," said CeeCee. She sounded different, tired perhaps.

Anne had anticipated a full-frontal assault, not a verbal one. Jumping Anne would have been CeeCee's best move. Still anticipating blows, Anne's eyes glanced about for something to protect herself from a nasty beating. However, a plastic trash container and a hardcover log book were the only "weapons" handy.

CeeCee still made no attempt to move, and Anne remained baffled, defenseless, and unable to make sense of CeeCee's words or intentions.

"I dragged it out of the boys. Now what are you really doing here?"

"What did they tell you?"

"That you caught them breaking into a storage shed. That you grilled them about Edgar MacAulay. That you kept your word and didn't turn them in. And so on. They also said you asked some pretty tough questions yesterday afternoon. Right?"

"Right," said Anne.

Anne remained guarded. So far CeeCee had kept her temper under control, but she had fallen short of any sign of détente.

"A little more than *chitchat*, right?"

What Anne heard was less the comment than CeeCee's change in tone. It was a poke at Anne's remark the previous day, but CeeCee had injected a lighthearted quality into it.

Anne nodded, and something in that nod appeared to satisfy CeeCee. A rare smile softened CeeCee's face, and Anne felt her muscles begin to uncoil.

"So I wanted to thank you, Anne Brown, for giving them boys a break."

"Everybody deserves a second chance, especially young fellas."

"And so do you. I guess we got off on the wrong foot these last few days. I read you wrong, and I'd like to make up for it, if I can. So if there's anything you need, or if anybody around here gives you a hard time, let me know."

"I'll do that... and... thanks, CeeCee."

"You still haven't answered my question: what're ya really doing here? The questions y'asked the boys weren't just chitchat and they had nothing to do with engineering..."

Anne remained silent.

"...and if you were a cop, you'd a' taken the boys into custody. That's all right, though. I understand. Just curious, that's all. By the way, I'm sorry to hear about that accident on the wharf this afternoon."

"That was no accident, CeeCee. Management didn't hire me to make the plant more profitable. That was a cover story. They were really interested in the thefts and vandalism that have plagued the factory for years. They asked me to look into it. I thought it best done on the QT. Apparently, someone else found out about what I was digging into, and tried to sideline me. Still, the fewer the people who know, the better for me. So, can I take a chance on your discretion?"

"As I said, you can count on me. By the way, I almost saw that accident... incident. I was on break, but I got tired of listening to my friends jabbering about this and that, so I came upstairs here and gabbed with Morgan while Vic was on her phone. I took a look out the window and saw a bunch of fellas running toward the wharf."

"But you couldn't see that part of the wharf from Morgan's office."

"No, but I saw something else that seemed queer. Everyone was running toward the wharf. But there was one guy heading the other direction."

"He was just walking away?"

"Kinda. He was walking, but he reminded me of a trotter that wants to break stride and run."

"Did you recognize him?"

"Didn't look familiar. He dressed like every other fisherman around here. Couldn't see his face. Wore a ball cap. The brim pulled down."

"Anything else?"

"He was making for the parking lot. A bit later a black sedan pulls out and heads up the lane toward Halkirk. Maybe that was him you're lookin' for... maybe not. What's that?"

"What?"

"Don't you hear it? A siren."

"Oh yeah. It's getting louder. Must be comin' down the lane."

"C'mon. Let's take a look. Someone musta got hurt."

"No, CeeCee, I think I'll pass. I've had enough excitement for one day. Just worn out. See ya tomorrow."

42.

Early Evening, Charlottetown

Jean passed on his father's movie offer. Michel didn't press him. He thought maybe he had stepped on his toes a few too many times already today. *Another time, then,* he suggested, and that seemed an acceptable option for Jean. Michel was satisfied with that. Jean had always been a forgiving child, and he had not changed. He had taken after his mother in that regard, and perhaps that was a good thing as well.

Michel walked along Charlottetown streets toward the cinema. It was too early for the movie, but he wanted to give Jean some space to think through his advice. He had grabbed a snack after his afternoon's work. So he was not yet hungry. Nevertheless, there was time to kill. He stopped at a new restaurant. A Moroccan immigrant owned the place and served Michel. He spoke French quite well, and that pleased Michel. He ordered a special blend of strong coffee and a snifter of brandy, and soon he found the stress of the day slip from his shoulders and fall into the oblivion of the past.

He was enjoying the oblivion course through his veins when his cellphone rang. The caller was unknown.

"Yes. Who is this?" Michel said.

"Just shut up and listen," said the caller. The voice was unfamiliar. It sounded distorted, as if someone were speaking from the bottom of a large steel drum. "I know who you are... I know what you've done... my silence will cost $100,000... get the money by tomorrow or face disgrace... more directions will follow."

43.

Wednesday Morning, Little Rose Harbour

Jean Gauthier took the stairs to the office two at a time. His
father Michel lagged behind. Jean waited impatiently at the top
for him. Then both men pushed through Bernie's closed office
door without knocking.

Bernie stood inside, startled. He was about to protest the
intrusion, but stopped when he recognized the two Gauthiers.
Tammy Wallace stood next to him. Her face reddened. She felt
ruffled, and her hands instinctively smoothed her blouse.

Bernie quickly read irritation in the faces of both Jean and
Michel.

"Tammy, we'll talk about those changes later, and thanks for
bringing them to my attention."

Tammy had scarcely cleared the room before Jean lashed
out, "Bernie, what the hell is going on with you? I told you I
wanted to be informed about everything that goes on here... and
I wanted to know about it when it happens, not to find it out on
the grapevine or a newscast."

The roar of Jean's voice filled the office and spilled into reception. Morgan, the receptionist, became embarrassed, abandoned
her desk, and fled to the bathroom up the hall.

Bernie thought about asking how he found out, but Jean left
no room to interject.

"And how did I find out? A CBC online news bulletin: 'Runaway forklift causes injuries and damage at Little Rose processing plant' and then something about a Workers Comp investigation that's pending. What the fuck is wrong with you, Bernie? Are you so busy playing with the help that you can't do your job anymore?"

Bernie's mouth opened to respond, but Jean motioned for him to shut up.

"Yeah, I know all about your history of extracurricular activities. I don't need elaboration or denials. I want to know why you didn't keep us up to date."

"That may have been my doing."

Everyone's head turned toward the doorway at the small figure of Anne Brown, just having arrived on site.

"You—"

"Yeah, I may have had something to do with it. Pull up a chair, and let's talk."

Anne sat down in front of Bernie's desk. Anne's arm extended by way of invitation to the others. Bernie, looking a bit confused and uncomfortable, took a seat behind his desk. Jean and Michel hesitated, but they pulled up chairs as well.

"Here's the story. There was an incident at the wharf, but it was no accident."

"What do you mean, no accident?" said Michel.

"Exactly that. Bernie and I found enough evidence to suggest that it was intentional. We put a lid on it because I wanted to investigate further without that complication hanging out there on public display. It wouldn't be good for the company, and it wouldn't be good for my investigation. And, yes, Bernie, you must have guessed by now that I'm not an engineer. I'm a private investigator."

Only Bernie's eyes registered surprise.

"So someone was out to get you," said Bernie.

"Or Fig," said Anne, "or just to do more damage to the company or its reputation."

"But you're the likely target," said Michel.

"Not necessarily," said Anne.

"Nobody would care enough about Fig to harm him. He's just a local character," said Bernie.

"Maybe... or maybe the targetting stems from a long-standing grudge against the company, and somebody doesn't want me to dig any further into that history. And that brings me to another question that's been bothering me lately: what can you tell me about George Livingstone? You would have had contact with him when he owned the place and you managed it for him."

"Actually, I didn't. I never met the man."

"How can that be?"

"I don't even know if he owned Big Sea Products. He acted as the owner, but he could have been a spokesperson for the owner. Big Sea Products was a shell company."

"I know that, Bernie. But you must have had some contact for him to run things."

"Everything ran pretty well the same as it did when I owned it. If he wanted to know the finances, I sent copies of the books to his accountants via a lawyer. If he wanted changes or an update, he'd go through lawyers or, on the odd occasion, he'd phone."

"And if something bad happened here, you'd phone him?"

"That's right."

"Didn't all that seem odd to you?"

"Of course it did. But why should I care? It's his property. He paid me a good price for it. Then he paid me a good wage to manage it, and, for the most part, I could manage it the way I wanted. He obviously was some kind of recluse or eccentric. But why should I care? Life was good. And, for that matter, why the hell do you care? That's ancient history."

"What's his phone number? His contact number. You must still have it."

"I did. And I kept it until the Gauthiers purchased the factory from him. There was no reason to keep it after that."

"Jean, do you have it?"

"No, I never had any contact with him. Papa handled the purchase for me."

"Mr. Gauthier, surely you must have George Livingstone's contact number?"

"I'm afraid not. I never had it. My purchase of the factory involved a get-together of my lawyers and his lawyers. He remained a complete mystery to me. I tried to reach out. I like a personal touch when I'm negotiating. Usually, I can make a better deal when I'm face to face. I was disappointed, but the asking price was fair, the books were in order, and there were no legal impediments to the purchase. And I think we've drifted quite a way from the topic at hand: the accident... or incident, whatever it was."

"The incident," said Bernie. "Anne and Fig both suffered injuries. Anne's were minor. Still, if it weren't for Fig, Anne wouldn't be digging into anything. We'd be digging a hole for her. Right?"

"What do you mean?" asked Michel.

"I mean if it hadn't been for Fig pushing her out of the way of that forklift, she'd be dead or seriously injured," said Bernie.

"Is that true, Anne?" said Jean.

"A bit of exaggeration, in my opinion."

"That changes everything," said Michel. "We can't have Anne risking her life over a bit of vandalism and theft, can we, Jean?"

"Of course not," said Jean. "I'm sorry, Anne, but we'll have to remove you from this case. There's too much at stake. We can't put you in harm's way."

"You can't do this. We had an agreement. You gave me two more days. This is the second day. You owe me today. Give me today at least. Then I'm done."

"Papa?"

"You already know what I'd say."

"I'm sorry, Anne, but we're done here. I can't take the chance."

"You promised two days. I need today. No more."

"No, I can't do that, but I will pay you for the time you would have worked up to the end of this week. How about that?"

"I bill clients for what I do, not what I don't do. So, if you don't have confidence in my ability to do this job, then I'm sorry."

"It's not a matter of confidence. It's a matter of safety," said Jean. "My safety is my concern. No one else's."

Neither Jean, nor Michel, nor Bernie uttered a reply. Silence spoke for them. Anne allowed the silence to stretch out a bit more before speaking: "You say, 'We're done here.' Fair enough, Mr. Gauthier. We *are* done here."

Then Anne rose, turned, and strode toward the door.

Anne felt the burn of embarrassment and humiliation at her sudden dismissal from the case. She felt tears not far off but fought stubbornly to keep them in check.

Crying like an offended little girl would be another humiliation, and she would never let that happen. The only antidote at hand, though, was anger and a burning desire to prove her worth, and she let that shape her thoughts and check her emotions as she left the office.

Anne closed the door firmly behind her. Morgan, the receptionist, had not returned to her desk. Anne gave it a quick once-over as she passed, then stopped. An old Rolodex gathered dust in the left corner on a small side table next to her desk. Anne picked up the phone as if to place a call with her right hand and fingered through the cards listed under "L" with the other. She looked furtively around and kept an ear for sounds in Bernie's office. She flipped through the listings, but nothing turned up. She hesitated, about to leave, but had second thoughts. She tried the Bs for Big Sea Products. Still nothing. Then she tried the Gs on a whim. Her first card in that section was plainly labelled "GL" and contained nothing but a single telephone number.

Anne thought she heard a shuffling of feet. She ripped the card from the Rolodex, stuffed it in her jacket pocket, and stepped quickly down the hall.

44.

Preferring not to be seen by the Gauthiers, Anne slipped into Tammy Wallace's office. As usual, Barbie Beaton was there, too. This time they appeared to be examining some records when her head popped around the corner.

"Am I disturbing you?"

"No, not really," said Tammy. "How are you feeling today?"

"Good," said Anne. "Not much damage done."

"Shoulda stuck to office work. Worst that's ever happened to me is a nasty paper cut and a pen that leaked all over a new pantsuit," said Barbie. "Well, at least you fared better than some."

"How so?"

"Didn't you hear? There was a dust-up down at the wharf yesterday."

"Never heard about that."

"Hec Dunne got throwed in the water..."

"...and broke his arm getting there," said Tammy.

"Who was fighting?" asked Anne.

"You'll never guess," said Barbie.

"It was Jack Pine, his hired man," said Tammy.

"Jack?" said Anne in amazement.

"Yeah, as I heard it, Jack caught Hec with his daughter," said Barbie.

"...in the icehouse of all places," said Tammy.

"Poor CeeCee," said Anne. "She'll be mortified..."

Tammy and Barbie gave Anne a simultaneous look of surprise.

"Don't ask," said Anne. "How's Jack doing?"

"He fared pretty well until the Mounties came and took him away."

"Guess that explains why he never showed up for supper last night."

"And somebody else didn't show up for supper last night."

"Who?"

"Hec. CeeCee kicked him out. He came home from the hospital with his arm in a cast and found the doors locked and his belongings in the yard. He tried to kick the door in, but she called the Mounties, and they took him in, too."

"Anne." Bernie appeared at the door and motioned for Anne to follow him. He led her down the hall a few metres, stopped, and said, "I guess this is the end of the road. I need the keys."

"The keys?"

"Mr. Gauthier wants the keys. You know what I'm talking about."

Anne backtracked to Tammy's office and dug into her jacket and passed him the master keys for the factory.

"Which Mr. Gauthier asked for them?"

"Jean."

"What was that all about?" asked Tammy.

"Guess my work here is done."

"A bit unexpected, is it?"

Anne nodded.

Then Barbie piped in, "I heard another fun bit of gossip, too. My sister saw Mr. Gauthier at dinner a few nights back with that same gorgeous girl. It must be serious."

"Where was this?" asked Tammy.

"At Red Shores casino. A lovely spot."

"Never been there," said Anne. Abruptly she got up and left.

45.

Bernie tossed the ring of keys to Jean and took a seat behind his desk.

"That's that, I suppose. Are you going to hire a real detective now?" asked Bernie.

"She may not look it, but she's got a good rep for getting results."

"What's next?" said Bernie. He looked first at Jean and then at Michel. Jean shifted uneasily in his chair.

"You want to buy the place back?" said Michel. This time Bernie squirmed restlessly, both at the question and the peculiar but unreadable grin on Michel's face.

"Not a chance," said Bernie. "Had my crack at it. Too many headaches. I agreed to stay on until you got used to the operations and the business end of things. Only four more weeks until the lobster season ends. Then you get the books and the keys, and I get time to enjoy life while I'm still young enough to do it."

"Where will you go? Charlottetown? Halifax?"

"Someplace warmer, I hope... with friendly ladies, and real rum... and where the work always starts *mañana*. Cuba... Mexico maybe..."

"Sounds wonderful," said Michel, "if you've managed to put away a nice nest egg over the years."

"I've always been clever with money," said Bernie.

"And you deserve a good rest, Bernie."

"Speaking of 'deserving,'" said Jean, "I've got something to do down on the wharf. Be gone half an hour. Want to come along?"

"No," said Michel. "One wharf looks like every other. And I don't care about a factory tour either, but... I might drive over and take a look at that new property of yours."

Jean headed for the wharf, more specifically for the Queens County Packers truck. On his way, he passed the mangled doorway of the warehouse. The gaping hole in the side must have been where the fork veered off course and pierced the corrugated-steel siding, he thought, and Jean gave a bit of a shudder. Then he spotted the big frame of Fig Grant leaning against the side of the truck box and staring out toward open water.

"Fig," he shouted. "Got a minute?"

Fig directed his attention toward the voice, said nothing, but turned, and waited for Jean's approach.

"Glad I was able to catch you here."

"Not hard to do. Not many other places I'd be this time of day." Fig's words were delivered with little enthusiasm or emotion, but the manner in which he spoke suggested a measure of irony that took the edge off them.

"I want to thank you for the courage and quick thinking yesterday when that forklift hit the warehouse. You saved at least one life when you pushed Anne Brown out of the way. That was impressive. It really was."

"When you've been around boats and machinery all your life, you get used to expecting surprises and keeping clear of trouble."

"Maybe so, but it's not a skill that most people I know would have mastered. Anne Brown is... was an employee and a friend, and we're very pleased she escaped serious harm, thanks to you."

Jean stepped back and looked at the truck Fig leaned against. "Have you worked for Queens County Packers long?"

"A couple years... whenever they're buying fish."

"Like the work?"

"It's work, and I can count on it. Not too many choices out here in the country."

"Did you ever consider working at the factory?"

Fig pondered his answer longer than Jean expected. Then he said, "I thought about it, years ago when Big Sea ran things. Bernie hired me as night watchman. Then Big Sea told Bernie they wanted somebody younger. So they let me go. I'm no younger now than I was then. So I've not thought about it since."

"What I'm sayin', Fig, is if you want a permanent job at the factory, you've got one."

"I'll think about it, but I'm doin' all right here. No hassles… and I have a little enterprise on the side that keeps me busy as well."

"The offer will be open."

"…appreciate it. By the way, have you been out mackerel fishin' yet?"

"No, I haven't."

46.

The perfectly round, nearly bald head of Luc LaVie swivelled when he saw Michel Gauthier heading for his car in the parking lot. Luc took note, some memory registered, and he rushed forward.

"Bonjour monsieur, comment ça va? Parlez-vous français?"

"Parfois..."

"If I may ask... are you Monsieur..."

"Gauthier. Yes, yes. Michel Gauthier."

"Luc LaVie," he said by way of introducing himself.

Luc spoke his name proudly. Then he took a step back, looked intently at Michel, and shaped his two hands into a rectangle. He held his hands up in front, arms extended, as if to frame Michel's head within them for a photo. Michel viewed him peculiarly and then began to walk away.

"I'm sorry, but I must go," said Michel.

"Please, Monsieur, please. You look just like... you remind me of... a cousin... my mother's grandnephew, I think. She was a Gauthier from North Rustico. I play with you when we were young. Remember?" Luc grinned excitedly.

"That's very interesting, Monsieur LaVie, but I really must go. You must excuse me, and I tell you that you are mistaken. I have no family from Prince Edward Island."

Michel continued toward his car without looking back. Luc LaVie remained there for a moment, his face clouding, his eager grin fading into bewilderment.

Luc walked back toward the wharf. As he did, he grew more sullen with every step.

47.

Anne was losing focus. Too much anger and confusion swirled in her head. Reason, emotion, and self-respect had been fighting for her attention until it became just too much. Then, any concentration Anne had managed to hold together fell apart. She needed to escape.

So she fled the proximity of the factory and, in time, found herself at the end of a deserted section of wharf. It was quiet there. No distractions. She wanted to cry, but no tears came. Instead, she just sat on a steel bollard at the edge of the quay and stared out over the water.

Minutes ticked, but she didn't count them. The southerly breeze was light and warm and as comforting as a friendly arm on her shoulder. The hum from the factory had become a soothing mantra, and the clutter in her mind began to slip away.

Still, no epiphany enlightened her, no intuition hinted a path forward, and no medicine show boasted a quick cure. Only time heals such wounds. She knew that.

So she idled at this remote arm of the wharf for a long while. Gradually, her racing mind slowed, her emotions calmed, and her hurt subsided, and she began to feel the return of well-being and wholeness, of professionalism and purpose, and at this point Anne reached out for what had always been the workhorses of her trade: logic and facts.

Anne had been undermined in her investigation, confounded by a case, and fired from a job. Argument wouldn't lead to her rehiring. That was out of her control. But the investigation itself was something she could tackle on her own—if she wanted to.

Anne recognized that the Gauthiers and Bernie White had the power to stop her pay cheque and access to the factory, but they couldn't keep her from working the case on her own dime and in her own way. It was matter of pride... self-respect, thought Anne. *The Gauthiers never saw me as a real investigator. They only saw what they wanted to see. But no one's going to tell me what I can or can't do.*

Anne's path forward now looked clearer; her hurt grew less painful, and her state of mind became less self-indulgent. She headed back.

Several wharves made up the harbour at Little Rose. This early in the morning they were clear of fishing gear. Most vessels were still offshore, working the lobster grounds. There were two lonely exceptions, though. One boat on the east wharf sputtered and revved unevenly as a mechanic sorted an engine malfunction. Several idle men stood on the open deck and watched or passed tools through a hatch into the engine compartment. Another boat, lonely and untended, lay against the west wharf. The boat's name, *Hell to Pay*, was clearly stencilled on the stern.

As Anne drew near *Hell to Pay*, she heard rattling from somewhere inside the cabin. If that's Hec Dunne with his fractured whatever, she thought, I hope he doesn't stick his leering face up soon enough to see me. The thought of his glib tongue rekindled a bit of her previous anger, but, as Anne passed, she looked back quickly enough to see a blonde head pushing a swab across a watery cabin floor. She stopped.

"CeeCee?" she called out. "Is that you?"

CeeCee's head turned sharply toward the sound, her face showing surprise and humiliation. Even in the emptiness of the wharf at this time of day, CeeCee seemed reluctant to speak or unable to find suitable words, so she simply uttered, "Guess you heard, huh?"

Anne nodded. "Sorry."

"No need to be," said CeeCee. "Got everything in hand."

"You and Hec made up?"

"Hell no! He's gone, and, as far as I'm concerned, that man won't be in the picture anymore. I'm done with him."

"Then why are you cleaning up his boat?"

"Funny how things turn out," said CeeCee. "The boat is mine, actually. It'd been my Dad's, but when Dad was thinking of retiring, he gave it to me for next to nothing just before Hec and me got married. It's still in my name."

"So you're going to sell it?"

"Not going to sell it either. I'm going to fish it for the rest of the season with Jack Pine. Me and Jack are going halves on the profit. Hec had a big plan to buy a second boat and lobster license this fall in his own name. But one fisherman with one boat can't hold more'n one lobster license, ya see. So he transferred this license into my name a few months back."

"Think you can handle that kind of work?"

"Did some fishin' with Dad years back. It's hard work, but I liked it. I still have to get clearance from the Department of Fisheries, but that shouldn't take more than another day or so. And you? What are you busy at?"

"I've had better days. I got fired ten minutes after I got here this morning. My employer thinks the job's becoming too risky for a woman. Then I heard that a guy I'd been seeing is two-timing me."

"Ouch!" said CeeCee. "That's gotta hurt. You have a game plan?"

"I'm workin' on it."

48.

Luc LaVie smouldered as he walked away from Michel Gauthier. He trundled along, muttering in French under his breath, and every so often his arms would spring up to underscore some fervent point that no one heard.

"What the hell's got into you?"

Luc looked up from his indecipherable grumblings and found himself heading toward a wharf to nowhere. Fig Grant stood a few feet away, and he wore a mischievous grin at having caught the little Frenchman unawares and somewhat confounded. Luc stopped suddenly, his articulate arms fell to his sides, and his language switched to English, as if it had never strayed, and as if Fig had been privy to his grievances about the erosion of French culture and language.

"So, what would you do?" said Luc.

"What on earth are you goin' on about, Luc?"

"How do we keep French when everything slip away from us?"

Fig's amused expression annoyed Luc.

"You English... what if you lose everything that make you English: your past, your custom, your language? What d'you do then?"

"Well, first of all, I'm not English. I'm an Islander, and the Grants have been Irish for as long as I recall. We had nothin' in Ireland when we came, scraped together next to nothing here, and I lost all that in short order. That's the way life is, Luc."

"It still make me mad," said Luc. "It just not fair."

"No point bein' mad if you can't put a face to it. You wind up punchin' shadows... 's not so much fun. Who are you mad at today?"

"That Gauthier fella. I talk to him in French, and he want to run away. Too embarrass to be French, maybe."

"Seemed like a friendly enough young fella to me."

"I talk about th' old one, th' father... and he—he is my second cousin by marriage, I think."

Fig gave out a hearty laugh. "Never had much use for my relatives," said Fig.

"My mother tell me all 'bout it. Her aunt, Frederique Gauthier, goes work in Nova Scotia and get pregnant. Her boyfriend, Michael MacDonald, run away. She give th' baby name, Michel Gauthier."

Fig chuckled again, more politely this time.

"You've got a helluva imagination, Luc. I bet you could look at a goat and see a side of beef... half-cooked. There must be five thousand Gauthiers in Atlantic Canada and god-only-knows how many in Quebec. What makes you think he's your cousin?"

"Frederique... Frederique..." said Luc, becoming exasperated with Fig's tone. "She visit us in Rustico in '58. Michel come with her. I was ten. Michel twelve. We argue all th' time 'bout who is better, Elvis Presley or Chuck Berry."

"That don't prove much, Luc."

"Though I suppose I should not have expected too much from him. After that, his father come back, and he and Frederique marry."

"A happy ending," said Fig, his expression hovering between a snicker and a tease.

Luc countered it with a quick scowl and went on: "It wasn't *Snow White and Seven Dwarf* happy. Th' father... he went overboard in a blow off Sou'west Nova. Never found his body. But before he go, the father adopt Michel and give th' boy his own name, Michael Macdonald. He was already half English by then, I bet."

Fig went silent. His face turned sour.

49.

Old Grant Homestead

Michel Gauthier turned off and followed the dirt lane toward Sullivan's Point. For decades overhanging tree branches had crowded that passage. The lane was narrow and had been little used until Jean had bought the property and marshalled an army of vehicles to begin construction of his new home. Then dump trucks and flatbeds beat the foliage down as they barrelled through the narrow corridor. Damaged branches hung limply. Stripped leaves peppered the roadbed.

He followed the fresh tracks made by the trucks. Their presence struck him as a desecration. That feeling, blended with sadness and melancholy, lasted until Michel's car broke into the cleared acreage of the point, and he saw the remnants of the Grant homestead. There, the sun shone brightly. Warmth nurtured and lifted his spirits. He felt whole again. He felt young again. He felt love again, and he recalled the first moment he saw her so many years before.

At twenty-nine, Michel was an active, resourceful young man. A friend working on the Caribou-Wood Islands ferry had told him of a job as deckhand aboard a lobster boat on Prince Edward Island. Michel had had experience as a seaman in Nova Scotia and had even worked the winter fishery off Sou'west Nova. He wanted to try something new. So fishing with Hap Gordon filled that need. Hap had been a fair man to work for, but now that job was done. He expected Hap to call him back for more work, but there was little to do but wait for Hap to decide whether to set trawl for cod or put up his A-frame and drag for groundfish. Meantime, Michel thought, maybe he could make few dollars harvesting bar clams or other shellfish along nearby tributaries. That's where he saw her.

His first glimpse found her barefoot and padding though the sandy shallows near Sullivan's Point. She was pretty. Quite pretty, actually. However, a blend of grace and sensuality, of which she seemed entirely oblivious, drew his attention even more intensely. That, coupled with a contradictory mix of youthful awkwardness and sophistication in her manner, transfixed him.

It took some time for Mary Grant to notice Michel, or "Michael MacDonald," as he called himself, but, when she did, she abruptly stopped, and quietly stared. It was as if she had come upon a deer drinking from a brook, had become fascinated, and wished not to frighten it away.

In the few weeks that followed, Michael found more than a promise of shellfish in the vicinity of Sullivan's Point. He and Mary met often and always in a secret rendezvous. They talked; they kissed; they touched. Neither, however, spoke of families. It was a subject that seemed unimportant at first. Later, however, Michael became suspicious that she was concealing something: a boyfriend, a tyrannical father, or a husband even. Michael could have asked her for the truth, but he didn't. In his heart, he was afraid that truth would snuff out the dream and end the blissful illusion of their future together.

Michael's fears became prophetic the third week in July. At that time, the two lovers had secreted themselves in a spot east of Sullivan's Point. It had become their favourite meeting place, a hollow amongst a stand of old pines. A thick, soft coat of needles bedded the hollow, and from this refuge they could look out over the water and watch the ebb and flow of boats, the flights of herons and osprey, and the lazy drift of puffy clouds. And from this refuge they could share dreams, imagine plans, and talk of futures from the vantage point of unspoken pasts.

The sound of heavy boots lumbering through the brush extinguished all that.

Fig Grant's long powerful arms reached down, grasped Michael by his shoulders, and hauled him out of the hollow. Michael never gained his footing. Fig dragged him by his neck. Mary screamed.

"Fig! Don't hurt him. Please don't hurt him! We weren't doing anything."

"I know what you was doin', and it weren't nothin'. Now tuck yourself in, and get home. Now!"

"Don't hurt him. Please!"

"Get… before I give you the back of m' hand."

Mary turned and ran. Tears streamed down her face.

"Don't hurt him," she shouted back.

Michael heard her desperate plea, but he never saw Fig's fist slam like a hammer into his face. He never felt his head slam back against a rock.

And he never saw Mary Grant again.

***

Michel Gauthier wandered through memories and, almost unknowingly, found himself at the Point. A few mature and stately trees stood near the hollow where he and Mary had met and made love so many years before, and it was there that Michel felt an uncontrollable flood of emotion and regret and anger and longing rise up from a recess he had forgotten had ever existed.

Then he turned and hurried away, no longer able to remain at that place with the guilt that still haunted him, and he didn't stop until he reached the yellow police tape that surrounded the pioneer graveyard near the Grant homestead. There, a spray of yellow crocuses bloomed near a poorly marked, recently tended gravesite. Tears welled up and streamed down his cheeks. His hand lowered gently onto the sun-warmed earth of her grave. He could feel the solitary pulse of his own heart. Then his eyes grew cold and dry, and his countenance, bled of emotion, became lifeless and stony. Compassion fled. Forgiveness had been driven out.

The incessant ringing of his cellphone forced him out of morbid introspection and self-indulgence. He grabbed at his phone and answered. His bark into the receiver was irritable and snappish.

The voice of the caller reverberated from the depths of a metal barrel, and Michel had no doubt who had rung him up.

"No need to get testy, Michel. I presume you have the money in small denominations."

"Yes."

"Listen carefully. I'll say it once. Tonight. Eleven o'clock. Callie's Road in Montague. Gibb's Snack Shop. It's closed now. You know it?"

"No. But I don't like the sound of it. We'll have to meet somewhere more public, where I won't get mugged... and in daytime, not night," Michel said, his tone obstinate and firm.

"You're in no position to bargain. Either you follow my instructions, or I'll pass my info on to that nosy woman that's been snooping around your factory. She might find it illuminating. Or your son? Maybe even the cops."

Michel's lip curled into a snarl, but no untoward sound followed it. Michel took a long, quiet breath and regained composure. He continued: "All right... all right. How do I know you'll keep quiet and not try to shake me down later?"

"You don't, but that's a risk you'll have to take. Come alone. Bring the cash in a sports bag. Behind Gibb's place there's an outside set of stairs leading up to a large storage loft. The door will be open. Put the bag inside. Wait inside for five minutes. I want to check that you haven't brought any helpers. Then leave, drive away, and don't double back. Got it?"

Another long pause followed.

"I got it." As he ended the call, Michel felt anger welling up. It nearly raged out of control as he spun the wheel of his car toward the factory at Little Rose. Then, in the lapse of just a few moments, the fire of his hatred fluttered, died down, and slipped into cold revenge.

Now Michel knew the extra work he had to do.

50.

Anne's game plan was hardly that. It seemed more of an inclination. She could have stopped, but she didn't. She didn't want to. It wasn't her nature. Once someone described her as being part terrier, but she always imagined herself being more formidable, a Doberman maybe.

She'd added one tactic to her game plan as soon as she stuck her hand into her jacket pocket and felt the crumpled Rolodex card, her only link to the mysterious George Livingstone. As she trudged the last few yards along the wharf, the possibility of a breakthrough energized her.

Anne wasn't entirely sure how to set everything in motion but, when she chanced to see Jean and his father and Bernie exiting the factory together, she seized the opportunity, entered the numbers for "GL's" phone, and hoped for a bit of luck.

Anne's phone began to ring GL's number. In the distance Michel broke stride and appeared to fumble for something. Bernie's phone began to chime, too. Both men walked away from each other for privacy. Jean stood halfway between them and waited.

Anne's pulse quickened at Michel's grab for his phone but, when Bernie also responded, she grew confused. Her phone continued to buzz for GL. Anne's confusion turned into deep disappointment when she viewed Michel speaking into his phone and punctuating his remarks with gesticulations. Then, her own attempted phone call forwarded to a message centre with a prerecorded, generic salutation. It was not the great stride forward she had hoped for.

Not until after they had pocketed their phones did the men notice Anne standing near the foot of the wharf. Michel headed toward her. Bernie followed. Jean went elsewhere.

Michel looked impatient; Bernie, somewhat aloof.

"You're still here," said Michel.

"Yes," said Anne.

"I don't understand. Your involvement with the factory was terminated. There's no reason for you to be here."

"I understand that, Mr. Gauthier, but I personally am not quite done with it. There are questions I want answered, whether I'm paid or not."

"That's foolish. It's too dangerous."

"I'm aware of the risks, and I'm not a china doll. I don't break easily."

"You're not making sense," said Michel, his voice scarcely masking his growing anger and frustration.

"He's right, you know," said Bernie.

"It's no skin off his back if I push a bit further… or yours, Bernie. Nobody's losing money. Nobody's losing sleep, and nobody's inconvenienced but me… and sometimes I like being inconvenienced. It gives me peace of mind."

"You'll regret this," said Michel, wagging a finger in her face and glowering at her defiance.

Michel spun around and headed toward his car. Bernie followed for a bit but fell behind Michel's stride and turned off toward the door to the office.

Well, that was interesting, thought Anne. I've never had anyone mad at me because I insisted on working for nothing.

For a few moments, Anne's rebuff of Michel and Bernie's plans tasted sweet, and she savoured it. Later, though, as she recalled their outburst, she realized that they had come close to threatening her, and the sweetness of her triumph slipped away.

51.

Despite her defiance in the face of Michel Gauthier, Anne knew she had drawn a worthless hand. Her hunch about George Livingstone's identity had led nowhere. Now she was out of leads and left to wonder what next. Or even if there was a next.

Was it time to fold? Or should she press ahead with some kind of bluff? Either or? This or that? No preferable choice at any turn. Then, she thought, maybe there was no need to decide now. Maybe there was no need to decide at all. She could just let events unfold a while longer and see what turned up.

Anne headed toward the factory. The girls would be taking their break soon. Maybe, she thought, just maybe she could pick up a scrap of information there, but, as she rounded the corner of a building, she collided with a small sturdy wall. The wall was Luc LaVie.

LaVie had been head down, not paying attention to anything but the argument roiling in his head, and Anne had been too self-absorbed with choices to be alert to anything around her. Their collision, however, brought both of them stumbling into the present.

After a flurry of awkward "sorrys," they slipped into another confusing exchange.

"I just do not understand," said Luc who had not quite stopped conversing with himself. "Why would he do it?"

"Who? Do what?" said Anne, her forehead wrinkling in bewilderment.

Luc leaped once again into his account of the 1958 family reunion at which he met young Michel Gauthier. Her eyes glazed over as he dove into the complexities of genealogy. It made little sense to Anne, but it did remind her of the name quest she'd embarked on earlier. So she trod down an old road one more time.

"Have you ever heard the name... George Livingstone?"

Luc was disappointed that Anne had not grasped the significance of his own finding, but he suppressed his dismay.

"Of course," he said. Anne brightened.

At last, she thought. "Tell me about him."

"He owned the factory for many years."

"Did you know him?"

"No."

"Have you any idea where he'd come from... where he lived or worked?"

"No."

"Do you know anybody who might know more about the man?"

"No... well... maybe Bernie."

"Don't you think it odd that no one seems to know anything about Livingstone?"

"Yes," he said and shrugged.

Anne gave Luc a halfhearted wave as she left. Both headed in different directions, each disappointed: Luc in her lack of empathy; Anne in his lack of information.

52.

Something in the look on Fig's face disturbed Spit. Fig was too quiet. He sat motionless on an overturned lobster crate in the back of the Queens County Packers refrigeration truck, hunched over, staring at a blank wall of the closed-in truck box. Spit imagined he could discern a menacing cloud hovering above his hulking form.

Spit knew something was amiss. He wanted to say something, ask something, but that might provoke an angry rebuke. So he kept silent. Squeak joined them later. Spit said little to Squeak, but he cocked his head in Fig's direction to signal that trouble might be brewing.

The brooding silence lingered like the stink of a spring thaw. Spit could bear such discomfort, but the protracted weight of it distressed Squeak. He had always fretted when his wife harboured some petty complaint and suffered it unspoken. Finally, he could take no more.

"Are we bottling tonight?"

"Up to you," said Fig. His head turned toward Squeak and, as if he had been betrayed, he said, "I'm going over now."

Squeak expected more, but no more came. Fig stood, dropped down onto the wharf, and headed for his own boat.

"What do you make of that?"

"It's queer business. I don't know. I don't like it."

"Maybe we should head over early."

"One more boat to come in. Then we'll go."

53.

Fig's bootleg operation was on Dill's Arm, a bump of land across the bay that stuck out with a view of both Little Rose Harbour and Sullivan's Point. It was isolated except for access by boat. The land was acidic and hid a layer of clay that made it wet and unsuitable for growing most everything but spruce and wild rose bushes. A tangled and rutted logging road had beaten its way into the area twenty years before. Now only a hint of that road remained.

Dill's Arm was as isolated a spot as one could find, but it was Fig's home—not that he owned it. He had been squatting on the land since his family homestead had been seized and put up for public sale many years before. The real owners of the land were absentee landlords from somewhere in Upper Canada. They had inherited the property but had seen no value in it, nor had anyone else. Even locals with a few dollars to invest failed to find a silver lining in such a purchase.

Fig, however, saw something others would not. He found the ideal site to keep an eye on his family's land, land he still thought his. He built a small cabin there. Later, in financially bleaker times, he viewed the location as a near-perfect hiding place for making bootleg whisky: virtually inaccessible by land and with fine visibility across the water for snoops, police, or would-be thieves. Most people in the area, though, minded their own business and left Fig & Co. to its own devices.

The police were not much different. Unless prodded by politicians or some public outcry, RCMP concentrated on more serious matters—unending break and enters, tenacious and inventive pot growers and, more recently, newly arrived biker gangs with reckless interests in chemistry. So a couple of old bootleggers became low priority.

Fig put the gears in neutral and let the boat's momentum carry it just inside the point to a pool of deep water near shore. He tied the bowline to an ancient wharf post, remnant of an abandoned private wharf that once stood on that site. He tied a stern line to another post, pulled out a couple of planks lying on the working deck of his vessel, stretched them across from boat to the shore, and clambered across them.

The cabin he had built was further up the shore, but he didn't head in that direction. Instead, he made his way a few yards up the embankment to another old shack. He and Spit and Squeak had floated it in and hauled it up twenty years before. Over the years the old shed disappeared from public sight among hardy shrubs and thick bush that grew up the bank. Fig transplanted a few more bushes here and there. They flourished and eventually screened all the bare spots that nature had not managed to obscure.

One time that shack had been a private station where some fishermen salted herring and mackerel. Fig never meant it to be used for that purpose or even as a shelter. It had a roof, a front door, and sides, but no back except the steep bank. Its sole purpose was to conceal the workings of their whisky-making enterprise from public view. It hid the furnace, made of rock and red clay, half-built into the side of the bank, as well as a fifty-gallon copper still, the cooling barrel, worm, and other gear. A nearby freshwater spring bled a small but steady stream out the slope of the bank. Spit and Squeak had diverted part of that water into a pipe to fill the cooling barrel.

It was still early afternoon when Fig settled in at the shack. The sun shone. There was strength to its heat. The view to Little Rose Harbour was clear, the water calm, the tide rising. It was by all local accounts a glorious day. Still, nothing could lift the cloud of dark thought that weighed him down.

Fig grabbed an empty one-litre plastic milk container from a shelf. His pocketknife carved away the spout and top half of the container until all that remained was a kind of pitcher, handle and all. A large barrel stood nearby. He lifted the top and scooped up a generous pitcher of moonshine. He sat outside on a stump and leaned back against the wooden door. He stared at the colourless 'shine as if it were sacramental wine—a remedy for suffering, the answer to lifelong mysteries—and took a long slow sip. This was his first drink in twenty years.

The homemade whisky burned. Fig grimaced. A warm, familiar pain coursed down his throat and into his belly. Tears came to his eyes, and a surge of heat broke like a wave and spread throughout his entire body.

Fig felt profound relief. It felt good... but not good enough. He needed profound oblivion.

He took a deep swig, one that could kill if it came to that. Then he took another.

54.

It was noon by the time Michel mounted the stairs to the office. His legs felt leaden, and he became weary even before reaching the landing. He had been feeling himself grow older by the hour. The upstairs offices were empty. Morgan had gone to lunch. He had sent Bernie off on some wild goose chase. No one was about.

For the past few days Michel had been making use of Jean's factory office space whenever he needed it. He gave the door a nudge, and it swung open. There was no sign of Jean. It's what he had expected. Jean usually spent the noon hour chatting with the workers. Good for morale, he had said.

Michel had counted on an empty office. He needed quiet and solitude. He needed to collect his thoughts and make a plan. He had to protect himself—from whom, he wasn't sure. But he knew damned well that, once an extortionist gets hooks into you, you're trapped forever, and going to the police was out of the question.

The first thing Michel intended to do was safeguard his money. He had worked too hard all his life to throw away a hundred thousand dollars. It just wasn't going to happen. He had an idea, though, but he needed the means to carry it out, and he was sure that the essentials could be got here.

In Morgan's office, Michel rifled through her supply cabinet. Her window's view showed approaches to the outside stairs, and that gave Michel a perfect vantage point to spot visitors and still snoop about.

In the cabinet Michel located a stockpile of computer paper. He placed one bundle into the printer tray. He raised the printer lid, neatly placed a handful of twenties and fifties on the glass, and pressed the button for multiple colour copies. He looked at his watch. He could count on no more than a half hour to print copies of the bills. *Ample time*, he thought. He spotted a paper cutter in a narrow slot between the storage and file cabinets. Michel took it to Jean's office. He returned to Morgan's office, and stood watch while the printer completed its run.

It was one o'clock when Michel heard footsteps and the voices of Tammy and Barbie. They were loud and rollicking and rife with fresh gossip to nourish their curiosities. Morgan arrived not long after them.

By then, Michel had locked himself behind Jean's office door. Cutting fake money to match the dimensions of regular bills would be the most time-consuming job. Michel worked slowly and accurately. He would put off assembling the fake bundles of cash until evening. He would have time for that later.

Job number two was to phone his lawyer in Halifax. He wanted a quick, thorough background check on some employees, and he wanted it done PDQ.

"I want your investigative contacts to look hard at Anne Brown, Barbie Beaton, Tammy Wallace, Bernie White, Morgan Sark, and Luc LaVie."

Michel bided his time patiently while Chris Nott, his lawyer, squirmed in his Halifax seat and described the enormity of such a task. Chris was a perfectionist. That's one reason Michel had developed a professional relationship with him.

"Yes, criminal, civil lawsuits, financial stability, and vices," he said. "I know it's a tall order… yes, and I know you can't get everything… yes, yes… just do your best. If you need to prioritize, put Brown and White at the top of the list. I need it today. Use my cellphone."

Michel hung up and turned his attention to something else.

Already he had deduced that the extortionist was not a professional. He or she had lowballed the figure demanded. To Michel, that suggested the culprit needed money. The second error was naming the drop site too soon. That was something that Michel hoped he could take advantage of.

He opened Jean's computer and keyed in a search engine with a mapping site. One site provided street views of most communities. Montague, PEI, was one of them, and Michel navigated to the location where he was to leave the cash.

Callie's Road was a central location in the town. Numerous exits existed, and three or four of them accessed roads out of the community. Michel stared at the picture of Gibb's Snack Shop. He stared, and then he smiled.

One more item to pick up, he concluded.

55.

Less than an hour later Fig watched a small powerboat approach from the direction of Little Rose Harbour. He recognized the boat. It was Spit's runabout. It slowed and pulled alongside Fig's vessel. Squeak made fast the lines to Fig's deck, and the two men trudged up toward the still. Each of them had two large bags filled with small plastic containers.

Spit and Squeak joked and laughed as they scrambled up the embankment. They looked like gnomes from Santa's workshop, raggedy white stubbles of beard and untrimmed hair sticking out from shapeless caps, jolly old elves with enormous bags of toys over their shoulders. They were Fig's best friends, probably his only friends, and they were a comic sight. Now Fig hated them both. They had betrayed him. His life had been ruined because of them. He did not know it then, but he knew it now. That night was the turning point in his life, and he remembered it as if it were yesterday.

***

"...in news today the Soviet spacecraft Soyuz successfully docked with America's Apollo spacecraft. This joint venture was a first in US-Soviet relations... more details later tonight, but now for a bit of music..."

The radio in Squeak's fishing boat picked up American stations in Boston and New York on most nights. This night was especially good reception. It was late enough and clear enough for a strong signal.

> "...Drums beatin' cold, English blood runs hot
> Lady of the house wonderin' when it's gonna stop
> House boy knows that he's doin' all right
> You should have heard him just around midnight
> Brown Sugar, how come you taste so good
> Brown Sugar, just like a young girl should..."

"W-would ya turn off that g-goddam music and put s-somethin' else on?" said Spit. "It's sp-sp-puttin' me off."

Squeak spun the dial until a furious fiddle pounded out a traditional Scottish jig on a Cape Breton station. Squeak turned the volume down.

"What's got into you?" he barked. Spit looked back at him angrily.

"Ya know d-damned well. We shouldn't be d-doin' this."

Squeak cocked his ear when he heard a series of sharp thumps in the cabin forward of the wheelhouse. It could have been flotsam striking the hull as they plowed ahead on their easterly course. But it wasn't.

It was Michael MacDonald, bound and gagged below deck. He must have regained consciousness, thought Squeak. Fig had beaten him brutally before he loaded him aboard their boat for his trip to nowhere.

Squeak turned up the radio to drown out the racket MacDonald was stirring up.

"Didn't have much choice about it, did we? Fig caught 'em in the act. Fig woulda killed him right then if Mary hadn't been there to see it, and we hadn't stopped him."

They had been steaming south for about an hour. Squeak looked at the Loran. The numbers put them east of Fisherman's Bank. The tide was about to turn.

"What else could we 'ave done? Let him beat the man to death?"

said Squeak, adding, "We woulda done the same if it was our kid... or sister. Right?"

"W-wouldn't go this far. W-where did Fig say to d-dump him over?"

"A bit east of the Bank in deep water... where the body won't snag on rocks or catch in trawl gear. Fallin' tide will take him out."

"Then we're g-gettin' close now. Are ya sure we want to do this?"

Squeak said nothing, but Spit could read the concern in his eyes—fear of going against Fig, dread of getting caught, the burden of killing—but there was no further conversation between the two men. Each stared out over a moonless sea, brightened by stars and rimmed by low grey outlines of Prince Edward Island to the west, Nova Scotia to the south, and Cape Breton just east of them. Pinpoints of red and white and green and amber light blinked out a Morse-like identification. Each beckoned warning or welcome and safe passage.

Michael MacDonald writhed and kicked wearily. The motor droned on for another twenty minutes. The irregular slap of small waves beat out the time, and silence between the two men thickened until it created a foreboding sound of its own.

"So... what then?" said Squeak.

"...Can't go back..."

"No. Can't do that."

"B-but I have an idea. Head for the Cape George light."

"...and Ballantyne's Cove?"

"No. K-keep the light to port 'til it disappears behind the headland. A couple of small wharf lights will pop up. M-make for them. We'll dump him near the c-coast."

An hour elapsed before Squeak's boat approached the western coastline of Nova Scotia. The moon had begun to rise. The mountains behind Lismore and Arisaig loomed to starboard. Then Squeak found the lights Spit had mentioned. They were dead ahead, and their vessel stood maybe a mile offshore. In the moonlight Squeak discerned a distant wharf.

Squeak left the engine in neutral. The two of them went below and hauled their passenger up on deck. He was still bound by his legs and arms, and gagged as well. They let him drop and stepped back. Michael struggled up onto his knees and stared over the dark watery expanse to see where he was. He was facing Prince Edward Island, about thirty miles away.

"That's where we're supposed to be tossin' ya over... for your misdeeds, Mikey... about ten miles that way. What d' ya think?"

Spit saw the rise of fear and panic in his eyes. Michael wriggled and squirmed, but the bonds held firm. His chest heaved in desperation. The gag stopped words or pleas from escaping or a fresh supply of air from relieving the ache in his lungs.

"Now it's deal time. Here's your choices. We can dump ya out there... or we can dump ya in here," he said pointing behind him.

Michael struggled around and saw the harbour lights. He shook his head eagerly.

"You've got a chance to make that shore from here. But if you're found, you don't know anything about PEI. You've never been there. Make up whatever excuse you want to... but never come back. Never. You understand what I'm tellin' ya? Fig'll kill ya for sure."

Michael nodded.

Spit cut the rope on his ankles and pulled the gag from his mouth. Squeak grabbed his arms and held them until Spit cut away the bindings on his hands. Then Squeak pushed Michael over the side. He sputtered when he rose to the surface. The wharf appeared farther away at water level than it had from the deck of Squeak's boat. The chill of the water had sharpened his senses, but he felt more keenly the damage that Fig's beating had inflicted on him. He stretched out his arms and pushed himself off toward the shore. The pain in his side suggested a broken rib and shortened his swimming stroke. He knew, too, that it would be difficult to reach shore and fight a current as well.

Squeak swung the wheel over. The boat steamed away. Its wake led back toward Michael MacDonald. The bow pointed up toward Little Rose Harbour and home. Fig would be there, and both Squeak and Spit hoped he would believe their story.

56.

The jolly old elves laughed and joked their way along the water's edge and up the short slope to the still. The huge bags, filled with plastic containers, rattled softly on their shoulders, but, when Squeak and Spit looked up ahead, they saw Fig, and his demeanour struck a chord of alarm.

Fig wielded a plastic dipper. He wavered on his feet. His mouth seemed to hang on his face.

"I think he's been into the brew," said Squeak.

"It's been many a year s-since I seen him at it, but I th-think he's drunk."

"Wonder what set him off?"

Their cheery spirit dimmed as a cloud of uncertainty loomed in front of them. In fact, they stopped moving altogether.

"What's the matter?" shouted Squeak up the hill to Fig. Fig's torso rose up like a threatening wave.

"Ya didn't take care of him, did ya? All these years you've been lyin' to me. All these years he's been alive. And all these years..."

"Fig, what are you j-jabberin' about?"

"Michael MacDonald. He's alive... and he's here. You lied to me. You both lied to me. You let him go."

Squeak felt a surge of panic but fought back against it.

"We did what we told ya we did? We took him out and dumped him over."

"You're lyin'. You're both lyin' to me."

"There's no way he could have survived. No way."

"You musta got it wrong somehow. We did what we told ya we done, and that's that."

"Yer lyin'. He's Luc's cousin. Luc recognized him. He told me all about him. I should kill you for what you did."

Fig took a few faltering steps toward them. Squeak and Spit panicked, dropped their bags, turned and ran back the way they'd come. Fig attempted to go after them, but he stumbled on a root and fell headlong down the muddy slope.

Fig lay there feeling helpless and deceived. He grasped at his plastic makeshift pitcher. It was empty. The contents had spilled. He looked back up the hill but didn't have the energy to return.

Squeak's little boat roared to life and sped away.

Fig lay motionless, facedown on the muddy slope below his still. He looked dead and, as the minutes ticked away, even the birds on the hillside bushes shed their fear and ventured close enough to snatch a small insect or draw a worm from the soft, freshly exposed soil near him. In time they grew bolder and bolder, until a twitch would frighten them away. Fig persisted in his drunken sleep until the awkward position into which he had fallen became uncomfortable and painful. The sun had lowered a bit as well, and now the glare of it shone more fully and directly onto his face and eyes.

Eventually, he roused himself, now only half-drunk, and sat up. His overalls were wet and covered in mud. He made a vain effort to brush the muck away but was unsuccessful and only managed to dirty his half-clean hands.

Fig remained there for some time, his hands folded in front of him, elbows resting on his knees; his head slung forward, dipping wearily toward the ground; his eyes staring at nothing; his mind speeding in circles of sane and rash deliberation, and, for the most part, landing on convincing half-truths.

Then some spark illuminated his brain and revealed an awesome improbability, something almost beyond comprehension and which, if true, would be a ghastly reality.

A kind of wild sanity finally motivated the man to rise to his feet, steady himself, and trudge in the direction of, not his still, but his cabin. Repetitive mutterings that only Fig could make sense of accompanied his unsteady strides along that path.

"Nobody else knows... but I know... I know... the sonofabitch... two and two... and I know why."

***

Fig's cabin was really a small old house that had been vacant for many years, but, when Fig lost his homestead to foreclosure, he claimed it for himself. No one seemed to care about his squatting one way or another. For all intents and purposes the place was worthless, but it had almost everything an old bachelor needed. There was one main room and a loft for sleeping. Over the years, he had repaired the roof, replaced the wood stove, and dug a new outhouse. A well pipe rose up from the root cellar under the house, passed through the floor, and fed into a washbasin in the kitchen space. Only the leather valve on the hand pump had needed replacement. The water was clean.

A universal dinginess clung to everything in Fig's house. The smell of old clothes drifted into musty corners and mingled with whiffs of forgotten stains. It was not appalling, but it was not fresh either; yet it suited his simple needs, and that's all that mattered to Fig.

The only things in the cabin that gleamed with cleanliness and regular care shone from a gun rack on the wall above a sagging upholstered chair. The rack held two firearms: a twelve-gauge, double-barreled shotgun for rabbits and partridge and a .22 bolt-action rifle for squirrels.

Fig took the shotgun from the wall rack and pocketed a half-dozen shells. He wrapped the gun in a blanket and made for the door with an unsteady gait. He worried he might be a bit too late. It was nearing four o'clock. The factory would be emptying soon, and he would miss his quarry.

Fig's old fishing boat growled to life. He cast off, and the vessel moved slowly and deliberately across the bay toward the harbour. Just west of the harbour, where Rose Creek trickled into the bay, trees grew close to shore and several large willows drooped limbs nearly to the waterline. Fig drifted in as close as he could get, anchored the boat out of sight, and waded ashore. Land behind the creek was too boggy for a home or cultivation, but it allowed Fig a secure avenue of approach to the factory and its parking lot.

Fig's heartbeat quickened when he spotted Michael's fancy black sedan in a reserved parking space. Fig moved closer, but it was not close enough. The brush along the parking lot was thin, and he still wasn't close enough. The effective range of a shotgun greatly limited the distance he could risk. Wounding wouldn't satisfy him. He needed two close shots to finish the job. And he was bent on doing just that: finishing.

He glanced at his watch. The factory shift would be over soon. Then there'd be five or ten minutes while people punched out, cleaned up, changed clothes, gathered their gear, and left the building for home. Michael would want to be out of there before the main exodus, or the road would be clogged with cars all the way to Halkirk and beyond, and some of the older workers were annoyingly light on the gas pedal. Not much time left. And although Fig wanted Michael dead, he was not fool enough to leave himself exposed to suspicion.

First, though, he needed to get closer. Several stacks of large holding tanks along the wall of the factory not far from Michael's car would do. Little foot traffic or vehicle traffic would interfere. No one could spot him behind the tanks. So that made it a perfect vantage point for killing.

Fig had barely got into his new hiding place before Michael, Jean, and Bernie stepped out the door. Fig clutched his shotgun with exasperation, but even half-drunk Fig knew that to fire at any of them now would be reckless. He hadn't expected so many at one time.

Fig held his fire, but, as the seconds ticked away, he sensed opportunity slipping from his hands. He cursed under his breath and railed in his mind at his unending bad luck. He felt himself tip toward rashness. Reason was losing its grip on madness.

Without thought his finger slipped inside the trigger guard. He took aim at Michael. His cheek pressed into the small of the stock. Then the bell for end of shift rang loudly above his head, and it startled him so much that he flinched and nearly jerked the trigger.

Fig's eyes grew large as they peered down the barrel, but at the end of it he watched Bernie say his goodbyes and head inside the factory. At this point, Fig didn't care which of the Gauthiers he killed. Michael was preferable, but Jean, dead, was almost as good. Michael would suffer almost as much, maybe more, knowing that his son had been murdered because of his own misdeeds.

The barrel of the shotgun swung from one Gauthier to the other twice, as Fig deliberated his decision. But just as Fig made his decision, Jean turned, waved toward someone around the corner, and moved quickly away and out of his line of sight.

Fig had tarried too long. In another second Michael would move. He raised the shotgun one final time, aimed, took up the slack in the trigger, and saw the white flash of a car entering the parking lot.

It was an RCMP patrol car. It moved methodically down each row of cars and trucks. It was moving slowly enough for a second constable to check license plates for up-to-date registration stickers.

Michael toted a small sports bag in one hand and waved to the constables with the other. Fig leaned back against the wall. He wrapped a blanket around his weapon and slipped into an all-too-familiar abyss of disappointment and failure.

57.

Anne figured that she had done all she could at the wharf. The chance of uncovering something at the factory remained, but she was barred from there now. Her only other refuge was home away from home: Halkirk Manor. Maybe she could pry some useful tidbit out of Dearie.

It was less than a five-minute drive from Little Rose Harbour to Halkirk, but when she got there Dearie was nowhere in sight. Her car was gone. The coffee pot was cold. That left one final spot to bide some time: the local café. But that would be an unnecessary distraction, she thought; so she dismissed the idea and retreated to her room.

Anne lay back, her head resting on a pillow. She closed her eyes and tried to imagine another route to follow with her renegade investigation, but her brain would not cooperate, and, in just moments, she fell into a sound sleep.

Anne snapped awake when the front door bang shut. Voices trailed down the Halkirk Manor hallway. Enid's, for sure, and the low rumbling tones of Jack... or Tom, perhaps.

She roused, but she still felt groggy and heavy-eyed. She splashed water on her face, smoothed and straightened her clothes, and ran a quick brush through her hair before heading downstairs.

Anne found Enid in the reading room. Tom followed Anne in, took a chair by the window, and became absorbed in the daily newspaper.

Anne passed the time in the reading room with Enid, who told her that her secret was out. Everyone now knew the real reason for Anne's hiring. That was mostly Bernie's doing, she said, and most speculated about why the company hired a private investigator. A few took offense. They grumbled and conjured outrageous scenarios that set off a firestorm of rumour and discord.

A bark from Dearie sent the boarders scurrying to the dining room. Silence weighed heavily on the diners throughout the first half of supper. Jane was in a foul mood. The jangle of forks and scrape of knives amplified in the stillness until it mimicked a clash of swords and ringing of shields. It was a discomforting assembly of diners.

Enid was first to cut into the silence. "Jane, these biscuits are lovely. Did you bake them yourself?"

Dearie looked up at her. Her scowl faltered as she tried to assess whether or not there was an ulterior motive or double meaning in the compliment.

"I baked them myself," she replied.

"They're some good," said Tom. A broad grin splayed across his face. "Got any molasses to go with 'em?"

"I'll see," said Dearie, getting up and heading toward the pantry.

By the time she returned, a lively conversation had sprung up among the others.

"Put new strings on m' fiddle today," said Jack. "Might try 'em out tonight."

"Thought ya restrung it a few weeks back," said Tom.

"Did," said Jack, "but a new skipper and a new start tomorrow... and new strings fer luck."

"So you've got clearance from Fisheries?" said Anne.

"Not quite, but they said they'd phone or drop down to the wharf tomorrow morning if we got the okay. Shouldn't be a problem, says CeeCee. Besides, can't leave traps in the water any longer without haulin' and rebaitin'."

"Can't say as I envy ya," said Tom. "Don't miss them days a bit."

"Did you fish?" asked Anne.

Tom nodded.

"I fished for a few years when I was young, but it wasn't my cup o' tea. Not regular work. Just boom and bust. My last fishin' job was 'cork' aboard old Hap Gordon's vessel. That woulda been... let's see... back in '75, I think, the year Michael MacDonald run off. Old Hap took me on to replace him. After that I learned how to weld and operate a metal lathe."

"So I guess good luck found you then," said Anne. "By the way, I got a question. I've been hearing the name George Livingstone in regard to the factory. Know the man?"

Jack was first to reply. "Can't say as I do. Heard the name, o' course. But never met the man."

"Tom, What about you?"

"No more 'n Jack here."

"Who's this Michael MacDonald?" she asked.

"What nonsense is this?" said Dearie, pushing her way into the room with dessert dishes of lime gelatin topped with whipped cream. "You've no dealings with the factory anymore. What gives you the right to poke your nose into other people's business?"

"No more right than anyone else with a curiosity," said Anne. "No more right than you, I suppose, Jane."

"Can't say as I know that name," said Jack.

"Where did he go?" said Anne.

"Never heard," said Tom. "He just disappeared."

"Yes... I remember that," said Enid.

"How can you remember that far back?" said Jane.

"I remember he was a good-lookin' young fella, and there was a shortage of them 'round here about that time."

"Hmmph," said Jane.

"Do you remember anything about him?" said Anne.

"I guess he'd 'a been at least ten years older than I was. Not much else. Then he was gone."

"Probably saw you gawkin' at him and fled the country," said Jane under her breath.

Enid ignored Jane's comment. Anne ignored their entire interchange. A few new ideas had taken root.

"Hap Gordon?" said Anne.

"Yep, Hap Gordon," said Tom.

"And where would I find him?" said Anne.

"Well..." said Tom, "That would be a problem. He's a hard man to get to."

"I'll give it a try. Which way would I go?"

"Well..." said Tom. If you're that set on seein' 'im... head up that road. It's quite a piece. Eventually, you'll come to a big set of gates. Ring the bell. An old fella might come out to see what you're after. Tell him who yer lookin' for. He'll check his guest list."

"Is it a retirement home?"

"Something like that."

"Ya think he'll be there?"

"There's only a couple places he could be. That's the first one I'd check out."

"What's the old fella's name?" said Anne.

"Peter... yep... Don't know his last name. Most people 'round here just call him St. Peter," said Tom. "Ya see... old Hap's been dead these last fifteen years or more."

Everyone but Anne had known where the story was going, and, at the drop of the punchline, their straight sober faces dissolved into hoots of mirth.

"You got me good that time, Tom," said Anne, wagging her finger at him.

58.

After dinner Anne returned to the reading room. She was alone there for a while. Then Tom joined her. Tom paged through an old copy of *Popular Science*; Anne scanned the *Eastern Graphic* newspaper. Both seemed engrossed by their reading material as Jane flitted about the kitchen and lobby and periodically hovered behind the dimly lighted doorway like a moth.

A faint clatter of dishes and pots signalled Dearie's presence elsewhere, and that was indication enough for Tom to speak freely.

"She doesn't mean to be a snoop. It's her nature. Just like mine's mechanical configurations and such."

"I'll have to take your word for that, Tom. She seemed a bit touchy when I mentioned Michael MacDonald, wouldn't you say?"

"I did notice her feathers ruffle a bit, but I don't know why. She woulda been too young to have known him."

"What can you recall about him?"

"Long time ago. So not much. I took his place with Hap a day after he run off. Hap liked him, but he didn't know what spooked him."

"Spooked him?"

"Yeah, that's the word Hap used. He said the boy just up and left. Suddenly. He boarded with Hap and the wife, and there wasn't a 'by yer leave' or 'goodbye' or nothin'. He didn't even take his things... just left them and never came back. Strange, eh? The first couple days Hap figured he just went off on a drunk or somethin'. Hap thought he'd be back to get his belongings, but he never did."

"Did he make any friends here?"

"He wasn't in the village long enough to do that, I should think. He was the industrious sort, too. Spent most of his extra time diggin' bar clams and steamers to make a few extra bucks. He'd get the loan of Hap's punt and row across the bay. Used to see him now and again walkin' the shore over near Sullivan's Point."

"I see. Anyone else still around who might have known him? Anyone at all?"

59.

It was an old house, typical of the area: small, one-and-a-half storeys, a long sloping roof, and painted wood shingles. It had been the home of Wesley and Gail Peake. Now it was just the residence of Wesley, better known locally as Squeak.

Squeak sat at the kitchen table in one of four wooden chairs. His oldest friend, Spit, sat in the chair facing him.

"What are w-we gonna do about him?"

"Nothin' until he sobers up."

"He's still gonna be p-pissed."

Squeak nodded. "Do ya think there was any sense to what he was ravin' about?"

"Well, he was right about one thing. We d-didn't kill Michael MacDonald."

"Fig said Luc LaVie brought up Michael MacDonald's name. So Luc must know something. I wonder what that is."

Spit looked somber and worried. "Maybe we *shoulda* f-finished him."

"You're talkin' crazy! We couldn't a' done it then, and we couldn't do it now." The sharpness of Squeak's rebuke jarred Spit.

"D-don't get in a twist about it. It was just talk… just t-talk."

"Your crazy talk might just lead to crazy thinkin'… and crazy actin'."

"Just sayin'… if it comes out, we'll be goin' to prison."

"It's been too long. Nobody would care now, not even Michael… if the man's still alive."

Their talk of murderous intentions, police, and imprisonment had unnerved the two men. They remained silent in each other's company but, all the while, a circus of unspoken arguments and reconstructions tumbled through their minds until a sharp, loud rap on the door snapped like a cross dog at the heels of their thoughts. It alarmed both of them, and they shrank from the sound. Like mice in the cupboard, they froze in place.

Anne Brown stood on the doorstep. It had begun to shower. Light raindrops fell on her hair. A gust of wind picked up. She had heard noises inside. No one came to the door. She rapped on the door again, this time forcefully and with an annoyance bounding toward anger.

It had been a hellish day for Anne. When you work hard, your life shouldn't fall apart, she fumed, and here I am standing in the friggin' rain, while no one will answer their friggin' door.

Anne felt the cold rain soak her hair and trickle down the nape of her neck. The breeze carried a chill.

Anne hammered the door and gave it two kicks. She felt a throbbing in her toe and that provoked an angry shout, "Open the damned door, Squeak. I know you're in there. I heard voices. I mean it. I'll kick this friggin' door in."

Anne heard a clatter of boots and a flurry of mumbled words. The door opened. Squeak stood in the doorway.

"What d' ya want?" he said.

Annoyance permeated Squeak's greeting. At least that's what Anne drew from so paltry and impolite a greeting, and, at the same time, she missed the alarm in his eyes and the timidity in his bearing. Squeak just stood there waiting for a reply. The anger that had been building in Anne climaxed with Squeak's poorly chosen words. Her temper flared. She lashed out.

"Don't invite me in out of the rain or anything so polite," she said. Then she pushed by him and strode all the way into the kitchen where Spit cowered at the sight of her. Both men viewed women as a separate and unpredictable species.

"Good. You're both here. That'll save me the trouble of another rude welcome later on. You," she said, pointing to Squeak who trailed in after her, "sit down. Make yourself at home. I've got a few questions, and I want straight answers. No bullshit. Understand? Or you will regret it. You *will* regret it."

Neither man spoke.

"Good. Dust off your memories. We're going back thirty... forty years. I want to know everything you know about two men, George Livingstone and Michael MacDonald. Start now."

Both men shuddered as if they had come upon a ghost. Squeak was first to recover his voice.

"Heard of George Livingstone. Something to do with the factory years ago," said Squeak. "Don't recall any Michael MacDonald."

"S-same h-h-here," said Spit.

"You're bad liars, the pair of you. One more chance," she said. "Otherwise... I call the authorities."

Anne's boldness was more bluster and bluff, but she caught a mark of panic in their eyes.

"Well... the name seems a bit familiar, but MacDonald is a common name around here. You can't turn over a rock without finding a MacDonald under it."

"You're hiding something, aren't you Squeak... Spit. What is it? What's the big secret here? You say you don't recall him? How could you forget? Hap Gordon woulda wondered and talked every day about what happened to the boy. That boy that just disappeared off the face of the earth, and you woulda heard Hap."

"He weren't no b-boy. He was twenty-five, twenty-six y-year old," said Spit.

"Memory's comin' back, is it, fellas?" Anne said. "And what did Hap Gordon say about him? Both of you, and probably your buddy, Fig, would have exchanged gossip with the other fellas at the wharf around that time. What stuck in Hap's mind that he came back to it again and again? I heard that he missed the boy, that he was a good worker. Remind me what Hap said. Prove that you aren't holding out on me. Prove that it matches what I know from some others that said they didn't know him too well either... and then admitted otherwise."

"It was all so long ago. I can't remember details. But Hap went on and on about Michael leavin' so sudden and never comin' back. He left his personal gear."

"What else?"

"Hap said he never come back for his wages either."

"Isn't that odd?" said Anne, looking at Squeak suspiciously and then at Spit.

"S'pose it is," said Squeak.

"And nobody reported his disappearance to the police?"

"No need to, I guess. No relatives here. No friends. He didn't owe anybody money. No ties to the place. A person can come and go as he pleases without involving police, can't he?"

"Who would benefit by his disappearance?"

"Nobody that I can f-figure," said Spit.

"What about one of your old buddies?" said Anne. "Maybe somebody with a temper."

"Maybe Old Hap did somethin' to him. Maybe Hap run him off," said Squeak.

Anne laughed. Her laugh disquieted Squeak like a feral cat's frozen stare.

"You goin' to blame it on a dead man. That's ridiculous. I heard he treated Michael like a son. Didn't he? And he was good to him. Didn't he let him use his punt for something? What was it?"

"Diggin' clams," said Squeak.

"Where?"

"Out Sullivan's Point way," said Squeak.

"He shoulda s-stayed clear of th-there," mumbled Spit.

"Why d' ya say that, Spit?"

Spit mumbled something incomprehensible under his breath. Squeak glanced at him dismissively.

The silence in the room grew heavy and substantial and seemed to weigh down the two old men sitting in the wooden chairs across from her. Anne let the silence and her last question thicken in their imaginations. Anne was grasping at straws and bluffing with generalities, but she knew that something was taking place in their heads. She knew she had hit some raw spot.

Behind Anne were cupboards, a counter, and a kitchen sink. To her right was the electric range, in front a large wood stove, to her left a refrigerator. A panel of framed photos filled the remaining wall space.

"Your wife?" asked Anne.

"Gail," said Squeak. "She passed twenty-two years ago."

"I'm sorry," said Anne. "She looks like she was a pleasant, good-natured lady."

"A good cook," he said, "and a good person, too."

"A r-real g-good person," repeated Spit.

"Then it must have been quite a burden when such 'a good person' like her learned that a well-liked young fella like Michael disappeared... without a trace. A woman like her would have heart. She and her friends would have talked and talked about it for weeks and speculated about what could have happened to the poor young fella. You must have heard her, both of you. Did Michael drown? Did somebody kill him? He must have been killed, she'd say. He left everything he owned behind, she'd say. How would she have felt if she knew the truth... when she learned what really happened to Michael MacDonald. It would have broken her heart."

Squeak's face blanched, and his hands clutched the edge of the table.

"We never killed him... never... if that's what you're getting' at. Couldn't do somethin' like that. No, sir... no, sir."

"Did he drown then? Maybe an accident? Maybe you couldn't help him."

"No... no..." said Squeak.

"What else could I believe? No one abandons their personal property and wages. Nobody but dead men."

"No, that's not what happened."

"You have no other explanation? Then, at the very least, there's a missing person that was never reported," said Anne.

Anne pulled out her cellphone and started to enter a phone number.

"W-what are ya d-doin?"

"I just said. There's a missing person not reported... and probably dead."

"But you don't know that."

"No, Squeak, but the police will have to be notified. They'll sort it out... even if it happened years and years ago. And, coincidentally, I heard the strangest thing today from Luc. He swears he saw Michael MacDonald in the area. Isn't that a laugh? Thinking he's here somewhere. If that's true, I wonder if he's here to get even. You know, an eye for an eye. Of course, maybe that's just rumour... my guess. Still... I should call the police. They can sort it out."

Squeak's eyes widened. Spit froze in his seat. Anne continued to enter digits into her phone.

"Wait," said Squeak. "We did it. Spit and I... I mean, we didn't do it. We didn't kill MacDonald. Listen..."

Anne had been pleased at how well the interview was proceeding, but, when Squeak and Spit intermittently retold their story of Michael MacDonald's beating and rough expulsion from the Island, Anne was speechless.

At the end of it, a gulf of silence enveloped the little room, and each of them contemplated what tomorrow would bring.

Then Squeak broke the stillness with a warning.

"Wish we'd never got involved. Bad luck's trailed us ever since. As for vandalism and theft, we've nothing to do with that."

"What about Fig?" said Anne.

"Don't know. Fig has no love for the factory—never has—but he keeps things to himself. I warn ya, though. Stay clear of 'im. He can be dangerous if ya cross 'im... And he's started drinkin' again."

"No t-tellin' what he might do."

60.

Anne pushed through the heavy front door to Halkirk Manor. Her mind raced through the information she had learned through her encounter with Squeak and Spit, and she was processing it into the skeleton of a plan. It was nearing ten o'clock. The men had slipped off to their rooms over an hour before. Enid was preparing to head off when Anne entered.

"There was a letter for you," she said.

"A letter?"

"Dearie found it on the entry floor. Someone pushed it through the mail slot and rang the bell. She opened the door, but he had gone. I couldn't be sure what Dearie would do with it. So I made sure she pushed it under your door."

"What time did it come?"

"Early, around seven-thirty, I'd say."

Anne thanked her and ran upstairs. Sure enough, the letter was there. No stamp. Poorly typed envelope. Inside was one sheet of paper, also typed.

Interested in George Livingstone?

I can help. Meet me. Gibb's Snack Shack. Callie's Road in Montague tonight. 11:15 sharp. Black pickup. Come alone. Stay in your car.

Curiosity killed the cat.

An invitation and a warning, thought Anne. She looked at her watch. It was already ten-thirty.

Anne was curious about the timing of this invitation... right on the heels of a breakthrough. It could be a coincidence, it could be some kind of trap, but it certainly was the right kind of bait.

Anne quickly changed into dry clothes: jeans and a bulky pullover. It was a twenty-minute drive to Montague. She could just make it. She climbed behind the wheel and drove a few hundred yards down the road. Then she pulled over onto the shoulder. She took her S&W.38 revolver and holster from the glove compartment, fixed them to her belt, covered them with her sweater, and swung back onto the road to Montague.

61.

Michel Gauthier drove into the parking lot at the Cineplex movie theatre in the Charlottetown mall. He looked at his watch. Nine o'clock. *Black Panther* was playing. He purchased a ticket, bought some popcorn and a drink, and paid with his credit card. The theatre lobby was crowded, a bustle of kids and parents. Action poses of King T'Challa and Nakia leaped from life-sized cardboard stands.

He passed the usher collecting tickets and stuffed the returned stub into his pocket. Then he headed toward the theatre doors, passed them by, tossed the popcorn and drink into the garbage, and exited through the side door. He was on his way to Montague within ten minutes.

He took the Pooles Corner exit off the Trans-Canada Highway, slowed as he passed the RCMP detachment, gave it a discerning look, and reviewed once more the timing and actions he had already reviewed a dozen times.

A river ran through the town. A pretty park, a marina, and a fishermen's wharf crowded the banks below the bridge, but, before crossing it, Michel turned left. Just beyond the park and marina a large inn rose above the skyline. Michel pulled into its parking lot, and filled a slot between several other vehicles from out of province. The Nova Scotia plates on his rental would draw no interest whatsoever. He looked at his watch. It was shortly after ten. He had less than hour, but he had much to prepare, and timing was important.

The area around the inn was residential. An occasional car drifted quietly by, and an infrequent pedestrian strolled past Gibb's Snack Shack a block away. Michel could see part of the store from his vantage point in the parking lot. It had not yet opened for the summer.

Michel stepped from his vehicle. He had dressed casually in black sweatpants and a lightweight navy windbreaker. A black ball cap and sneakers sported a popular logo. Michel popped the car trunk, removed a small pry bar, and slipped it into his waistband. Then he casually strode along the sidewalk leading to Callie's Road and the Snack Shack. Michel paused at the corner, bent down as if to tie his sneaker, and scanned the street for foot traffic and nearby windows for faces. Then, satisfied, he moved unhurriedly alongside the building to a rear door. He forced the pry bar between the door and jamb, gave it a firm quick jerk, and the lock broke loose.

Inside were empty shelves and bare racks, a few small tables, and the basic equipment for a small commercial kitchen. Propane fuelled a three-burner stove. He gave the valve a twist and waited for the hiss of gas. No sound or smell escaped, and Michel felt a stunning rush of dread and imagined his plan falling into disarray. He stared out the small side window toward the road and wondered what else he could do. It was far too late to change plans without the possibility of some oversight landing him in prison.

Then it struck him. Nervous relief almost made him laugh, but he stifled it. That would be premature, he thought. Still, Michel indulged a small bubbling of hope as he left the building and moved toward the large propane tank alongside the shop. Another look around for passersby or faces in windows and his hand grasped the valve of the tank. It turned, and he smiled grimly as he opened the gas feed.

To be certain, Michel stuck his head back through the shop door to hear the hiss of gas seeping into the room. He closed the door behind him and retreated to his car.

At ten minutes to eleven, Michel retrieved the sports bag with fake money from the trunk of his car and started a second slow walk toward the Snack Shack. The stairs to the second-floor loft, strangely enough, were on the Callie's Road side of the building. Several trees in full foliage obscured movements close to the store. A distant street light cast the shadows of trees onto the face of the building. So there was little chance of anyone seeing him climb the stairs.

As the extortionist had promised, the upper door was unlocked. Michel stepped in cautiously. The room was large and empty except for an odd collection of furniture at the far end. Michel sniffed the air. There was no hint of gas from the lower level. Ambient streetlight and eyes adapting to the dimness allowed him to find his way to the far end of the storeroom, where Michel set down the bag.

Michel spent no time loitering. He headed for his car and sped away, but he didn't travel far. He made a believable show of leaving but, after reaching Main Street, he doubled back along a riverside lane toward the marina, parked his car at a lookout, and hurried along a walking trail that parallelled the river. He moved through a thicket next to the inn, found an advantageous spot, settled in, and waited.

Michel waited for Bernie. He had suspected him of being the extortionist, but he needed to be sure, and Michel's call to the lawyer had verified his suspicions. Bernie was not only broke, but deeply in debt to an unsavoury fellow in Charlottetown, one who had no misgivings about breaking bones or carving scars. It was a shame, thought Michel. He had liked Bernie. They had had a long relationship, but now Bernie had gone too far.

62.

Anne was invigorated at the prospect of learning more about George Livingstone, but the energy she experienced was heightened awareness and fear of the unknown. The offer was unexpected, out of the blue, and suspect.

A number of reservations raced through her mind: Why now? Have I unknowingly stumbled upon some fragment of truth or poked an old wound? Has my digging prompted a need to confess a misstep or a long-repressed crime? Or is it simply a trap? Something too good to be true, dangling like bait in front of me? Some diversion from Spit and Squeak? Or a wasteful distraction during my last few hours at Halkirk and Little Rose Harbour?

In the long run, it didn't matter. Anne knew she would be driven to follow up on it anyway. Expect the unexpected. That's what she had to do. That's what her Uncle Bill Darby had taught her, and those words had been prudent and useful before.

Anne pictured her uncle sitting behind the big desk in his office at Darby Investigations, and it brought a smile to her face. Uncle Bill had prided himself on readiness for any situation, and, toward that goal, he had kept a foot locker in the trunk of his big old sedan. He had filled the locker with assorted tools, ropes and cords, tape, chains, and assorted odds and ends that might be useful and at hand when needed. Anne had followed his habit of preparedness.

Anne refocused on the present... and preparing. The note she received had specified eleven-fifteen. In this instance Anne's prep called for an early recon of the meeting place. She'd had a late start already, and, with that in mind, she pushed the accelerator down another twenty kilometers per hour. She turned onto Callie's Road. That street was dark and quiet. She passed the address the note had identified. Gibb's Snack Shack was closed. No cars, no people, nothing. She continued on a short distance to where the road began to turn rural, pulled over, turned off her lights, and looked back. Anne still had a clear view of the rendezvous point. She looked at her watch. It was eleven o'clock.

So far, so good, she thought. She'd wait a bit longer... see what happens.

***

It was exactly eleven o'clock when a car passed Gibb's Snack Shack. Michel craned his neck to see if it were Bernie. It wasn't, but illumination from the street lamp on the corner showed a young woman, and the car had looked like the one belonging to Anne Brown.

Damn it, he thought. Damn... damn... damn.

Michel had not expected Anne to show up so early. He'd hoped her punctual arrival in the aftermath would be enough to scare her off the investigation, not injure or kill her. But her early arrival changed nothing. There was no stopping, and he accepted that. He was too far into it. Any change would foul his plan, his entire charade would be exposed, and it would all end in failure. If she got in the way, that would be her bad luck, not his doing.

At that moment another set of lights shone, a second car slowed and stopped in front of the Snack Shack. Its lights went dark, and the hunched figure of Bernie White stepped out. He looked around. Then he mounted the stairs.

***

As soon as Bernie entered the second-floor loft, Michel leaped from his hiding place and rushed to the side of the Snack Shack and the entrance to the kitchen. Michel counted seconds in his head. He guessed it would take Bernie at least ten to locate the sports bag and reach out for it. Bernie would unzip it and check the money. That would take another five seconds, and five more to leave the room.

In less than ten seconds Michel ran past the kitchen door. He turned, pulled a flare gun from under his jacket, pulled back the hammer, aimed, and fired a projectile through the glass pane on the door. There was a sharp report. As the glass shattered, Michel ran back into the brush beside the inn. His mind was a shambles; his careful counting of seconds had faltered; he had lost track of time altogether.

I've failed, he thought. It was a dud.

***

Anne had seen a vehicle slow down and stop on Callie's Road. So she began another drive-by, but the car was not the black pickup she'd expected, so she coasted past again.

At that moment Anne caught a flash in her rear-view mirror. A vehicle turning? Reflection of a street lamp on a fender? The flicker of a porch light? It coupled with the sound of an engine backfiring. An explosion followed.

Anne's first awareness that something had gone very wrong came with the concussion. The blast struck the left rear quarter of her car just after she'd passed. The force swallowed the vehicle with enormous jaws. She felt the car lift and shake like a dog tearing at a squirrel. Anne's head snapped to one side; the rear of the car fishtailed and plunged ahead. She braced herself, her right foot frozen to the accelerator. The car hurtled, leaped a curb, and careened through a hedge. By then Anne's foot had freed itself from the gas pedal.

The car rolled a few more yards, then stopped. Anne's eyes fixed on the horrifying conflagration in her rear-view mirror. Then she turned around. Gibb's Snack Shack was gone. The explosion had blown out all four walls. The loft had collapsed into the debris. Flames fed on wreckage. They burned furiously, almost vengefully, on shattered boards and shingles and beams.

Sirens sounded in the distance. Fire engines, ambulances, police. All were en route. There was nothing Anne could do. She put her car in gear and moved farther from the scorching flames and made way for the emergency vehicles.

She looked back. Her rear window had cracked. Fortunately, little debris from the blast had struck her car. She had been shaken and still trembled, but fortune had smiled on her. She felt that, too. At the same time, she wondered wildly if the explosion been an attempt to kill her... and perhaps an informer, too.

As the wail of sirens grew, Anne tapped the gas pedal and drove away. If she had to deal with police questions, she'd do that later. Not now.

***

Michel had reached a dense growth of bushes beside the inn when the gas ignited and blew the building apart. He whirled around, dropped the flare gun, and stood there aghast. The thundering noise and blinding flash of the explosion caught Michel by surprise. Only a few moments before he believed that his attempt to kill Bernie had failed. Now he felt relieved.

In the light of the blaze he suddenly felt naked and vulnerable. Fear and instinct snagged his mind back to the magnitude of his action. He snatched up the flare gun and walked briskly downhill and then along the darkened walking trail. He looked ahead and back, neither saw nor heard footsteps, and, with a mighty effort, hurled the gun into the black, slow-moving Montague River. He heard a soft plop mid-stream, and then he heard sirens.

In the distance he heard the sharp crackle of burning wood, the shouts and screams of nearby residents, and the ringing of emergency alarms. Michel drove less-travelled roads away from the chaos and slipped into the indifferent murmur of highway traffic leading to Charlottetown. He gave little thought to Bernie. Bernie had got what he deserved. He knew he'd been pilfering for quite some time, and while Michel could tolerate a little graft,

Bernie had gone way too far. Anne was a different story. He had liked her. He admired her, but she had been the author of her own destruction. His thoughts moved back to a remote memory of an old family dog that wouldn't stop chasing cars and had been struck and killed in its fanatic pursuit.

Sad, he thought. *Unfortunate.*

63.

Thursday

Anne was shaken by the explosion in Montague and couldn't sleep on her return to Halkirk Manor. For most of the night she lay on her bed turning over the series of events that had led to the tragedy. Half-consciously she reviewed the wording of the message she had received. Who had sent it? To what purpose? Was she the target? What happened to the occupant of the car in front of the building? Was he killed? Who was he? Did he live nearby or could he have been the one who had arranged to meet her? There were many questions, but no answers, and sleep never really came.

Sound carried in the old rooming house, and, when Anne heard a small rattling downstairs, she dressed and headed in that direction. The dining room was empty except for the rummaging around of Jack Pine.

"You're up early," said Anne.

"I'm up late. Old habits. When I'm fishin', I'm out the door by four-thirty… and some are long gone before that."

"You shoulda slept in then," said Anne.

"No hope of doin' that."

"Did CeeCee get her okay from Fisheries?"

"Not yet. Maybe Hec jammed a wrench in their gears. I don't know."

"So what's her plan?"

"We'll call in a few hours. If that doesn't do it, we'll ask a few friends to haul our traps for us. Not much else we can do. Can't leave the lobsters any longer. They'll start feedin' on each other."

Anne cringed.

"That's what happens when you're trapped or desperate— every man or lobster for himself. What about you? Headin' back to the big city?"

"Later. I have a few friends to say goodbye to and a couple of things to tidy up."

"Prob'ly the best thing. There's cereal, coffee, and a dish of cinnamon rolls over there. Have a feed before you go. Dearie won't be roamin' about for another hour, and maybe I'll see ya down on the wharf."

Anne took a quick shower to rinse away any hint of smoke. After that, she packed her belongings and made her way to the car. The cracked rear window was a grim reminder of last night's misadventure. The smoky odour added to it. So she lowered the windows and drove toward Little Rose Harbour. It drove well enough, but she noticed a tremor in the front end, probably the result of hitting a curb the night before.

It was too early to go straight to the factory. She needed to kill some time. So she headed for Sullivan's Point. She didn't know why she pointed her car in that direction. At least she wouldn't admit a reason to herself. Spit and Squeak had planted the idea in her head that the seeds of Fig's disappointments and anger and failures had taken root on these grounds. Fig's hatred for the factory must have been related to it in some way that was not entirely clear to her. The link between the two eluded Anne. She had been close to learning that connection last night, but the explosion had killed that prospect. George Livingstone probably was the key. But now she was no closer to learning about him than she was at the start of the investigation.

Anne spent the next half hour roaming the grounds of the Grant homestead. Not much had changed there, but Anne sensed something was different. Perhaps the weather had coloured her opinion. Summer had taken a step backward. The air had grown damp, the sky grey. Mist hung over the trees and waterways, and fog cloaked the horizon. The elements had ushered a dreary presence that spoke of hopelessness, and Anne felt as if she were being enveloped in a slowly closing fist.

She ventured past the clearing and farther east toward the shore. She came across a hollow near some old weathered pines, perhaps the last meeting place of Michael MacDonald and Mary Grant. Then she turned back and headed for her car. She passed the graveyard, and there she saw something that was different... something new. A small rose bush, the buds of which not yet opened. It was growing next to the small patch of crocuses that she remembered from her previous visit.

64.

The first shift at the factory started at eight o'clock. It was closer to seven-thirty when Anne arrived. The parking lot was beginning to fill.

"I saw your room door wide open when I walked by this morning and thought you musta cleared out for home," said Enid.

"Thought this would be a better place to say goodbye, Enid. You've been a good friend this past week. I'll miss your company."

"Yours, too. And you know where I spend my evenings if you want to chat," she said with a wave goodbye.

"And give my regards to Kate."

"Kate's around. I'll tell her." That night at the dance now seemed impossibly far in Anne's past.

While she was chatting with Enid, Anne watched Morgan pass and unlock the office door. A few minutes later, Barb and Tammy passed and mounted the stairs to their offices. Then, strangely enough, Michel Gauthier's car pulled in. He had made a rare appearance at the Little Rose Harbour facility in the past week, but to find him here again, so early in the day, and Jean not with him, was exceptional.

Anne ignored him and continued toward the stairs to the office.

"Anne. Anne Brown!"

Anne turned. Michel Gauthier was striding toward her, his hand raised to catch her attention. He nearly broke into a trot to catch up.

Uh-oh. He's going to bar me from the factory parking lot, too, Anne thought.

Anne stopped at the door. The idea of him slapping her with a restraining order flickered in the moment. Her thoughts raced through a list of responses—personal appeals, civil rejoinders, and legal challenges.

Michel was puffing when he caught up. Anne planned to verbally strike while he was still out of breath, but, as she was about to voice her indignation, Michel put his arm on her shoulder and said, "It's good to see you again, Anne."

"What do you mean by that?" she said and stepped back.

"Just that... that you're not taking our actions personally... that you know we're only concerned about no harm coming to you."

"Perhaps you don't know, but I've got Irish on both sides and a drop or two of German blood a bit farther back. I've got stubbornness galore, Michel. It just ain't goin' away."

"No doubt," he said. "I don't intend to stop you from doing anything. I... we just don't intend to enable you to carry on or pay you to do it anymore. We want to be civil. Fair enough? Now... can I buy you a cup of coffee?" he said, motioning up the stairs.

Anne led the way up. She heard Michel's feet moving unsteadily behind her. She couldn't help wonder about Michel's sudden change. So she kept a steady hand on the railing in case he had a wild urge to grab her and hurl her back down the steep flight of stairs.

Anne stood at the crossroads of offices at the top of the staircase. She was unaware of where Michel would lead her. Michel took in a few more puffs of air behind her, then took Anne by her arm and drew her into Morgan's reception area.

Michel looked at Bernie's office door. His access was via Morgan's workspace. His door was closed.

"Is Bernie free now?" Michel asked

"I don't know," said Morgan. "He's not come in yet."

Michel watched Morgan sip coffee from a large paper cup.

"No coffee here," he muttered. "Let's try down the hall." Michel passed two offices and turned left. There, Barbie Beaton and

Tammy Wallace were hovering over their burbling percolator. It had almost filled with fresh coffee.

The smell was delightful. Barbie and Tammy were always upbeat. Michel had mellowed. All of that prompted Anne to consider dialing back some of her guardedness.

"You two make up?" Barbie asked. Tammy cringed at her boldness.

"Not quite," said Michel.

"Somewhere between a Mexican standoff and an unratified peace agreement," said Anne.

"Let's drink to that at least," said Barbie, pulling out two extra mugs from a discreet place and filling them.

"Will Jean be negotiator?"

"Hardly," said Anne. "He's an interested party. By the way, where is Jean?"

"He said he had a few things to do here early this morning. So I'm surprised we haven't seen him yet," said Michel.

"Haven't seen Bernie this morning, either," said Barbie. She looked puzzled, then brightened. "Have you heard the news? There was an explosion in Montague last night. Propane tank exploded."

"Anyone hurt?" asked Michel.

"They recovered one body," said Tammy, "and a few residents were cut from broken glass."

"That's unfortunate," said Michel. "People don't realize how dangerous propane can be if they're not careful."

Tammy nodded in agreement. Barbie nodded as well. Then both stared at the open doorway. Morgan had appeared there. Her face was ashen. Her lips moved soundlessly. She seemed unable to speak.

"What is it?" said Michel, turning around impatiently.

"Uh... RCMP phoned. They... they found Bernie's car. It burned out near the explosion in Montague. They're coming here... for something."

No one saw it fall, but Barbie's favourite mug, one inscribed "Luv Thy Boss," slipped through her fingers and broke on the floor.

Morgan retreated to her cubicle to ponder the arrival of the police inquiry.

Michel stood. "I think I'll take a walk along the wharf and clear my head."

"Maybe I'll tag along a bit. There's still a few people I want to see down there," said Anne.

65.

Neither spoke as they made their way down the staircase and into the dank morning air of the wharf. By mid-June one would have expected warmer, sunnier weather, but conditions continued to be unsettled. Anne looked up. There was a luminous patch where the sun ought to be, but it was ill-defined, bleak and ominous.

Michel quietly separated from her and walked toward the concrete incline of the boat ramp where he stood staring reflectively into its darkening waters. Anne saw a boat or two up the wharf. One of them was *Hell to Pay*. The boat hadn't moved since Hec's injury. It looked abandoned. Then Anne caught a movement in the shadows of the windbreak behind the cabin. She hallooed and strode over. Jack Pine and CeeCee waved back.

"Got the okay," shouted CeeCee as Anne arrived.

"Just waitin' for Harry's boy to run some fresh bait down here from the cooler."

"Then we're off," said CeeCee. She was both excited and pensive about her new undertaking.

"Good luck with it," said Anne.

CeeCee nodded, let out a long quivering sigh, and looked out through the misty opening in the breakwater. Light fog drifted across the inner channel.

"How's weather today?" Anne asked.

"It's foggy outside," she said pointing toward the sea. "But we've got radar, and we have points marked on the plotter where our gear's set, and Jack knows the waters hereabouts anyway."

Anne nodded approvingly. In the corner of her eye she saw Michel walking toward them. It reminded her, and she asked, "Look, you haven't seen Jean Gauthier down around here today, have you?"

CeeCee shook her head.

"I seen him," said Jack. "He passed by, said hello, just before CeeCee came down. He had an armful of rain gear and rubber boots. Said he was goin' fishin'... with Fig Grant."

"What's this? Are you talking about Jean?" said Michel.

"Spoke to him me-self," said Jack.

"With Fig?" said Michel.

"Yep... out jiggin' mackerel, I expect. Bit of an odd pair, if ya don't mind my sayin'. And Fig... he's not been known to take anyone out fishin' just for the hell of it."

No one noticed Michel's face grow pale or his countenance turn to stone. The morning was too grey to perceive such subtleties. But his voice carried authority and resolve when he said, "I've got to get him off that boat."

"It's safe enough," said Jack. "It's an old boat, but it's still sound... and the radio's not callin' for any kind of weather. I wouldn't fret about him."

"I have to get him off that boat... away from Fig," he said. Michel's words laboured with desperation. Anne looked at him queerly.

A pickup truck pulled alongside the boat. Harry's boy stepped down, lowered the tailgate, and said, "Fresh gaspereaux. Last tray. Still want it?"

"Bring 'er aboard," said CeeCee.

Jack and Harry's boy lowered the heavy tub down onto the deck.

"I guess we're off now," said CeeCee.

"I need a boat," said Michel. Urgency and desperation coloured his words.

"We got work to do. Can't help ya. Got lobster to haul. Long overdue."

"I'll pay... I'll pay anything."

"Ya don't know what you're askin'," said Jack.

"I'll pay anything. I mean it... anything."

"What the hell's the matter with you, Michel?" said Anne.

"Jean is in danger. I know it. We've got to get him back off the boat *now*, Anne." Then he turned to CeeCee. "It's your fleet. Name your price. Just name it."

CeeCee thought for a moment. "Okay, the cost of two full days' charter, plus losses to our lobster catch or wear and tear or any other nonsense because of your side trip."

"Fair enough," said Michel. "Cast off. Let's go. Any idea where he might be?"

"Other times I seen him over on Willy's Bump," said Jack. "It's a bit outa the way. Most boats don't bother with it, and lobsters don't favour them grounds much."

The boat engine roared to life when Jack hit the ignition. CeeCee tossed two life jackets toward Michel and Anne. "Put these on. Don't want ya fallin' over before we get paid," she said with a laugh and retreated under the windbreak behind the wheelhouse.

Anne and Michel struggled into the bulky orange jackets. It was cooler in the morning's air in the open stern, but that's where Michel preferred to position himself. He was comfortable there. It was where he had stood as the hired man so many decades before when traps were hauled up from a hydraulic wheel.

Anne stood beside him, not out of loyalty or thirst for fresh air, but because she was piqued with curiosity at Michel's behaviour. He was acting erratic. It made no sense. It was uncharacteristic. Yet it smacked of necessity and a fear that was tangible, and she wondered what scenario could compel it.

66.

Anne reflected a moment on the best way to deal with Michel Gauthier, but there was no clear path.

Bluntness won.

"Why do you think Fig's a threat to Jean? How can you know that?"

"I don't like the look of him, and I don't like his reputation."

"Bullshit, Michel. You've come out to Little Rose twice, maybe three times. How could you know anything about anyone around here?"

"I know," he said. His denial was cold, confident. His eyes glared with fierceness and contempt.

"More bullshit, Michel. I'm tired of it. Now I'm getting the feeling that you've been blindsiding me all along..."

"You've no business interfering in our affairs."

"...and I'm getting the feeling that maybe Luc LaVie may have been right."

"I've heard enough from you."

"You *are* his cousin."

"I said 'stop.'"

"A check for name change in Nova Scotia is easy to prove. One call to Vital Statistics should do it. Then you'll be found out... and whatever schemes you've been involved in will be out in the open."

"Stop it."

"And just last night Spit and Squeak confessed to what they did to you... that beating... their boat ride to nowhere... your abandonment... your... your affair with Mary Grant..."

"Stop!"

"...Mary Grant... a fifteen-year-old child..."

"No more. No more!" he shouted, loud enough to be heard near the wheelhouse.

Michel lunged at Anne. He grabbed her throat, and pinned her in the corner between the washboard and stern.

Anne's torso bent backward. She felt her feet lift from the deck. She could hear the rush of water from the wake. Droplets of spray showered her face and blurred her vision. She caught the greasy scent of diesel exhaust. She felt the vibration of the engine radiating through every fibre of the vessel. Then she heard a gasp, the sound of pain and surprise. The stranglehold on her neck loosened, and through bleary eyes, she watched Michel crumble to the deck.

When her vision cleared, Anne saw CeeCee holding a lobster crate. Two coils of rope inside had added weight to it. CeeCee had slung it like a battering ram and was readying to drive it home again, but there was no need. Michel had struggled out of his life jacket and was trying to rub the pain from his legs and thigh. He did not attempt to get up.

"Shall we head back?" said CeeCee.

"Please... no... please." The begging of such a proud and self-sufficient man struck Anne as pitiful.

CeeCee looked puzzled.

Anne looked at Michel, still in pain. He looked tired, very tired, and wore the cast of one who has given up.

"Please. I'll tell you everything. Nothing matters now but Jean. He's in real danger. He is. And I need your help."

Anne nodded to CeeCee and added, "Michel and I are going to have a little heart to heart. Meantime, don't be in a hurry to put that crate away. It may still come in handy."

Anne took a look around. Until then, she hadn't realized that the fog had thickened as much as it had. As soon as they had cleared port and made it through the slot into open water, visibility dropped to a few hundred yards. The land behind them faded into grey. The path over the bow led to everywhere and nowhere.

"Are you able to find this place... Willy's Bump... in this fog?" asked Anne.

"Not a problem," said CeeCee. "We have an electronic plotter. We can get to it straightaway. Another five... ten minutes is all. Got radar, too. The mark from Fig's vessel is already showing up."

"We've got to hurry. Fig plans to kill Jean," said Michel.

"What makes you say that?" said Anne.

"Revenge... revenge... for things I've done to him."

"What things?"

"I destroyed his life... and others, too."

67.

It was slack tide when Fig's boat settled over the top of Willy's Bump. Fog had settled in, too. Far off in every direction Jean heard faint rumbles of lobster boats moving unseen from one string of lobster traps to the next. Fig took little note of them, but, in the emptiness of that lonely vault of fog, Jean found them comforting.

The knowledge that others were not far off, fearlessly working in the same half-blind world as he, gave Jean a measure of security. Unlike his father, Jean had never spent any time aboard fishing vessels. As a result, open decks made him ill at ease, and the way they rolled and tossed in confused seas terrified him. He had heard the stories. He had read Conrad and Slocum. He admired the spirit of such mariners, but he desired none of it for himself. Instead, he preferred well-appointed cabins of yachts and cruisers he'd played on with friends and business associates from Halifax yacht clubs on pleasant summer afternoons. Many of these vessels rarely left the dock. They were not intended to. They served their captains quite well enough as floating cocktail lounges and social venues, and less as vehicles for adventure or sport.

Jean gathered some reassurance from Fig's presence, though. Fig had been at this game for over fifty years, and he was still alive. So he must know what he's doing. Jean could have turned down Fig's invitation to go out, but that would have been bad-mannered. After all, he had saved Anne from serious injury when the forklift rammed that storage building and done so much damage. And Fig had seemed eager to take Jean out for a short fishing trip, and Jean believed it was the least he could do to thank the man.

The trek to Willy's Bump had passed with little talking between the two men. The roar of the engine discouraged conversation, and Jean was still barely awake from his four o'clock wake-up in Charlottetown. Fig had advised him that mackerel were best fished at the change of tide, and, if Jean wanted a "proper" catch, he would have to be on time, and so he was. When they reached Fig's fishing ground, Fig killed the engine and hauled out a pair of small wooden frames around which heavy line was wrapped. He handed one to Jean. Jean had been expecting a pole, and he inspected this device with a baffled look. At the end of the line were several hooks, each nesting near a feather. A lead weight was fastened to the line's end.

"It's a jig," said Fig. "Feed out enough line to reach bottom. Raise it a foot or two. Then give the line a little jig up and down a few times to make it look like it's got some life in it. If there's a mackerel around, she'll strike. Then haul 'er aboard."

The first fish to strike was on Jean's line. He felt a dull hit. Fig hollered for him to haul it in, and he did, hand over hand. At first Jean didn't think he had anything, but, when the fish broke the water, it flung about violently. Jean couldn't control it. Fig with a laugh scooped it quickly up between calloused fingers, squeezed firmly to keep it from flopping violently about, backed the barb from its mouth, and tossed the gleaming fish into a large bucket.

"A nice one," said Fig.

"My first," said Jean.

"Hopefully, not your last," said Fig. He smiled, but his smile was curiously empty. "Ya look cold."

Jean had been quivering a bit. The sun had not burnt off the fog. His oil clothes protected from the spray, but he wasn't prepared for the clamminess that came with it.

"Shoulda worn a sweater or something underneath. It's always colder offshore. 'Specially if you're just standin' around not workin'. Here, this'll do ya some good."

Fig slid open a wooden panel near the wheel and pulled out two pint bottles.

"This'll take the chill off." He took a drink from one and passed the other to Jean.

"Moonshine?" said Jean noticing the absence of commercial labels.

"Made it myself and been doin' so since before you were born. There's some bite to it, but that's just the good of it nippin' at the heels of a chill... or whatever else is ailin' ya."

Jean felt the burn and winced. Then he felt a trickle of heat swell into a wave that threaded its way through passages in his body he thought immune to alcoholic stimulation. He smiled appreciatively and slipped the pint into a pocket of his oil clothes.

In the next half hour, the two men had caught a dozen blue and white shimmering prizes, and, when Fig inspected the large bucket of fish, he said, "That's enough for a good feed. Maybe we'll try somethin' else for fun."

Fig pulled his pint from a pocket under his oil clothes. He looked at Jean and took another pull on the bottle as if toasting some grand event.

"Up the republic!" he said.

Jean followed the example, raised his own bottle, and downed a healthy swig himself.

Fig read the puzzlement in Jean's face and said, "It's an old saying that my grandfather brought over after the First War. 'What the famine couldn't kill, the English trenches took care of,' he used to say."

"Thank god those days are gone," said Jean.

"They're gone for some..." Fig looked away. His response had been acidic.

Jean missed the insinuation. He started to speak, but thought better of it, and kept silent.

"D'ya know anything about setting trawl?" said Fig.

Fig's change of subject made it clearer.

"No, never have," he said.

"Nothin' to it," said Fig. "I'm goin' to let you try your hand at it like a real fisherman. See this tub," he said, pointing toward the stern. Jean nodded. "This is how we caught cod and haddock before the fishery collapse in the seventies. Want to give it a try?"

"I never did anything like this before."

"It's not complicated... and not hard work, either. The setting is quick and easy. Haulin' up the catch by myself tomorrow will be more of a chore, though. See that big tub near the stern? It holds a couple hundred feet of rope. Every few feet a lighter line's made fast to it. There's baited hooks at the end... maybe a hundred in each tub. When I get the boat in place, I'm goin' to ask you to toss that buoy over first. Then the anchor next to it. The current will carry the boat along, and the line and hooks will start to feed out of the tub. The fisherman at the stern, you, can use this short stick to fling coiled line from the tub as the boat drifts down current. When the rope reaches its end, toss the second anchor. Then the second buoy."

"That's it?" said Jean.

"That's it. If somethin' fouls up, just holler. I'll back her up... take the pressure off."

"I think I can get the hang of it," said Jean. "Is it legal?" he asked cautiously.

"Let's put it this way. I don't sell the catch. I salt it for personal use over the winter."

"Just say when..."

Fig returned to the wheel, put the transmission in gear, and turned the boat around. He headed at a certain bearing for a minute or two. Then he slowed and checked the number on his sounder.

"We're getting close," he said. "Are you ready?"

"Ready," Jean said.

"All right... Now. Toss the buoy!"

Fig dropped the gearshift into neutral. The drift of the boat took up the slack on the buoy line.

"Toss the anchor!"

The sound of the splash sank into the wall of fog.

"When you see the slack on the anchor take up, fling the line overboard a little at a time."

Fig's ears perked a bit when he heard a boat engine growing perceptibly louder and perceptibly nearer.

"There. You're getting the hang of it."

It didn't take long for Jean to get into a rhythm of flicking the stick under the arc of barbed line and sending more streams of line overboard. He began to feel useful in a way he hadn't before. It felt good.

Every once in a while, Fig would drop the engine into gear and take up slack in the line and then idle again. His ears were still attuned to his surroundings. The course he'd set. The speed of his small boat. The fog. Shifts in wind. And the sounds of other unseen vessels.

It was the sound of other vessels that most caught his attention—one especially. It was getting slowly louder. It stood out from the fishing boats whose engine roars were intermittent as they moved from one string of traps, hauled and cleared their catch, ran it off again, and moved to another string. This one was consistent in sound and course as well. Fig became concerned. He knew that the time had come to do what he needed to do.

Fig glanced back at Jean. He had got the hang of it, thought Fig. He noticed that, even when Jean hit a snag in the coiled line, he was nimble enough to clear it quickly without calling for help. The tub of trawl line was about half payed out. The time was now.

Fig slipped the engine in gear, swung the wheel counterclockwise, and jammed the throttle forward. The boat lurched to port. Jean lost balance and fell hard against the washboard. The trawl line jerked. Hooks snagged Jean's oil clothes. The anchor on the bottom held firmly. The engine roared. He felt himself being dragged toward the stern.

"Fig! Fig!" he screamed. "I'm caught! Stop the boat! I can't get loose!"

Fig ignored him. Jean felt his torso slip over the top of the washboard. His fingertips clutched at every scrap of resistance, but the force of the anchored line was too immense to resist. In less time than he could imagine, he was pulled over the side. The cold water seeped inside his oil clothes. His boots filled with water, but he wasn't sinking.

I'm not sinking. The concept rather than the words themselves registered in Jean's mind. Then, he thought, *Fig must have heard me.*

Fig had heard him, but he had ignored his plea for help. Something else had forced Fig to stop the boat. The quick, sudden manoeuvre that had carried Jean over the side had also fouled the rope flying out from the tub. Several hooks had not cleared the washboard. They caught the edge, dug in, and kept Jean from going under. Jean's clothing was too sodden and heavy, though, to let him to clamber back onto the working deck.

The sounds in Fig's ears told him that he had to be quick.

"Fig, gimme a hand! I can't get up."

Fig said nothing. He grabbed the half-filled trawl tub and heaved it overboard.

"Fig! What the hell are you doing?"

"Your father destroyed my sister's life. So I'm takin' yours. I want him to know what it feels like. I want him to feel the pain and hatred I've had for him all these years!"

Fig grabbed a knife and quickly cut away the last few hooks that kept Jean tethered to the boat.

"Fig, don't do this. You'll regret it. Please. I've done you no harm."

Fig cocked his head attentively. He heard something, but he said nothing. He tossed the last anchor over the side. The buoy splashed dully.

A bow appeared out of the heavy mist. Fig downed the throttle and fled into another wall of fog.

Jean disappeared beneath the surface.

68.

"That's him. We got him," said Jack. He was at the wheel of *Hell to Pay*. CeeCee stood beside him in the wheelhouse. Michel and Anne had remained behind her on the open deck.

"I see him, too," said Anne.

Jack swung the wheel in pursuit of Fig's vessel. Fig knew his was no match in power and speed with *Hell to Pay*. They could bear down on him quickly and disable his smaller boat if need be. In spite of that probability, Fig and his vessel slipped into the fog and out of sight.

"Hold it, Jack. Stop," said Michel. "Stop!"

Jack slowed the boat hesitantly. He looked back, perplexed. Michel's face turned grave and dissolved into a grotesque mask of horror.

Jack slipped the transmission into neutral. "What's wrong?" he said.

"Fig was alone. Jean wasn't with him."

"Where would he be then?" said Jack.

Michel pointed toward a red buoy just to starboard.

"Oh my god," said Jack.

"He's killed him. I know it."

"We'll see 'bout that," said Jack. "CeeCee, grab that boathook."

Jack swung the bow around and headed for the red buoy. When it passed alongside, CeeCee gaffed the line and hauled the buoy aboard. Jack flipped the lever for the hydraulic hauler. Michel guessed what Jack had planned to do, and he manned the hauler himself. The hauler whined under the strain of the rope feeding through it. Michel kept his hand on the lever and his eye on whatever rose up from the murky depths. When he saw the anchor drawing up, he slowed the machine and eased the anchor aboard. After that, the hauler laboured under stress. Its moan deepened. Suddenly Michel hit the lever and stopped the haul. The trawl tub and a knot of fouled gear broke the surface. It took both men to hoist that knotted mess up and over the washboards, and every moment of that effort worried Michel because, if Jean was snagged on the line below it, he had no time left. The remaining rope and hooked lines howled through the wheel effortlessly now, but many long seconds passed before Jean's body surfaced alongside the boat.

Jack and CeeCee stood by to drag the body aboard. With grim faces, they cut his clothes loose from the hooks and stretched him out. Anne and CeeCee pulled off his rubber oil clothes and stretched him out on the deck. He lay limp. He appeared lifeless. A peculiar blue cast rested like a pall on his face. He showed no response to voices, and shaking him sparked no reflexes.

Anne rolled him to one side, managed to expel some liquid from his lungs, and checked for pulse and breathing.

"I got something..." said Anne. "Yes... a pulse. A pulse," she repeated, more excitedly.

"Thank god," said Jack.

"Amen to that," added CeeCee.

"...but he's not breathing. Get on the radio. Have an ambulance meet us at the wharf."

Anne began mouth-to-mouth resuscitation.

Jack rushed to the wheelhouse, grabbed the mic for the VHF, and made the emergency call. Suddenly, his ears perked to the rumble of an engine. Somewhere beyond the veil of fog stood another fishing boat. *More help... maybe a faster vessel*, he thought.

"Canada Coast Guard, Canada Coast Guard... This is MV *Hell to Pay*. We have a medical emergency aboard and request assistance at Little Rose Harbour wharf. We'll need police, as well, over."

"Your location, *Hell to Pay*?"

Jack rattled off the numbers.

As he spoke, he peered out the portside glass panel. Again, he still heard the slow manoeuvring of a boat somewhere nearby. Then he caught the rev of an engine. It was a gas engine, not diesel, and the only person he knew who still owned a gas-powered fishing boat was Fig Grant.

At that moment of frightening illumination, he saw the bow of Fig's boat burst through a veil of fog. Jack's mouth drew open, dumbfounded, and it was then that Fig jammed the throttle full-down and made straight for the side of *Hell to Pay*.

"Standby! He's comin' in!" Jack shouted. On deck, three heads popped up and stared aghast and frozen at Fig's vessel bearing down on them.

In the seventy-five yards of visibility, Fig gained considerable speed. His bow was pointed for a broadside impact, but *Hell to Pay* was still caught up in Fig's longline trawl gear, which anchored them in place. They couldn't flee. They couldn't take evasive manoeuvres. They were trapped.

"Maybe he's had second thoughts," said CeeCee. "Maybe he's coming back to help."

"He's coming back to kill us all," said Michel, "...to kill us all."

"Brace yourselves," said Jack. "Stay low!"

Fig's old boat was smaller than newer fiberglass fishing vessels like *Hell to Pay*, but it was heavy—solid wood construction—and Jack and CeeCee stared helplessly at the approach of its bow, knifing through the water and hurling sheets of spray, its engine shrieking, and a madman at the wheel.

With only seconds left, though, Fig's vessel slowed and half-circled *Hell to Pay*. Jack poked his head up at the drop in rpm. As he did, he watched Fig hurl a container of some sort into the air. A fiery plume flickered. A faint trail of smoke trailed it. The projectile arced through the air and struck the top of the wheelhouse. The container split. Flames spilled out, leaped up, and roared like something vicious escaping through a fissure in hell. A wall of heat and flame flowed along the slope of the foredeck. Jack and CeeCee and Anne, trapped in the wheelhouse, recoiled at the fiery concussion and covered their faces. Anne dragged Jean farther away from the searing flames.

Jack recovered quickly, grabbed a fire extinguisher inside the cabin, and scrambled forward toward the peak of the bow. He lifted the forward deck hatch a crack. It was not aflame and Jack climbed through, fire extinguisher in hand, and worked his way with methodical sweeping motions farther and farther aft.

Jack had nearly doused the flames when Fig's boat began another pass. A second incendiary cannister sailed through the air and crashed onto the middle of the working deck. The gasoline bomb flared and billowed. It illuminated the fog that surrounded them, and the concussion and heat drove CeeCee and Anne back inside the wheelhouse again.

Jack was about to drop down onto the main deck when Fig loosed a blast from his shotgun. The shot went wild, but Jack lost his footing and tumbled off the top of the wheelhouse cabin. He winced. Then he lurched toward the flames with his extinguisher.

There was little chance that the fibreglass deck would burn, but the fuel tanks were aft, under the stern deck. He emptied the extinguisher. Halfway to the stern, he hollered to CeeCee. She brought a second extinguisher, and it held enough retardant to quench the blaze.

In his desperate attempt to control the fires, Jack had become oblivious to Fig's whereabouts, but in the seconds that followed, Jack realized the sound of Fig's engine had diminished and was fading into some hidden place in the fog.

Anne scrambled back to her resuscitation of Jean.

In the confusion, however, no one had noticed Michel. No one had seen him fall back onto the hauler and the mess of rope and line and hooks piled on the washboard. Several hooks had dug into his clothing, and, when he wrenched himself away, he dislodged the trawl line from the hauler. In the melee, no one had heard his scream for help as the freed line payed out and dragged him overboard.

Jack Pine gripped his side. He felt a stab of pain. *Mebbe just a cracked rib*, he thought. He stood up. He winced. "Life jackets, get 'em on... just in case," he shouted and began tossing them from a storage bin back onto the deck. Then he shouted, "Where's Michel?"

Anne looked toward him with uncertainty. Jack's eyes shifted to the hauling wheel. The displaced trawl line, still slowly feeding out, answered his question.

CeeCee stumbled toward the VHF radio and made a second mayday call to the Coast Guard. Then she stepped back from the radio. A bewildered look swept her face.

"Radio's out," she shouted to Jack. "No electrical."

Her hand reached toward the ignition switch for the engine.

"Don't touch it," shouted Jack. "There might be fumes in the bilge."

"What'll we do?"

Every movement and every word he spoke brought pain to Jack's side.

"There's an... air horn... forward. Second drawer... inside cabin. Seven short... one long blast. That should get... some notice."

69.

Heart's Desire took *Hell to Pay* in tow, and they headed slowly back toward Little Rose Harbour.

Neither CeeCee Dunne nor Jack Pine had ever witnessed such a gathering as appeared along the dock at Little Rose Harbour that morning. The chatter over the VHF had driven the rumour mills, and the factory emptied. Most of the workers spilled onto the wharves to see firsthand what had taken place. The fact that none of the bosses had been there to crack the whip contributed to their lack of discipline.

Rumours had spread like brush fires. Truth struggled to find a place at the gossip table, but the most imaginative spinners carried the day with grist that was juicier, more sensational, and too compelling to ignore, as well as more difficult to believe.

Flickering racks of lights on two RCMP cruisers signalled an official presence on the scene. One car had arrived earlier to inquire about Bernie White. The other had responded to the emergency call relayed from the Canadian Coast Guard station.

The number of newspeople on the scene was unusual as well. Ordinarily, a couple of vessels banging into one another during fishing season would not qualify as news, but the mayday broadcast and the request for police had whet reporters' curiosities. Most of the journalists had already been in Montague covering the explosion and death there. So it would be just a short run from there to Little Rose Harbour for a second story.

The first reporters on the scene cornered local residents for background colour. That would be enough to tease the palates of a news-hungry public; the facts would trundle out soon enough. TV camera people gathered film footage and commandeered elevated positions to record the damaged vessels limping through the channel.

By the time *Heart's Desire* and *Hell to Pay* made their appearance, though, RCMP constables had moved the crowd back from the main wharf and opened a broad passage for the ambulance and paramedics.

Jack Pine and CeeCee felt a wave of embarrassment at the hubbub they saw waiting for them. Neither craved the limelight. They wished they could shrink away, but they couldn't. Paramedics they had hoped for; police they had expected. They even looked forward to familiar faces lending a hand with mooring lines when they tied up, but no—the size of the gathering was disconcerting. Even more intimidating were the TV cameras, following their boat's sluggish progress toward the dock like shotgun barrels tracking winter partridge.

"Fer god's sake, it looks like half of Kings County's waitin' fer us," said Jack.

"Helluva way to start a fishing career," said CeeCee. "Dead in the water before we landed a single canner."

Hell to Pay was pumping a steady stream of water from her bilge when she reached the wharf under tow. Paramedics and RCMP swept aboard as soon as the boat tied up. Jean Gauthier was conscious but uncommunicative, dazed, and probably in shock. Moments later he was taken up, slipped into the rear of the ambulance, and transported to hospital. Anne had planned to accompany him, but she was held back by a constable, who insisted she remain until she had given her account of the morning's events.

The first constables to arrive at the factory already had taken statements from office staff regarding Bernie White. They confirmed that Bernie's had been the body recovered from the explosion. Tammy Wallace broke down at the news, and, after the company's accounting ledgers were seized, she admitted that she and Bernie had concocted a scheme to skim from the company's business account, and that they intended to go away together once his contract ended in a few weeks. She admitted, too, that Bernie was trying to get out from under some gambling debts. He told her he had a plan to leave them "sitting pretty" on some tropical isle.

Police arrested Tammy on suspicion of embezzlement. All the while, however, she insisted she had no inkling why Bernie was in Montague on the night of his death.

An hour later Anne emerged from the factory office, where her interview with police had taken place. She walked into the fresh salty air to a different setting than had greeted her when she came ashore. The fog over the land had partly burned off. The sun had grown stronger and threw a peculiar tawny cast over the harbour buildings and landscape. Offshore, however, a wall of fog remained. The strange ambience gripped her. She felt trapped in a way. Cut off from reality. So many dead, so much hatred, so many questions. Still so many questions.

The sickly sepia-coloured waterfront contributed to Anne's discomfort and unease, but she seemed the only one so indisposed. Others around her—fishermen and dockworkers, buyers and warehousemen—moved about the scene unaffected by the unnatural milieu. For them life went on, and work continued. Perhaps a few more sensitive souls reflected on their own mortality after the morning's tragedies. Few would have mourned Michel Gauthier; he was a stranger. Jean, young and handsome and personable, would have garnered sympathy and perhaps a few prayers. Others may have given a moment or two to Fig Grant. Perhaps he would even have been the subject of a memorable story or two passing between some of the old-timers.

Wesley Peake and Sampson Pitt sat along the edge of their box truck and warmed themselves in the dull glow of a weak sun trying to wear away the yellow fog. Squeak set down his pencil and the crossword puzzle he'd been labouring over in *The Guardian* newspaper. One of the inshore boats had slipped through the curtain of fog at the channel entrance and was making for the wharf. He recognized it as one of their customers.

The *Brenda Jane* swung alongside the wharf next to the Queens County Packers truck.

"How is it outside?" asked Squeak.

"Not so much fun. Too damned crowded. Tried to run off some gear and had a near miss with another one haulin' 'is own traps. Decided I had enough fer today. Fog locked in solid. Any word on Fig?"

"Nothin' yet," said Squeak.

"There's quite a few at it," said *Brenda Jane*'s skipper, "and they're pretty heated up 'bout what he done. Me... I'm waitin' till the fog lifts some. Then I'll give them a hand. So many boats doin' a grid search in this weather is too dangerous. You know him pretty good. Do you think they'll find him?"

"Only if he wants to be found," said Squeak.

"...'n' that's not l-likely," added Spit.

Spit nodded, and Squeak went back to his puzzle. The *Brenda Jane* gunned her engine, swung around, and headed toward her berth.

***

"Don't think I've ever seen you without a crossword in your hand," said Anne, passing by the Queens County Packers truck and stopping.

"It passes the time... and winters can be long around here. I read a lot and do these," he said, lifting up and showing the paper.

"Looks like you got most of it."

"You do the puzzles?" he said.

"When I have a few minutes to spare. Any news?"

"One of the boats radioed they come across a buoy. Old Mr. Gauthier was at the other end of it. They're bringin' 'im in."

"You mean Michael MacDonald, don't you?" said Anne.

Squeak looked up stonily, but said nothing.

"I'm sorry," said Anne. "That was cold."

"No matter. It's true, and now there's an end to it. It answers a lot of questions... fills in a lot of blanks."

Spit's head bobbed in agreement.

"J-j-just that it t-took two udder deaths t' tell the whole t-tale. Mebbe three."

"What do ya mean?"

Squeak stared with alarm at him. Spit balked and sputtered. Then Squeak's face softened. His shoulders drooped. Then they shrugged.

"What Spit means is that there's an older story to tell. After we got rid of Michael, Fig tells us that his sister is pregnant. Michael MacDonald's doin', we suppose. She drops outa school a few months later to stay home and take care of the homestead. See, by then it was just Fig and her to keep care of the place. Fig wanted her t' get rid of it, but she wanted to keep it. Kept sayin' that 'Michael was coming back.' They managed to keep everything secret. Fig delivered the baby himself. Even then no one knew."

"Then the b-baby died," said Spit. "Mary lost her senses, I guess. A few weeks later she walked out into the channel and drowned herself. Mary was his pride and joy, and he blamed Michael for her death."

"Did Fig have something to do with the baby dying?"

"D-dunno," he said.

Anne pondered the story quietly. Then she said, "That's at least two. You said three."

"H-hate grows on ya," said Spit. "I... we 'spect it st-started with old Declan. He was a mean sonofabitch. Real mean. M-most gave him a wide berth. Fig couldn't."

"Fig had to fish with him," said Squeak. "Declan pulled him outa school to do it. Lobsters in spring. Then trawl. One day Declan fetched up in a trawl line and went over. Fig wasn't able to bring him aboard in time 'n' 'e drowned."

"Do you think that Fig was slow on purpose?"

"I don't know. I woulda been if it'd been me," said Squeak and tossed his crossword carelessly onto the floor of the truck.

Anne stared down at it. A long silence weighed down conversation.

"Done or stuck?" said Anne finally.

"Both," said Squeak.

"What's the clue?"

"*Stanley found him*," said Squeak. "Stan Musial, Stanley Kubrick, Stan Rogers, Stan Laurel... nothing registers."

"What about *Livingstone*," said Anne. "Would that work? How many letters?"

"Eleven," said Squeak.

"Never heard of him, but it fits," said Squeak. "*Livingstone*," he pondered.

"It's about a lost African safari," said Anne, "and there was an old movie about it, too."

Squeak smirked.

"Something funny?"

"No, just that you've been askin' all over about some George Livingstone and the name comes up in a crossword."

"So that's funny?" said Anne.

"Kinda. Livingstone Harbour is the place we cut Michael MacDonald loose. It's a little hole-in-the-wall port on Cape George. You know, over in Nova Scotia."

"I guess that is kinda funny," said Anne. "A real coincidence."

70.

Friday

Charlottetown

Anne left Little Rose Harbour late Thursday afternoon. She hoped she wouldn't have to revisit that place for a long, long time. The memories and terrors and frustrations of the past few days took hold, and the forty-five-minute drive from Halkirk to Charlottetown seemed endless.

She also dreaded her first stop in Charlottetown. It was professional and obligatory—a check on Jean Gauthier's condition at the Queen Elizabeth Hospital. Circumstances, however, muddied that effort when she learned that police had barred visitors other than immediate family from entering his room.

All for the best, she thought and turned toward home, deeply relieved.

As she pulled into her driveway, a local radio station broadcast a news update:

> Earlier today, an incident at Little Rose Harbour, near Halkirk, PEI, prompted responses by RCMP and Coast Guard personnel. Unofficial sources report that an assault left one man dead and another in hospital. One fishing vessel was heavily damaged. A second is missing. Fog is hampering the search for the missing boat. No names have been released.

Anne closed her bedroom door and plopped onto her bed. She fell into a peculiar, dreamless sleep in which she felt as if she were conscious but in a coma, and she remained in that state until the next morning, well after Jacqueline had gone to school.

A long, hot shower relaxed Anne. A suds-filled stream flushed the scent of smoke and stale fish bait and fuel oil onto ceramic tiles and down the drain, and, when she finally emerged, she felt renewed in body but emotionally spent.

She glanced at the clock. Then she dressed in fresh jeans and a casual top, and headed downstairs, not unmindful that the soiled clothes she had dropped at the foot of her bed the night before were churning in the washing machine. *Jacqui's doing*, she mused, and Anne's spirit brightened at her daughter's thoughtfulness.

***

Queen Elizabeth Hospital was a sprawling assembly of wings and levels west of the Hillsborough River. Several grey-haired volunteers staffed the information desk at the entrance. One especially cheerful woman jotted Jean Gauthier's room number on a slip of paper, pointed up the busy corridor, and assured her that the patient was allowed visitors. A thought flashed through Anne's mind: What visitors? Who, if anyone, would visit Jean? Who was left? Bernie was dead. Jean's father had killed him. Michel was dead. He had no relative or friends on the Island that she knew of. No doubt the police would have stopped to take a statement about the incident on Fig's boat and maybe gather more details about Michel's movements, and Jean's, too. As far as others who cared about Jean, not a one, she thought.

That last thought made Anne uncomfortable. She struggled with memories of her personal relationship with Jean. She felt somehow guilty. She felt sad, then ashamed. Then she felt a flash of anger that prodded her to make a quick about-face and leave, but she didn't. Anger shifted to hurt. Then it resolved itself in a cold professionalism. At the far end of the lobby, several kiosks sold coffee and tea and takeout sandwiches and muffins. Beyond them stood a glass-enclosed gift shop.

It would be appropriate to bring something up, she thought. She looked over the choices. *Flowers? Too personal. Chocolates? He could read something into that.* Anne moved to the magazine stand and thumbed through the rack. Anne snatched up a lobster-shaped ceramic ashtray and the latest issue of *Canadian Yachting* and made her way toward Jean's room.

*** *** ***

"Thanks..." said Jean, accepting Anne's gifts. He looked curiously at the ashtray and reached out to set both presents on the side table. It was too long a stretch. Anne helped put them aside. "...and thank you for the first aid on the boat. The medics say your quick thinking and persistence saved me."

"I couldn't let you drown, could I? I hadn't been paid yet," said Anne. She smiled. It lacked warmth.

"I'd hoped there would have been more to it than that."

Anne shrugged. Jean looked suddenly rather tired and feeble.

"Perhaps at one time," she said, "but I know how it goes. New toys are more amusing than old ones."

"I don't follow."

"You've got more important things to concern you, I'm sure. Were the police here? Did they explain what happened?"

"They were short on information and long on questions."

"What kind of questions?"

"Mostly about Dad and the business... and why Fig tried to kill me."

"What did you say?"

"Not much to say... just that Fig ranted on and on about how Dad ruined his life and about some girl named Mary. I thought he'd gone off the rails. Made no sense whatsoever."

"Did the police mention Bernie?

Jean nodded. "They enquired about my business dealings with him... and Dad's."

"What did you say?"

"Not much I could say. I knew him for a few months before the purchase. Dad scarcely knew him at all."

"Did they tell you that Bernie was dead?"

Jean looked stunned. He stared at Anne for a long while before his lips twitched, and he asked, "What happened?"

"An explosion in Montague" was all she said. "Did the police tell you anything else?"

"They found Fig's boat. Three or four miles offshore. They guessed he'd set it afire. It was mostly sunk."

"He killed himself?"

"That's what they think. Not possible to swim that far. Too cold. Strong currents."

"So it's over," said Anne. Jean nodded gravely. "Good. That puts an end to a number of things," she said. Anne ended her declaration with a peculiar finality. Jean looked up puzzled. Anne rose from her chair.

"I know that you are seeing someone else." Anne stared down at him. He looked uncomfortable. "I know all about it."

"...but..."

Anne turned and walked out the door.

71.

Saturday evening
Holland College, Charlottetown

Anne had been surprised at just how much distance a day or two could take her from the ordeal she had gone through. If she or a news report didn't conjure it up, then her frightening experience at Little Rose Harbour lay uneasily in the past.

That evening she and Ben and Sarah and Mary Anne had gathered together in the Holland College theatre, where Jacqui's high-school theatre group was performing a 1920s-style revue, a collection of humorous skits, vocal harmonizing, readings, and lively musical pieces. It was a year-end production, and it would mark Jacqui's last stage performance before graduation.

Jacqui had done her best to keep a low profile the last few days, but her eagerness to take on uncustomary household chores had raised Anne's suspicion that Jacqui was treating her with kid gloves. On the one hand, it was amusing; on the other, it was touching. It was also a reminder that everything had not returned to normal. Her best friend, Mary Anne, had been the picture of tact. That in itself was out of character. Sarah, on the other hand, was best at letting the past fade into the past. Her husband, Ben, was the least tactful. His cop perspective and bluntness were too ingrained to suppress, and, every so often, his sentence would begin with a cue that Sarah guessed would drift toward events in Little Rose Harbour. At those times, her elbow would jab Ben's rib—a reminder that he was about to go too far.

Anne, of course, was mindful of the delicate handling by friends and by Jacqui, too, and she pretended to be oblivious to their gaffes, as well as their goings-on to shield her. She felt protected in the warmth of their good intentions.

Anne spotted Jacqui's face poke between a break in stage curtains, smile toward her, and quickly disappear. The house lights faded. Anne fumbled with her program in semi-darkness and found Jacqui's name on the list. Jacqui would recite her Hamlet soliloquy after a choral group chirped out a tune from *The Mikado*.

The program was a pleasant diversion—mostly upbeat, vintage twenties vaudeville with a sprinkling of headier fare. It was fast-paced, too, leaving patrons less time to cringe at the scratchy bow of a viola or squirm at the bad timing in a comic routine. As the show progressed, the audience grew to expect talented performers outnumbering the ordinary.

It was during a rendition of a Ma Rainey blues song that Anne's cellphone shuddered. The vibration startled her, and a bothersome light flickered from the small screen. She glanced at the caller ID and the message. She looked annoyed and puzzled, then turned it off and buried the phone deep in her handbag.

Applause, smiles, and giggles followed singing of "Three little maids from school are we." Then the lights dimmed on an empty stage to indicate a change in pace and tone. Jacqui walked out, dressed as Hamlet. Anne caught her breath. She thought Jacqui looked a bit dumbstruck and unprepared—a bit lost, perhaps. Anne felt a pang of concern. Her daughter had known the words. She had heard Jacqui recite at Ben and Sarah's dinner. Had she frozen up because of the large crowd?

Jacqui wandered onto her mark. A spotlight pinned her. Her head lowered as if to examine herself standing there. Then she spoke:

"O that this too solid flesh would melt," she said, and began to wind her way through Hamlet's wilderness of logic, emotion, morality, and deed. Anne relaxed. Jacqui's voice was strong and inflective. She knew what she was doing, thought Anne. Jacqui had been setting up the audience.

Anne closed her eyes and listened, but she scarcely perceived Jacqui's performance. Through it all she felt pummelled with certain of Hamlet's words and phrases that Jacqui poured out. They evoked another stage and another tragedy, the one at Little Rose Harbour.

Out of Hamlet's reference to an "unweeded garden" Anne's imagination summoned up the overgrown plot, once the Grant family burial ground on Sullivan's Point. She remembered the scant flowers that struggled to survive there amid the unchecked, wild growth. Anne recalled the stories Enid Clements told her of old Declan Grant's greed and cruelty and the hard-heartedness that smouldered within him—dreadful gifts he passed on to his son, Fig. She imagined Mary Grant's youthful spirit, destroyed by Michael MacDonald's exploitation and Fig's hate for him, and how those men ruined each other's lives in order to feed cravings for revenge.

Jacqui's performance lasted less than five minutes, but, by the end of it, Anne felt tears making their way toward her cheeks. Ben glanced at her with feeble unease. Mary Anne squeezed her hand. Jacqui took her bow and, looking quite pleased, bounded into the wings.

72.

Monday

A six o'clock run on the boardwalk in Victoria Park and a quick shower both relaxed and invigorated Anne. She felt fresh. She had risen before Jacqui, who still had exams to complete before her final day at school, and decided to spoil her with a breakfast of waffles, whipped cream, and fresh Island strawberries.

A thank you for such a wonderful performance, she told her daughter.

Anne wanted life to return to normal. She wanted her mind uncluttered. So she avoided local TV and radio programming. She ignored the telephone and let her messaging centre greet the callers. She had no intention of becoming a recluse. She just wanted the uneventful to soothe her like a warm bath and seep into her soul, and she thought she might find such a reprieve in the quiet of her office.

Anne's Victoria Row office was a second-floor walk-up, a quaint old brick structure in the heart of Charlottetown. The street was still quiet at nine o'clock, and the light was soft as a Monet painting. She opened her office window. A pigeon fluttered away; another bird twittered unseen from a perch in the trees that towered along the street.

Anne worked her way through the pile of mail that had accumulated during the last week. Most of it was trivial, but she gave each item the same attention she would have given a valued document.

By eleven she had made it through a tedious log of online messages and a stack of junk mail, and now she felt rather useless sitting behind her great oak desk with nothing left to do. But she was growing hungry. It might be early, she thought, but, if she headed down now, The Blue Peter restaurant would be less busy, and maybe Mary Anne would have time for a chat.

There was something else, though, that needed resolution: the text message she got at the concert. She pulled her cellphone from a pocket. It was still there. It was real. It wasn't going away, and she couldn't put it off any longer. It was from Jean Gauthier.

Nothing will turn the clock back. For that I'm sorry. Our personal relationship may be over, but we still have business matters to wrap up. Pick a time and place to meet, preferably over dinner somewhere, he had texted.

Anne was tempted to name Red Shores as their meeting place, the same spot Jean supposedly had a rendezvous with another woman. But Anne had second thoughts: that would be vindictive. And she didn't want to come across as petty and unprofessional.

Six o'clock this evening at Griffon Room, she texted back.

***

Mary Anne was disappointed that Anne hadn't stayed longer at The Blue Peter, but Anne insisted she had unfinished work at her office. She did. Now that her appointment with Jean was confirmed, she needed to complete her final report on the Little Rose Harbour investigation. That took three more hours, and by then she had grown physically weary, sick at heart, and depleted in spirit.

With the final report next to her, she drove aimlessly west out of Charlottetown and along rural, less-travelled roads until she found herself at land's end near the Blockhouse Point Lighthouse. It was an isolated spot at the narrow mouth to Charlottetown

Harbour. She parked, walked the shore, let the gentle lap of wave against sandstone mesmerize her, and shed much of the burden that had weighed her down.

An hour later, the sun grew uncomfortably warm, and the glare from the water became harsh. Anne pulled herself away from the shore and drove home.

73.

Anne arrived at the restaurant at six-twenty. She wore a red silk print dress, matching heels. She carried a small black handbag in one hand and clutched a thick document-size envelope in the other. Anne spotted Jean first. He looked anxious but brightened when he saw her and stood as she approached his table.

"You look lovely," he said.

"I'm sorry I'm late. Traffic..."

Anne sat, placed the envelope on a nearby chair, and surveyed the surroundings.

"You're feeling better," she said.

Jean nodded.

"Not a hundred per cent, but getting there."

Anne nodded.

"Have you ordered yet?"

"No, I thought I'd wait until you arrived."

"Whatever you're having, then..."

"Grilled salmon with lemon slices, asparagus tips with orange sauce, toasted hazelnuts, and a bottle of Chardonnay... for two," said Jean to the waitress he had signalled.

The Chardonnay melted a bit of the ice in Anne's demeanour, and Jean grew a bit more relaxed. During their second cup of wine Jean looked up with a bewildered expression. Anne thought she saw tears welling in his eyes. He swallowed hard.

"I still don't understand why Fig did it."

"The police didn't explain anything to you?"

"They asked questions but were reluctant to give information. When I pressed them, they said it was an ongoing investigation."

Anne took a long sip from her glass. Then she looked up at Jean: "So you had no knowledge of your father's past relationship with Fig?"

Jean shook his head. "There was no relationship. How could there be? He spent his whole life in Nova Scotia."

Anne refilled her glass and ran through the story as she had heard it: Michael's spring fishing at Little Rose Harbour, his relationship with Mary Grant, his beating and banishment at the hands of Fig, Spit, and Squeak.

"That's nonsense, and, even if it were true," said Jean, "that was so long ago... almost a lifetime."

Anne continued with Mary's pregnancy and the birth and death of her child, her devastation knowing that Michael would never return, and the despair that drove her to drown herself.

"Fig became bitter after that, drank too much, lost his boat and license. Then he mortgaged his land to buy his boat and gear back. But that didn't work out. Bernie's factory held the mortgage, but Bernie let him live there until he sold out to Big Sea Products. Your father owned that company by then, and he evicted Fig from his family homestead."

"No, you're wrong there! My father didn't purchase it, I did, and you know that was only recently."

"He did it under the pseudonym of George Livingstone and Big Sea Products, a shell company he'd set up. My guess is that he did it secretly to take revenge on Fig over many years. Consequently, Fig came to hate that company so much that he struck back at it with theft and vandalism. Your insistence on being independent and buying Big Sea Products' two PEI canneries threw a wrench into your father's plan. He was afraid that if you dug too far into the paperwork of Big Sea, you'd uncover his secret. That's why he insisted on negotiating the purchase with George Livingstone on your behalf. Of course, your father was negotiating with himself. Your father had taken the pseudonym George Livingstone."

"That's the wildest conjecture I've ever heard," he said, growing angry. "How could you possibly reach that conclusion?"

"He confessed most of it to me on the boat just before it was firebombed. Other information came from Fig's accomplices. His cover as George Livingstone came to me later when I learned that your father was tossed overboard just outside of *Livingstone* Harbour on Cape *George*, Nova Scotia."

"It still doesn't make sense. How would Fig know, after all these years, that my father was this Michael MacDonald fellow?"

"Well, they say 'you can't throw a stone on Prince Edward Island without hitting a relative,' and that's what happened. His cousin spotted him: Luc LaVie, your night watchman. Ask him. His mother was a Gauthier, and Luc had known your father when they were children. It's all in my report," she said, pushing the large envelope toward him.

Jean's hand reached out slowly and settled on top of the report. He left it there. His face softened, and he looked older. Anne imagined she saw his father's eyes looking back at her. Then Jean said, "Do the police have to know about all this?"

"I don't work for the police. They can come to their own conclusions," said Anne.

"Thank you."

"There's no one left who needs punishment now. Fig's gone... Michel's gone... Bernie's gone, and there's no one left to give evidence against Spit or Squeak. It's over."

"It won't be over for me until the wake's held... and the funeral's concluded."

74.

Tuesday

At her dinner meeting with Jean, Anne had not mentioned Bernie White. Anne suspected that Jean's father killed Bernie, but she had no evidence to support that notion and no reason to follow it up. That investigation rested more properly with the police and their great forensic resources. Maybe they would sort it out; maybe not. Anyway, she didn't want to dump more tragedy on Jean's plate. He already had an abundance of family history to process.

Besides, Anne felt sorry for Jean. His world of comfort, respectability, and privilege was unravelling, perhaps for the first time in his life. So, when Jean had asked Anne to assist him at his father's wake, she found herself conflicted.

His plan was to hold a viewing in Charlottetown for those who knew his father locally. He expected a modest number would arrive from Halkirk and vicinity, and perhaps a few more from west of Summerside, where his other factory was located.

He didn't think he could handle it all alone, in that receiving line, he'd said. He said he'd really appreciate someone else with him for support.

Anne hated the idea. She felt like a hypocrite, but she also felt Jean's helplessness at having no one else to shoulder the burden.

She agreed. The wake would be on Thursday evening, and she would stand next to him in the very short receiving line.

Jean also had planned a second viewing at a Halifax funeral home on Saturday with a burial service on Sunday. Distant cousins, aunts, and uncles would support him there. So Anne would be spared from attending those ceremonies.

Michel's death notice had appeared on the local newspaper's website listing on Tuesday and in Wednesday's morning paper. Workers at the plant had been given the afternoon off with pay to ensure a better than modest turnout.

75.

Thursday Evening
Highland Funeral Home, Charlottetown

Anne arrived at Highland Funeral Home a half hour early. Johnny Cassell, the funeral director, was making final adjustments to the wreaths and flower arrangements as Anne arrived.

"How does he look?" he said. Johnny Cassell was immaculately groomed, and his tone carried an impossible mix of pride and humility.

Anne nodded, and he handed her a nametag that identified her as "Friend." She fastened it to her blouse. As she did, she recalled the message she had received just before the explosion that killed Bernie, and she wondered if Michel Gauthier had intended to kill her, too, or if he had just been playing loose and free with her life. At that moment, anger welled up, and Anne felt a primordial urge to scream and run.

"You're here. Thank goodness. I thought you might not show."

"Why would you think that?" asked Anne. She spoke with confidence, but she trembled at her sudden impulse to escape.

"I know this must be difficult for you... that you're disappointed in him... and me."

"I try to be professional. I'm here to support my client... you. That's part of the job."

"Still..."

"There is no *still*, Jean. If I were a man, you'd expect me *to suck it up... get on with it*. I don't need patronizing. I didn't earn the respect I have by weeping in a corner, waiting for some guy to say, '*There, there, dear. It'll be okay.*' Right? Right," she said, answering her own question. "I think they did an excellent job, given the short time they had to prepare for the viewing, wouldn't you say?"

Jean glanced around the large room, satisfied to follow Anne's diversion, and nodded his head.

A corridor at the entrance to Highland Funeral Home had led Jean to where his father was waked. A visitors' registry stood by the doorway to the viewing room. The casket was centred along a short wall. Wreaths, family photos, and vases filled with flowers lined the route toward it. If visitors and relatives wished to sit and rest or chat and reminisce, then groups of chairs had been arranged for that convenience. Amid it all, the unending melody of a string ensemble wafted softly from hidden speakers, and after visitors had paid their respects, they could slip out through a second door at the back.

Anne and Jean waited awkwardly with each other as the rigid, powdered face of old Michel Gauthier stared blankly at the ceiling. They busied themselves over trivial tasks, and the wait for mourners seemed exceedingly long.

A rapid, chattering mix of French and English echoed down the hallway as the first visitors approached.

Luc Lavie's perfectly round, bald head bobbed like a metronome with each slow measure of speech he uttered.

"I am Luc Lavie... I, too, am a Gauthier... on my mother's side," he said.

"You remember Luc, your night watchman..." said Anne, seeing the fright of blank-mindedness cross Jean's face and suspecting that this was the real reason for her being present.

"...and your cousin... do you know that?"

"Afraid not, Luc. I know rather little about my grandmother's side of the family."

"Second cousin, once removed," said the woman alongside Luc.

"...and this is Jeanette... she was a Doiron... before I find her."

A host of other newfound relatives followed Luc. They numbered a dozen or more. Their relationships blurred in Jean's mind, but he kept up an interest that pleased them. Rather than simply filing out the exit, the Gauthiers and Lavies lingered, gathered about in small clusters of the chairs, and chatted and laughed quietly, all of which depleted Jean's dread of the staid rigidity of other wakes he had attended.

Jack Pine and Tom Bean were driven in by CeeCee with her son, Rufus, in tow. Both Jack and CeeCee thanked Jean for shouldering the cost for repairs to their damaged vessel and other losses. Both Jack and CeeCee gave Anne hugs for her help. Tom Bean offered condolences as well as news of his latest invention, a less expensive process for quick-freezing fish. Kate Chapman brought her new boyfriend along. Barb Beaton and Morgan Sark represented the factory's office staff.

By the time Enid Clements arrived, the line of mourners had become sporadic. As usual, Enid was sympathetic and kind as well as blunt and outspoken. She offered the usual condolences that she had uttered by rote over decades of wakes. Then she saw something in Jean's eye or in the expression on his face that prompted more.

"You're not your father. Remember that. You seem like a good man."

Enid stepped away. She took Anne's hand and nodded, but said little, and left the funeral home.

Out of the corner of her eye, Anne saw several new visitors approach the doorway to sign the register. She didn't know them.

"Washroom," said Anne and left for the accommodations that lay along the corridor just past the exit from the viewing room.

Anne dawdled there for five minutes. She checked herself in the mirror, glanced at her watch, and returned to the roomful of mourners.

There was no lineup for viewing. Jean was still standing alone and visibly uncomfortable, but smiled nervously when he saw Anne about to return.

A few of Luc's family stood near a photo display of Michel's family. They poked fingers at his resemblance to others in their Gauthier clan. Then they suddenly turned toward the entrance behind them. The hand of one woman clapped against her mouth. Another, startled, backed into a photo display. It toppled to the floor, taking a flower vase with it. Then a gasp and a weak scream! Every eye in the room turned toward them.

Fig Grant had stepped past the guest registry and stumbled into the viewing room. He looked like an apparition. He wore a weather-beaten cap, wet from the evening drizzle. He was dishevelled. A long dark raincoat draped almost to his knees, but it was not long enough to hide the double barrel of a shotgun concealed underneath.

Fig was tall and large. His face carried a wild, vacant gaze. His head swivelled toward the mourners and visitors. Many shrank back in their chairs. In those who didn't know him, his appearance provoked unease. In those that did, the awful vision standing before them belied their certainty that he had drowned. He provoked a vision from a horror show. He defied their reality and smothered their primal instinct to react. He stood before them as a dead man who had come to life again.

But whimpers and gasps of fright grew louder and broke the spell of incredulity when Fig uncovered his shotgun. He brandished it. The double barrel swung wildly and uncontrollably around the room. Mourners scattered; some ducked under the scant cover of chairs, others froze in place, and a few tumbled toward the far door through which Anne had just entered.

She, too, stared ahead in disbelief at the madman at the other end of the room. Fig had not died, and his nightmarish plan had not died with him. And his purpose now was… what?

The barrel of his gun swung in nearly another full circle, fomenting terror in everyone it passed. It stopped when Fig's rotation finished, and he was pointing toward the casket. He stared at the pasty grey pallor of the Michael MacDonald he had known so many years before. Memories flashed. Anger resurrected. Hate rose like an unstoppable wave. And then a simple lucidity settled over him, like the ominous quiet in the heart of a great storm.

"This is for Mary," he said, staring at the corpse of Michael MacDonald. Fig jerked the trigger.

The twelve-gauge blast in the closed room was overwhelming. The sound swept away any thoughts that had taken root in the stunned sensibilities of the people there, and into its wake rushed a swell of panic and a paralysis of movement.

Fig's ears were ringing, too, but old hurts, unforgotten history, and unquenchable revenge drove him toward a final resolution. He turned toward Jean, who was staring at the maimed body of his dead father. The impact of the blast had jolted the corpse like an electric shock from a resuscitator. Pellets had peppered his father's suit coat and blown away half his skull. Fragments of grey matter clung to the raised coffin lid. Jean's mouth gaped like a simpleton, and his eyes bugged like a stunned bird.

Anne saw Fig shift his attention from Michael to Jean, and she knew immediately where his mind was headed. Fig's side-by-side shifted slowly toward Jean. The shell in one barrel had been spent. A final lethal barrel remained.

"This is for you, Michael."

Anne leaped forward. Along the ten metres between them, she snagged the back of a chair. Fig raised his shotgun. His finger touched the trigger. Anne's arm carried the chair forward in a long swing. Fig's cheek pressed into the small of the stock. His finger tightened. His eyes saw Jean's face droop in bewilderment, and he jerked the trigger. His last picture of Jean dissolved into a blurry image, the shotgun's roar, and the recoil of the gun-butt pounding his shoulder.

Anne saw little, but she felt the cluster of lead balls strike the chair that blocked the way between Fig and Jean. Her momentum carried her tumbling and sliding forward, past Jean, past the casket, and into the wall. The impact stunned her. She was disoriented, and her hand felt numb and weak. She looked down. A stream of blood flowed from her right arm.

Jean struggled to regain his senses. The wood chair Anne

had wielded had taken the brunt of the lead shot and saved his life. Now it lay tattered and split apart. Jean's eyes blurred. He rubbed them. His hand was covered in blood from several scalp wounds. He saw Anne lying helplessly in the corner and stumbled toward her.

Jack Pine, CeeCee's fishing partner, found his moment. After Fig discharged the second and last shell in his gun, Jack heard a familiar click, the latch to the shotgun's firing chamber. Fig had started to reload.

While Fig's eyes focused on reloading, Jack bolted toward Fig. Jack grabbed the shotgun with both hands. He was strong and able and much younger than Fig, but Fig was large and still powerful, and he was carrying decades of vengeance in his soul, and vengeance generates its own power.

Fig wrestled with Jack, each on opposite sides of the shotgun, pulling and twisting the weapon. Jack had a firm grip. He refused to let go. Fig had a firm grip as well, but he felt his energy waning, and he knew that others would come to Jack's aid, or the police would arrive, and that would be the end.

His thrashing about with Jack at the other end of that shotgun dredged up an old memory of himself. Fig. Thirteen years old... the end of lobster season... slinging traps... four hundred of them... heavy, sodden... four or five rows high... his slow progress... his arms like rubber... his father's backhand... mean-spirited rebukes...

With old wounds awakened and desperation in the wings, Fig braced and hauled back with a will. Jack kept hold but lost his footing. Fig swept Jack off his feet and slammed him into a corner of the wall near the entry. Jack's grip on the gun gave way. His consciousness dimmed, and he crumbled into a heap on the floor.

The room grew silent once again, except for the gentle music looping endlessly through ceiling speakers, and except for the mournful urgency of police sirens in the distance.

Fig deftly slipped two more shells from his raincoat pocket, chambered them, and snapped the action shut. He looked impatiently around the room. Jean Gauthier wiped blood from his forehead. Fig's attention fixed on him. Both men now wore expressions of dazed vacuity. Then Fig glared toward Anne who lay next to Jean. The barrel of his shotgun pointed uncertainly along the floor. Anne clutched Jean's arm. She knew the distance was too far, the outcome too clear.

Then Jean bolted. He broke from her protective hold, scuttled a dozen safe feet away from her, very near the spot he had greeted his father's mourners. He stared back at Fig.

Fig wasted no time. "This is for Michael..." he said, and jerked the trigger. The blast was enormous. Ears rang, minds emptied, bodies cringed, and eyes clapped shut. Almost no one saw the volley strike Jean. No one saw the jump of his torso. No one heard Anne's scream.

Fig's stare shifted to Anne. His eyes still dazed, a thought seemed to penetrate. Then it faded. In those confusing seconds, no one noticed Fig lowering his right arm, and elevating the barrel with his left.

"...and this is for me," he said.

Fig pressed the muzzle of the old shotgun under his jaw. He thumbed the trigger. Another blast, so quickly after, brought a chorus of screams from terrified mourners. Mouths fell agape and eyes clapped shut, but those spontaneous moves spared them the horror of seeing Fig's face disappear in a brutal volley of lead shot. Only the back of his head remained, as he dropped to the floor and fell forward.

Anne scrambled toward Jean. He was badly wounded. He gasped for air and tried to speak.

"Shhhhh, don't talk," she said.

Anne loosened the tie around his neck, unfastened the top buttons on his shirt, and opened his suit coat. She saw the wound. Upper-right side of his chest. Jack Pine joined her. He grabbed a jacket from the floor. Anne used it as a compress to stay the flow of blood. Then Jack left to ensure that emergency medical units were on their way.

Jean's breathing was laboured. His chest rattled as he gasped for air.

"I have to... tell you," he said, chest rattling.

"You don't have to tell me anything," she said. "We'll have plenty of time for that... later."

Blood seeped through the compress she held against his wound. "The ambulance will be here in a minute. I can hear the sirens. We'll sort things in a couple of days. I don't give up that easily."

City police officers burst through the entrance with guns drawn. Some mourners whimpered and shrank back at the sight of more weapons. The police quickly assessed the situation, holstered their pistols, and approached Anne and Jean.

"Ambulance just arrived," said the one officer. "How is he?"

"He's..." she said, looking down at Jean's tilted head...

76.

One week later, Anne Brown's Home

> *You don't know what love is*
> *Until you've learned the meaning of the blues...*

The bathtub is old, cast iron, deep, and filled with water warm enough to generate a ghostly vapour that clings to the surface like a timid child clutching her mother's skirt. Anne Brown lies motionless in the bath. Wind buffets the house. A mid-summer storm. She imagines boats tied to the wharf at Little Rose Harbour. She sees them tugging against mooring lines like willful pups.

> *Until you've loved a love you had to lose...*

Lyrics from a Chet Baker song drift freely from the CD player on a side table. A half-empty glass of wine rests alongside it. Her arm reaches out slowly, lifts the glass to her lips and empties it.

Anne slowly submerges. Only her face is visible. A rush of intoxication runs through her veins. She senses no past or future. Water trickles from her hair. Tears slip onto her cheeks. She knows that neither water nor tears will replenish her spirit or numb her pain.

You don't know how hearts yearn
For love that cannot live, yet never dies,
Until you've faced each dawn with sleepless eyes...

Jacqui taps gently on the bathroom door. "Mom, are you all right?"

How could you know what love is...

"Just a bit more time, dear... just a bit more time..."

The end

Acknowledgements

In the film version of his life, the writer hunches over his type-writer. A blank page stares at him. He gazes out the window for inspiration and, though it is night, through the darkened window pane of his chilly room, an idea forms. At first, his typewriter rattles hesitantly. Then it grows fluid and strident as charming fictional characters mount his pages. Cliques form and clash. Struggles ensue, but over several months of privation and determination, the writer pens a story that both breaks hearts and soothes torn spirits. Then the beginning and the end and everything in between, are bound up into a tidy package and posted to some respected publishing house. A week or two, perhaps even a month passes, before copies of his novel fill shelves in bookstores everywhere.

Would it were so simple!

In reality, a writer will burn up one or two years in finishing his novel. Sometimes more. And while it is mostly a solitary task, many others along the way will have provided invaluable information, insight, and skill to bring it to a finely-tuned completion. Here are a few to whom I offer thanks:

To Kent Bushey and his staff at Beach Point Processing Plant for a tour of their facilities and for technical info about processing and packaging lobster.

To Terrilee Bulger, publisher at Acorn Press for her on-going confidence in my literary endeavors.

To editor Jane Ledwell, whose eagle eyes, even at a hundred yards, can spot a "purple patch" in need of trimming or an error in fact that needs righting.

To editor Laurie Brinklow, who does the fine tuning, and with fresh eyes, hunts down and draws a bead on minor slip-ups and oversights that had escaped the twenty or thirty readings which preceded her.

To Matt Reid for a layout and cover design that catches the mystery, eeriness, and sense of place that shapes my tale.

To various archives, oral histories, and PEI government databases which added realism and depth to the story line of this novel.

And most of all to my wife, Brenda, for her support of my writing and her input into rural life on PEI. There is a rumor around that she locks me in the basement where, for several hours each day I do my writing. I believe she may even have started that rumor. Nevertheless, she feeds and waters me on a regular basis. Life is good. Thanks, Brenda